8

AUTHOR OF THE GOOD HOPE SERIES

CINDY KIRK

Reunited in
Good
Hope

REUNITED IN GOOD HOPE

CINDY KIRK

WAVERLY
HOUSE

CHAPTER ONE

When Cassie Lohmeier was fifteen, she never imagined she'd spend her thirty-fifth birthday dressed in a donkey costume schlepping drinks in the Good Hope town square.

Of course, back then, thirty-five had been so old, just visualizing herself at such an advanced age had been impossible. Coffee shops like the Daily Grind, where she currently worked, hadn't been in vogue. In fact, there hadn't been a single coffee shop in town. If you wanted a cup of joe, you made it in a percolator or grabbed a cup at Muddy Boots.

If shops like the Daily Grind *had* existed, she'd have likely considered working at such an establishment temporarily, or perhaps as a job to come back to during breaks from college. At fifteen, she had a dream. A dream that included graduating from high school and going on to the University of Wisconsin with the goal of getting a degree in finance. She'd wanted to eventually run her own business.

If Cassie had to describe herself back then, she could do it in three words. Serious. Stubborn. Naïve.

All three characteristics had contributed to her downfall. A slide into darkness that had started after a fight with her mother, when she decided to attend a party at the beach. When she'd—

"I wondered when our paths would cross."

Cassie whirled, and the blasted tail of her costume hit the front of the wooden booth. It knocked her just enough off balance that she stumbled. Or perhaps it wasn't the tail at all that had her fighting to right herself.

It was the boy from that long-ago beach party who'd played a starring role in the destruction of her hopes and dreams.

The benefit of being old—okay, so maybe thirty-five wasn't ancient, but these days she felt every year—was that she was in better control of her emotions.

She kept her face expressionless as she stared at Krew Slattery, NFL star and her crush from years back.

The years had been good to him. His body was lean and hard, honed from hours in the weight room and on the field. Though he had to be nearly thirty-eight, his wavy hair was still dark without a hint of gray.

That alone could cause her to despise him, as she'd found several wiry silver strands in her hair just that morning.

Though dressed casually, from the Italian loafers to his Oakley sunglasses looped around his neck, he breathed money.

When Cassie realized she was staring, she inclined her head and smiled politely. "What can I get you?"

"Coffee. Black."

Of course. No latte or cappuccino for Mr. NFL Superstar.

"Coming right up." Cassie knew Krew had returned to Good Hope for the first time in twenty years earlier this month for the retirement of his high school jersey.

She'd heard he'd been honored at halftime of the Homecoming game. Even with two boys in high school, there had been no reason to go. K.T. and Braxton weren't into sports, and she wasn't into setting eyes on Krew Slattery.

"How've you been?"

Cassie glanced around, coffee cup in hand, hoping Krew had directed the question at someone else.

No such luck. But then, luck had never been on her side.

Even though there had been a line at her booth all day, the traffic had disappeared. Probably because of the awards being given out.

The Daily Grind had set up a booth in the town square as part of the Howl-O-Ween celebration, where pets paraded through the business district and best-costume prizes were awarded.

"Great." To be wearing a donkey costume while he looked so…rich and happy was like a knife to her heart.

"I've been good, too," he said conversationally, though she hadn't asked. "Well, other than the injury."

A career-ending injury that had been talked about ad nauseum in Good Hope ever since it had occurred last month. When it had happened, Cassie had made no comments and contributed to no conversations for one simple reason. She couldn't care less about Krew Slattery.

"Momma." With arms open wide, three-year-old Axl—dressed in Spider-Man pajamas—flung himself at Cassie.

Trailing behind him, dressed as a gypsy, was her oldest child, Dakota.

"He insisted we come by to tell you about the weenie dog." Dakota cast a friendly smile at Krew, who still stood at the counter.

Cassie couldn't figure out why he hadn't left, then realized he was obviously waiting to pay.

After giving Axl a hug, she turned to Krew. "That'll be two dollars."

He handed her a five-dollar bill. "Keep the change."

She took the bill. Refusing the tip would only prolong the interaction. Still, she couldn't bring herself to thank him, so she settled for a forced smile and a nod before turning back to her children.

Cassie crouched before the little boy, not an easy task in a donkey costume. She wished for the thousandth time that she'd gone with the milk maid, the only other costume available. "Tell me about the weenie dog."

"He was wearing a hot dog bun. I touched it, and it was soft like a real bun." The boy had a slight lisp when he said his "s" sounds that she found adorable.

Actually, Cassie found everything about her youngest son adorable. Though he was high energy, Axl was kind and sweet. He was nothing like his father. Though the toddler had inherited the shape of his mouth from his father, Clint Gourley, thankfully all the boy's other features were from the Lohmeier side of the family.

"Did the weenie dog win a prize?"

Axl glanced up at his big sister.

Only when she shifted her gaze did Cassie realize Krew hadn't left. Her blood turned to ice when she realized the focus of his lazy gaze was no longer on her, but on Dakota.

At nineteen, Dakota was a dark-haired beauty with an unspoiled freshness. Her dark hair fell past her shoulders in loose waves, and her eyes were large and commanded attention.

"Frankie—that was the dachshund's name—did win a prize," Dakota confirmed, casting a hesitant glance in Krew's direction. "In the small-dog division."

Cassie rose and was ready to ask Krew to move along when the owner of the Daily Grind and her boss, Ryder Goodhue, strode up.

Dressed in his trademark black, Ryder had gone to school with Krew and considered him a friend. Of course, even if he hadn't played ball with Krew at Good Hope High, he'd have been just as friendly.

In Good Hope, strangers were considered friends you hadn't met.

"Nice to see you, man." Ryder clapped Krew on the shoulder even as he shook his hand. "I hope Cassie has been taking good care of you."

Cassie held her breath. She needed this job. Really needed this job. If Krew somehow screwed it up for her, she—

"Absolutely." Krew lifted his coffee cup in a salute in Cassie's direction. "I was just about to ask her for an introduction to this lovely young lady."

Krew's amber-colored eyes settled on the girl. "You've waited on me before at Muddy Boots, but I don't believe we've ever been introduced."

"I'm Dakota Lohmeier." Dakota extended her hand, fingers dripping with rings and wrists encased in bangles, all part of her gypsy costume. "Cassie's daughter."

Krew's gaze sharpened. He slanted a barely perceptible look in Cassie's direction before focusing his total attention on Dakota.

"It's a pleasure to meet you." Krew's voice oozed charm, and it took every ounce of Cassie's control not to give him a smack in the side with her tail.

Ryder's presence was all that held her back. That and not wanting to give Krew the satisfaction of knowing he mattered at all to her.

"I take it you live here in Good Hope?"

On the surface, the question appeared to be innocent. A polite inquiry that anyone would ask when meeting someone for the first time.

But Cassie didn't trust Krew. And she didn't like the way he was intently studying her child.

"I am for now," Dakota answered, apparently sensing nothing amiss in the question. "I was attending UWL—that's the University of Wisconsin branch over in La Crosse—but I ran out of money, so I'm waitressing and living with my grandmother until I earn enough to go back."

Krew nodded. "I know UWL, and I know how it is to be short of cash. Even if my family had wanted to help me back then, they could barely afford to keep a roof over our heads. If I hadn't gotten a football scholarship, I wouldn't have been able to go to school."

"That's how it is for me." Dakota appeared to regret her words the instant they left her mouth.

No apology was necessary. As the oldest in a family with four children and a single parent, Dakota had grown up knowing there would be no money for college.

"My mom still has three kids at home. My grandmother would like to help, but her money is tied up in her business. I don't mind. Earning my own way makes me take my classes seriously." As if determined to move on from the topic, Dakota shifted her attention to her mother. "I'd ask if you're having a nice birthday, but—"

Dakota gestured with one hand toward the booth.

"It has been a good day so far." Cassie spoke with a positivity that had been hard won. Several months earlier, she'd begun seeing a psychologist, and slowly but surely, she was pulling herself out of the dark hole that had been her home for what felt like forever. "The boys made me pancakes with chocolate chips for breakfast, and Axl drew me a lovely picture."

She tousled her son's straw-colored hair, then glanced up at Dakota. "Tonight, you and I will toast Lindsay and Owen."

Lindsay was Cassie's younger sister. This evening, Lindsay would marry Owen Vaughn in a small, intimate ceremony at Kyle and Eliza Kendrick's home. Cassie had no doubt the two would have a long and happy life together.

Despite having four children, Cassie had never walked down the aisle. Not once had she seen love shining in the eyes of any man she'd gone to bed with. She'd lived with Axl's father for a couple of years. Not having booted him out the door when he... well, not ridding herself of him sooner was her biggest regret.

"The wedding and reception will be a blast. I have a short shift today at the diner, so—" Dakota pulled her phone from her pocket and gave a little yelp. "I'm on duty in ten. You're off now, right?"

Dakota's gaze dropped to her little brother, who was running an ancient Hot Wheels car up the side of the booth.

"That's why I'm here." Ryder pulled his attention from his conversation with Krew. "I'm taking over now so your mother has time to get ready for the wedding."

Cassie didn't waste a second, pulling off the green apron in a single fluid movement. She hadn't realized it was so late. She had an appointment with hairstylist Marigold Rallis in fifteen minutes.

She was about to grab Axl's hand and bolt when she remembered her manners. "Thanks for letting me off early, Ryder. I really appreciate it."

"No worries." Her boss waved a dismissive hand. "I'm glad you agreed to take this shift. I know how busy you are today."

She only smiled and turned as she took her son's hand.

"Happy birthday, Cassie."

The deep rumble had her pausing for just a second. She should have known better than to think—to assume—that Krew would let her have the last word.

Unless she was prepared to dredge up dirty laundry—further sullying a reputation she'd only recently begun to rebuild—she needed to be civil. Besides, she was a mother, and it was up to her to set a good example for her children.

She took a second to turn back and smile with faux sweetness. "Thank you."

"Hey, maybe we can meet sometime to talk."

Cassie blinked. "Why?"

Krew slanted a glance at Dakota who, despite the need to get to her job, appeared to be listening intently to the conversation. "Old times."

"Thanks, but I'm pretty busy these days."

This time when she walked away from Krew, it was with her head held high.

~

Cassie gazed into the salon's mirror and blinked, not recognizing herself in the reflection.

She and her sister were both dishwater blondes. Lindsay had been highlighting her hair since high school. Most months, Cassie could barely scrape up enough money to make rent, much less have extra for her hair. But doing the hair of the wedding party had been Marigold's gift to Lindsay. The varying shades of blond and deep conditioning had Cassie's hair shimmering in the light.

"I love it." She touched the soft wavy strands that had been accentuated with a crown of baby's breath.

Marigold studied her intently, then gave a satisfied nod. "You look fabulous."

"You're a miracle worker." Cassie breathed the words.

"Hey, give me a little credit for the transformation." Delphinium, known to friends as Fin, glanced over from where she was applying makeup to her sister Ami's face.

"I never guessed that mascara and a little color could make me look…so amazing." Cassie shot Fin a smile. "Thank you."

She shifted her gaze back to Marigold. "From the bottom of my heart, thank you."

"Our pleasure," Marigold said with a decisive nod.

"You've always been pretty, Cassie." Fin's gaze remained sharp and assessing. "You've just never let that light shine before."

Cassie shrugged and cast a glance at Axl, relieved the toys she'd brought along continued to keep his attention.

"It's going to be an amazing wedding." Ami obligingly closed her eyes as her sister applied a light primer to her lids.

The Bloom sisters—Ami, Delphinium, Primrose and Marigold—had been a part of Cassie's and her sister's lives for as far back as Cassie could remember. Their parents had been friends and had frequently socialized before Sarah Bloom died of leukemia and Richard Lohmeier was felled by a massive heart attack.

Cassie would be Lindsay's maid of honor, while Ami and another friend, Eliza Kendrick, would be bridesmaids. Cassie was under no illusions that Lindsay had chosen her because she was her closest friend. Though never spoken, Cassie knew she'd gotten the top spot because Lindsay couldn't choose between Ami and Eliza.

"Are we still meeting at Eliza's house at five?" Cassie didn't want to mess up.

She'd planned to confirm the time with Eliza, but Eliza had already had her hair done and left by the time Cassie arrived.

Unlike her and Ami, Eliza preferred to do her own makeup. There wasn't a single doubt in Cassie's mind that the results would be flawless, just like the woman herself. While many in town spoke of a softening in Eliza after her marriage and subsequent pregnancy, the business owner still intimidated the heck out of Cassie.

"That's the plan." Ami's lids remained shut as Fin worked her magic with a brush.

"I can't believe I'll be the only one standing in front of the minister who isn't pregnant." Cassie laughed. "For once, I'll be the skinny minny."

Ami, Eliza and Lindsay were all expecting babies this spring. Since Ami already had one child, her baby bump was a little more pronounced than her two friends. In fact, because of the cut of Lindsay's wedding dress, her sister didn't even look pregnant.

"I'd give anything not to be a skinny minny." Marigold heaved a sigh.

Cassie immediately regretted bringing up the pregnancies. She knew Marigold and her husband, Cade, the town sheriff, had been trying to get pregnant for more than a year without success.

She wasn't sure if Fin and her husband, Jeremy, were trying. But then, Fin had never been as open about her personal life as Marigold was.

"It will happen," Fin assured her youngest sister, her eyes as warm and supportive as her voice.

Marigold lifted one shoulder, let it drop. "What I can't understand is how some women, ones who can't even afford the ones they have, can just pop another one out, while Cade and I—"

Marigold shot Cassie an apologetic look, realizing a little too late that the type of woman she was describing fit Cassie to a T.

Cassie had become pregnant the first time she had sex. After five years, when she had sex again, she'd gotten pregnant despite using a condom. Two years later, birth control pills hadn't stopped her from becoming pregnant yet again. Then, four years ago, Axl had been conceived.

"It's okay, Marigold." Cassie waved a dismissive hand and forced an offhand tone. "You're right. It isn't fair. Then again, what in life is?"

Cassie tried to recapture the joy she'd initially felt when looking in the mirror. She reminded herself what Dr. Gallagher had told her when she'd called herself a failure who'd never amount to anything.

The psychologist urged her to remember that her past didn't determine her future. She was smart and young and healthy. There was no reason she couldn't move forward and build a better life for herself and her children. Unless she chose to stay mired in the past.

Cassie was still working on forgiving herself for past mistakes and was determined not to get off track. This time, she would not get involved with a man just because she was lonely.

She'd learned her lesson on that score.

She was on the road to a new, better life, and nothing—and no one—would get in her way.

CHAPTER TWO

Cassie stood just to the left of the fireplace in Eliza's large parlor. While Cassie's cocktail-length dress was the same jade color and the identical chiffon fabric as the dresses Ami and Eliza wore, the bridesmaids' dresses were A-line, which worked for their expanding waistlines. Cassie's dress clung to her slender frame.

Jeremy Rakes, Fin's husband, sat at the piano in the adjacent parlor, playing the processional music.

Cassie's heart swelled when Axl suddenly appeared in the hall at the bottom of the steps, holding hands with Sarah Rose Cross, Ami's daughter. The wedding party had already descended the stairs before entering the parlor. All, that was, except for the ring bearer and flower girl.

Beckett Cross—Ami's husband and Sarah Rose's protective father—had worried his daughter might fall.

The thought of Axl holding hands with Sarah Rose on steps had also brought fear to Cassie's heart. She could visualize her son dragging the younger child down the steps in his eagerness to get to the bottom. Which was why she totally supported Beck's plan for the kids to enter in a different way.

Axl broke into a big smile when he spotted her and would have raced down the aisle, but Cassie raised the fingers of one hand. That was all it took for him to slow his pace.

They'd had a long discussion that morning about the importance of walking slowly to the front. Though she didn't like to bribe, Axl had been promised a new truck if he did as he was instructed.

Sarah Rose, dark hair curling about her face, her head topped with a crown of flowers, wore a dress the same color as the bridesmaids', while Axl's dark tux matched the groomsmen.

The two made it all the way to the front where, after giving their respective mothers a hug, they turned to sit in the audience. Sarah Rose sat with her father while Axl joined Cassie's family. Today, that family included her three other children and her mother, Anita Fishback.

As the music changed, Cassie felt a stirring of excitement. In a few minutes, Lindsay would marry the man she loved. So far, there hadn't been a single glitch.

Unless you counted the unexpected appearance of Krew Slattery.

Cassie had been shocked, had actually nearly stumbled, when she'd spotted Krew sitting beside Owen's parents and sisters. She wasn't sure why she was so surprised. Owen's first marriage had been to Krew's sister, and Owen and Krew were still friendly.

The man was sinfully good-looking. At seventeen, he'd been cute. At thirty-seven, well, he was a hunk. A classically handsome face coupled with broad shoulders, lean hips, long legs...and all that dark hair. In that moment, she did what Dr. Gallagher had been urging—she forgave herself for that youthful indiscretion.

She didn't forgive herself for all the other stupid things she'd done after that point, but this was a start. Everyone in the audience stood as Lindsay made her way down the steps on the arm of former Good Hope sheriff, Len Swarts. As Lindsay and

Cassie's father had passed away and their stepfather, Bernie Fish-back, had been a jerk, Lindsay had been faced with three choices.

She could walk down the aisle alone. She could let Steve Bloom, who'd been like a second father to them all these years, walk her down the aisle. Or she could ask Len, her mother's current boyfriend, to escort her.

Len had no children from his first marriage, and his wife had died several years back. From the second he and Anita had first begun dating, he'd treated Cassie and her sister as if they were family.

The pride Cassie saw in the eyes of the man many referred to as the Silver Fox brought tears to her eyes. Or maybe it was the look in Lindsay's eyes when she saw Owen that had moisture welling up.

Thank you, God, for bringing this wonderful man into my sister's life.

Cassie wasn't much for praying. For so long, it had felt as if the man upstairs had deserted her. But she was finally able to admit that poor choices on her part had contributed to her troubles.

Pulling her thoughts back to the present, Cassie focused on Pastor Dan Marshall. The minister had understood when Lindsay broke it off with him and seemed genuinely pleased that she and Owen were now together. His words about the power of love, promises made and building a future together touched Cassie's heart.

Lindsay and Owen had written their vows. Though tradition-ally the groom went first, Lindsay—worried she might break down when Owen spoke from the heart—had opted to go first.

When Lindsay said slowly, solemnly, her gaze never wavering from Owen's face, "I trust you with my heart, with my love and with my entire being," Cassie nearly lost it.

The old saying *Trust takes seconds to break but forever to rebuild* flashed through her mind, but Cassie immediately dismissed it as not relevant in this situation. Lindsay and Owen had rebuilt that trust. Her sister meant every word of her vows.

Cassie should have kept her focus on the bride and groom. Instead, she let her gaze wander. Only then did she discover the reason for the itch between her shoulder blades.

Krew Slattery's gaze was firmly focused on her.

He offered up a lazy smile that didn't quite reach his eyes.

Clamping her lips together, she pulled her gaze away just in time to hear Dan pronounce the couple husband and wife and to see Owen and Lindsay kiss.

They kissed for so long, Cassie heard Gladys and her two friends—Katherine and Ruby—titter. There was no other word for the sound they made.

Then the couple was striding down the aisle and Cassie was on best man David Chapin's arm on the short trek to the hallway.

"Congratulations, Lindsay." Cassie enfolded her sister in a hug, knowing this would likely be the only time she'd have a chance tonight. "I'm so happy for you."

"Thanks, Cass." Lindsay gave her a quick hug.

Her sister had barely stepped back before both Ami and Eliza were hugging her and offering their congratulations.

If things had been different, if Cassie hadn't made so many mistakes, she and Lindsay might have remained best friends. Or at least the kind of friends they'd been back when she was fifteen and Lindsay was twelve.

One night at a bonfire had changed everything. She wished—

"You look pretty, Mom." Fourteen-year-old Kaiden—more commonly known as K.T.—surveyed her with his artist's eyes, from the tips of her heeled shoes to the crown of baby's breath on her head.

"Yeah, you clean up pretty good." Sixteen-year-old Braxton, a computer guru, gave her the thumbs-up.

Though they were as different as night and day, the boys were best friends. The way she and Lindsay had once been.

"Where's your brother?" Cassie glanced around, worried when she didn't spot the youngest Lohmeier.

"Dakota has the brat." Despite the moniker, there was affection in Braxton's voice. Both boys adored their little brother.

"I better—"

"Who are these young men?"

Cassie froze, but only for a second. If Krew was expecting her boys to fawn all over him because of his NFL career, he'd quickly find out her sons didn't give a fig about football.

The boys, dressed in the dark pants and dress shirts she'd made them wear, stared at the dark-haired stranger. She could almost read K.T.'s thoughts. *Is this another one of Mom's guys?*

Despite the fact that there had been no man in her life since Clint went to prison, her boys were still wary. Cassie didn't blame them.

"These are my two older boys, Braxton and Kaiden." Cassie could have cheered when her voice came out sounding casual and offhand. "Boys, this is Owen's former brother-in-law, Krew Slattery."

"Hey," K.T. tossed out.

"How ya doin' man?" Braxton's tone came out slightly bored.

Normally, Cassie would have called the boys out on their poor manners. But she understood the origin of their animosity, and she didn't care enough about Krew to worry about his feelings.

K.T.'s gaze shifted to her. "There's no one our age here."

"Everyone's super old," Braxton agreed. "We scoped out the food, and the only thing to drink is punch."

K.T. made a gagging sound.

"There's champagne," Braxton added, "which you won't let us drink."

Cassie kept her attention on her sons, ignoring Krew. "What are you proposing?"

"Good one, Mom." K.T. offered a quick smile.

She lifted a brow.

"You know, wedding…proposing."

Braxton snorted. "That's lame even for you, bro."

Cassie waited, knowing one of them would soon get to the point. They were too eager to leave to draw this out much longer.

"Taylor said we could come and hang at his house tonight, you know, while you're here." Braxton turned persuasive. "Sheriff Rallis knows him, and so does Len. His family is normal."

"No arrests or convictions." K.T.'s comment and flippant tone had Braxton elbowing him.

"Take out your phone and call Taylor. Tell him I want to speak to his mother." Cassie made a do-it-quick motion with her hand.

K.T. shot a glance at his brother. "She might not be there."

"Taylor's parents go out on dates." Braxton's disgust made it clear what he thought of the idea.

"If no parents are there, you're staying put." Cassie saw her sister and brother-in-law were positioning themselves to make a comment to the crowd. "Get her on the phone now, or you'll be hanging with me and the other old people this evening."

Braxton had Taylor's mother, Heather, on the phone her sons shared in a matter of seconds. Heather confirmed that she and her husband would be home all evening and would love to have the boys come over.

Cassie handed the phone back to Braxton. "Your sister can give you a ride. She's—"

"We can walk. It's not far."

They were surely old enough to walk a few blocks by themselves. She nodded. "I'll text you when I leave here and am on my way to pick you up."

"What about the brat?" K.T. slanted a glance at his little

brother, who was playing ring-around-the-rosy with Sarah Rose and laughing like a maniac.

"Eliza set aside a space upstairs and hired a sitter to watch the kids. He'll be heading up there in a few minutes." Cassie had volunteered to toss in some money for the sitter, but Eliza had waved the offer aside.

Apparently, she considered it all part of hosting the event. Cassie had to admit she'd been relieved. Though Ryder had recently given her a raise when he bumped her up to assistant manager at the Daily Grind, the money she made barely paid the bills.

K.T. turned to go. "See ya."

"Yeah, see ya." Braxton cast a hard-eyed look at Krew before following his brother out of the room.

Cassie hadn't realized Krew was still hanging around. Why, she wondered, was he still there?

"Cassie, I know you're busy, but I'd really like to talk to you." Krew met her gaze. "There are things between us we need to discuss."

"Whatever you think we need to discuss, we don't." Cassie kept her voice low. "I'm not a teenager with a stupid crush anymore. I'm a different woman, you're a different man, and we have nothing in common."

"Well, I don't know if I'd say *nothing*."

Something in Krew's voice demanded Cassie's full attention. Was he challenging her? Teasing her? She tipped her head up to look him in the eye, but noticed his eyes weren't on her. Krew's gaze was on Dakota.

Cassie inhaled sharply as the realization washed over her. "Oh my gosh, is that what this is about? You want to get my permission to date my daughter now? That will never happen. You stay away from her. If you even try to sleep with her, I'll—"

"Hey, no way." Krew held up both hands, looking totally

repulsed by the idea. "That isn't it at all. She's just a kid. I don't want to date her."

Cassie's anger deflated like an untied balloon. Krew leaned in closer to her, so close she felt his warm breath against the sensitive skin below her ear. "But there is something I need—"

The piercing sound of silver pinging on crystal cut Krew off as Eliza clanged a spoon against a champagne flute.

"It's time for the best man and maid of honor to say a few words." Eliza's cool-eyed gaze scanned the room, settling first on David and then on Cassie. She motioned them forward.

With a reluctant sigh, Cassie did as Eliza instructed. First, because no one said no to Eliza Kendrick. And second, because Cassie had known full well that this speech was part of the deal when she'd agreed to be her sister's maid of honor.

As Cassie wove her way through the crowd, her mother's perfectly manicured hand closed around her arm. "Keep it clean."

The warning had Cassie's steps faltering for just a second. Despite the progress she'd made in the last year, her mother still didn't trust her to do the right thing.

It shouldn't have hurt, but it did.

The sting from the words was still present as Cassie took her place at the front of the room beside her sister. Lindsay glowed as brightly as the diamond Owen had placed on her hand only three weeks earlier.

When Eliza gave her the microphone, the same warning that had been in Anita's eyes shone in Eliza's.

Cassie was determined not to screw this up. She *wouldn't* screw this up. Thankfully, before her life had imploded all those years earlier, she'd taken a class in public speaking…and had excelled. And this past week, she'd googled wedding toasts and public speaking.

Talk about what you know. Well, that one was easy. Though she and her sister hadn't been close in recent years, they'd grown up together. She knew what made her younger sister tick.

Practice. Axl had giggled and pointed at her each time she'd stood in front of her bathroom mirror and read from her notes. Yesterday, she'd finally been able to make it all the way through without glancing at the sheet of notebook paper.

Of course, she'd hadn't been in front of a bunch of people who knew the old Cassie in that tiny bathroom with the cracked mirror and peeling paint. Now, she stood in front of a packed room filled with Lindsay and Owen's family and friends.

Her goal was to grab their attention by telling a story. As the audience moved in restless anticipation, Cassie took a deep breath.

"What I've always admired about Lindsay is her capacity for love. She is one of the most caring individuals I know, always thinking of others before herself. She lights up any room she walks into with her smile." Cassie paused and took a breath. "When we were girls, we could play for hours with our Barbies. Ken was always part of the picture, probably because our father was a big part of our lives. He and our mother had a happy marriage. There was passion and there was friendship."

For a second, thinking of her father had tears springing to her eyes. Ignoring the tightness in her chest, Cassie continued.

"The kind of marriage our parents had was what I always wanted for my baby sister. What started out as friendship between her and Owen soon morphed into love. I knew Owen was in love with Lindsay before she realized it. The way he looks at her…"

Cassie paused to blink the moisture from her eyes. "Such warmth. Such tenderness. Such love."

She shifted her gaze to Owen. "Lindsay looks at you the same way, which is why I know you will have a happy life together. Congratulations."

Lindsay gave her a fierce hug as applause filled the room.

Cassie clung to her sister, hoping that today would be a first step toward the sisterly closeness she missed so much.

～

One of the perks of being an NFL superstar was that you were invited to the best parties. Men wanted to pick your brain about strategy, and women wanted to jump you.

It was a good life, but Krew had found himself growing tired of the lifestyle even before the hit had ruptured his spleen and taken him out of the game for the rest of this season. Unlike his father, who'd never had a pot to piss in, Krew had invested the money he made, not only from playing the game but from endorsements.

Over the years, he'd seen plenty of guys squander the millions they earned. Knowing one injury could have the money train screeching to a stop had had Krew finding a financial adviser he trusted and investing.

Now, he had choices.

"What are you doing over here by yourself? I never pegged you as antisocial."

Krew turned and smiled.

In charge of greeting guests as they arrived, Dakota had followed the wedding's color scheme by wearing a green dress. But unlike her mother's and the bridesmaids', hers was short and sassy and more of a mint color.

It flattered her dark hair and olive complexion.

He realized two things at nearly the same time. He was staring, and she was awaiting his response.

"Just thinking about the wedding."

Dakota snorted out a laugh, causing several people nearby to turn and smile.

He arched a brow. "You don't believe me?"

"You don't seem like the marrying kind." Dakota studied him with the same intensity he'd studied her only seconds before. "So, no. I don't buy that you were thinking of the wedding."

Krew brought the crystal tumbler of whiskey he held to his

lips and took a drink. He ignored the twisting in his gut. The resemblance was uncanny.

"Can I have a sip?" Even as she asked, Dakota reached for the tumbler.

He pulled back, placing it just out of reach before her fingers could curve around the glass. "Are you legal?"

"Nearly."

"Then no. You can't have a drink."

Dakota rolled those golden eyes in a well-practiced move.

Krew had to admit that if he hadn't known better, he'd have thought she was twenty-one, or perhaps even older. With women maturing faster these days, it had become more difficult to pick out the underage groupies.

"Tell me about the classes you've taken at UWL."

Surprise had her kohl-lined eyes widening. "You don't want to talk about college courses."

"I do." The truth was, he found himself wanting to know all about her, and discussing things that interested her seemed a good start. "You and I have a lot in common. I was the first in my family to go to college. Tessa, my sister, ended up surpassing me in education when she obtained her JD, but I was the first Slattery to walk into a college classroom."

The confident façade slipped from Dakota's face. "I-I didn't feel as if I belonged. I really didn't know what to expect. I was so afraid of failing. You know?"

He nodded. Krew could identify with each of those feelings.

"I worked to save money for school, and because of our family income, I qualified for a number of grants."

Never taking his eyes off of her, he took another drink of whiskey. "What about loans?"

She shook her head, a rueful smile lifting her lips. "I know I could get them, and a lot of my friends have them, but I don't want the debt. For me, it'd feel as if, when I graduated, I was starting out behind. I've felt that way my whole life. I won't do it to myself."

"Fair enough." He finished off the drink.

Just listening to her brought back emotions he'd thought were in the rearview. Suddenly, the room seemed to close in.

Krew put a hand on her arm, not ready for the conversation to be over. "What do you think about continuing this conversation out on the porch? It's cool, but if you don't have a coat, I have—"

"Take your hand off my daughter."

Krew shifted his gaze from Dakota's horrified face to Cassie in full mother-bear mode. Her earlier reaction had made him wonder. This only confirmed it.

Cassie thought his interest in Dakota was romantic. She hadn't seen the resemblance. She hadn't pieced together what he had.

She had no idea he was Dakota's father.

He suddenly wished he had another drink.

Cassie stepped forward even as Krew wisely moved back. She took Dakota's arm in a firm grasp, ignoring the man beside her daughter. Keeping her voice low, she told her firstborn, "You and I are taking a walk."

"M-om." Dakota's cheeks pinked with embarrassment. "I'm not a child you can order around."

The last thing Cassie wanted on her sister's wedding day was to make a scene. But she, more than anyone else in the room, knew there was danger in Krew's charm. She would do whatever needed to keep her daughter safe.

You didn't protect her from Clint.

Guilt flooded her, the way it always did when her mind returned to that horrible period when she'd let Dakota down in a massive way. She should have stood up for her daughter and not been so willing to believe a boyfriend's lies.

Cassie shook away the image. The fact she'd made huge mistakes in the past only made her even more determined to do right by her daughter now.

"Dakota. Please. I just want to talk." Cassie met her daughter's eyes and didn't look away.

Not even when Dakota slanted a glance at Krew.

Krew didn't protest. Cassie could only hope that it meant he wasn't nearly as interested in getting together with her child as she feared.

The thought of Krew flattering her daughter and impressing her with his money and charm had bile rising in Cassie's throat. She knew how persuasive that smile could be to a naïve girl. Despite being in college, Dakota wasn't schooled in the ways of men.

She hadn't been, either, Cassie remembered. Look where she'd ended up.

Though attractive and outgoing, Dakota had rarely dated in high school. She claimed she was too busy with her studies. Cassie suspected her wariness had more to do with the poor example Cassie had set during her daughter's childhood.

"Okay. Sure." Without waiting for a response, Dakota whirled and stalked to the front door, leaving Cassie no choice but to follow in her wake.

After giving Krew a cold-eyed stare, she pasted a smile on her face and attempted to look relaxed while her insides trembled violently.

Dakota stood at the rail of the spacious porch, her arms wrapped around herself.

For the past week, the weather had been uncommonly warm, but tonight there was a decided nip in the air. Cassie ignored the gooseflesh that quickly covered her arms.

"You embarrassed me back there." Dakota's chin jutted up. "Why?"

Cassie wished she could chalk this antagonism up to simple mother-daughter friction, but the wall that stood between her and Dakota went beyond that. Dr. Gallagher had asked that she invite Dakota to one of their sessions, but so far Cassie had refused to take that step.

Her newfound strength was too tenuous.

"What were you and Krew discussing?" Cassie tried to keep her voice light and offhand, but failed miserably, the question sounding more like a demand.

"Is that what you wanted to talk to me about?" Confusion blanketed Dakota's pretty features.

"He's a lot older than you," Cassie began hesitantly, not sure where she was going with this, but knowing it was a road she must travel. "He—"

"I'm not going to hop into bed with him just because he gives me a couple of compliments." Dakota's brows pulled together in puzzlement. "Give me more credit than that."

"Good. That's good."

"Can you get to the point?" Dakota rubbed her arms. "I'm freezing out here."

While an exaggeration, it was close enough to the truth to have the words hurriedly spilling from Cassie's lips. "I want you to be careful with Krew. He's used to women throwing themselves at him. While he's rich and attractive, he's—"

"You can't be serious." Dakota frowned. "He's fun to talk with, but he's *old*."

Cassie controlled the urge to laugh aloud with relief. Dakota's confusion was too honest to be feigned.

"I'm sorry. You're right. I don't know what's wrong with me. Let's go back inside and enjoy the party." Cassie turned back toward the door.

"Wait." Dakota stopped her with a light touch.

Cassie looked from her daughter's hand on her arm to her eyes, fixed squarely on the worn porch floor.

Dakota lifted her gaze. "Thanks for the concern. I...I appreciate you looking out for me."

They walked back into the house together.

Cassie wanted to take comfort from Dakota's words. All she could think, though, was that her motherly concern had come a little too late.

CHAPTER THREE

Krew couldn't believe he'd gotten roped into being a celebrity judge for a children's Halloween costume contest. The event, being held at the Good Hope Living Center, was for children two to ten, with the grand prize being five hundred dollars. Apparently, the cash had been donated anonymously as a way to spark interest in the contest.

Even from all these miles away, Krew could practically hear his former teammates laughing. Instead of partying with friends, he was at a senior center waiting for a bunch of kids to stroll past his judging stand.

Gladys had cornered him last night at the reception and asked him to judge. Anyone else he could have brushed off. But he remembered how, when he and his sister had knocked on Gladys's door on Halloween, she'd always given them a big candy bar. One year, they'd each gotten two.

Gladys was still amazing. From what he understood, not only had she spearheaded this contest, she was in charge of the holiday craft festival going on in the gymnasium.

Though Krew tried to redirect his thoughts, they returned to his sister. Why hadn't he kept in closer contact with Tessa? At the time, he'd told himself she had enough on her plate with her split from Owen and their daughter, Mindy, dying from a brain tumor. He wished he'd made more of an effort to be supportive of Tessa when she'd needed him the most.

"Do you have plans for the evening?" The question broke through his thoughts as Gladys pushed a page with a list of contestants' names in front of him.

He recognized one name right off. Axl Lohmeier.

"No plans." He smiled. "What about you?"

"Several friends and I are drinking wine and watching horror flicks." She winked. "I like 'em scary."

Surprisingly, the idea held appeal, other than he'd substitute beer for the wine. Maybe Owen…

He immediately banished the thought. Though Owen and Lindsay had delayed their honeymoon, since the next couple of months were the busy season for her floral business, Owen would want to spend any free time with his bride.

"What movies do you have on tap?" Krew resisted the urge to check the time on his phone. Gladys had promised him the judging would take fifteen minutes tops. She hadn't mentioned the need for him to arrive early and pose for pictures afterward.

Gladys smiled. "I prefer the classics."

Krew raised a brow.

"*The Exorcist*, *The Shining* and *Nightmare on Elm Street*."

Krew covered his snort of laughter with a cough. "That's quite a mix."

"Ruby prefers *Psycho* and *Rosemary's Baby*." Gladys made a face. "Katherine is into zombies. *Night of the Living Dead* and *Braindead* are two of her favorites."

"Really." Krew found himself intrigued. "Tell me—"

A buzzing came from the watch on her bony wrist. "There's the signal. The children are ready."

"Top three," Krew murmured.

"Correct. Those in the second and third positions will win a gift certificate to Blooms Bake Shop. The grand-prize winner will win the five hundred dollars." Gladys's pale blue eyes locked on his. "Some of these parents are struggling. They could really use the cash."

Krew nodded and picked up the pen he'd been given to make notes.

The children—there had to be at least fifty of them—wiggled and jiggled past him to songs like *The Monster Mash* and *I Put a Spell on You.*

Krew smiled at the baby dressed as a taco and the little boy who looked like a miniature Prince, complete with purple jacket and microphone. There were the expected witches, zombies and Little Red Riding Hoods.

He had to admit Beck's daughter, Sarah Rose, with her dark hair and fair complexion, made a perfect Sleeping Beauty.

The baby taco and Prince were in the running for the top spot when Axl strode in. He was dressed in black leather with metal trim, and Cassie had darkened his hair and painted his face so his eyes looked sunken. Table knives protruded from his small hands instead of fingers. A perfect replica of Edward Scissorhands.

The child strutted, rather than walked, past the judging table.

Krew had to admit this one caught the eye. He moved Axl up on the list, beside baby taco and Prince.

Cassie stood, anxiously watching from the sidelines with the other parents. He thought about what Gladys had said about some parents really needing the cash. If there was ever anyone who fit that description, it was Cassie.

Though he owed Cassie more than he could ever repay, Krew told himself he would choose the winner based on merit.

Still, when all the kids had filed past and it was time to make the call, Krew couldn't help noticing that baby taco and Prince both had addresses on Millionaire's Row, a pricey area just off the waterfront.

Cassie's address wasn't too far from where he'd grown up. All three costumes were standouts. Any were worthy of the top spot.

He quickly listed his first through third picks and handed the paper to Gladys.

Dressed today as a witch in a long black gauzy gown with purple undertones, she cackled as she took the microphone and stepped forward.

"On behalf of the Good Hope Senior Living Center and the Giving Tree, I thank you for coming out and letting us ooh and aah over your children's amazing costumes. Your entry fee of twenty dollars will bring us closer to our annual goal of raising twenty-five thousand dollars for the Giving Tree. Thanks to your efforts we're now only three thousand dollars from that goal."

Krew wondered how he'd missed that this activity was raising money for the Giving Tree. Had Gladys mentioned that fact?

"Before I announce the top three, I'd like everyone to give a big round of applause to our celebrity judge, last year's NFL most valuable player, our own Krew Slattery."

He'd expected the applause. In this part of the country, everyone loved their football, but he was surprised at the hooting and hollering that came from the residents of the Living Center.

Gladys shoved the microphone into his face.

"Say a few words," she hissed.

He rose to his feet. Over the years, he'd done so many interviews that he'd grown comfortable speaking in front of crowds. "It was my pleasure to serve as the judge today, especially knowing money raised from this event will go toward the Giving Tree. Not too many people are aware of this, but one year when my father briefly left the family and my mother was struggling to pay rent, the Giving Tree stepped up to help."

Even after all these years, that particular holiday season was imprinted on Krew's memory.

"My mom was able to buy food, some much-needed clothes for me and my sister and even Christmas..." Krew paused and glanced at the children gathered around. "Well, Santa helped Mom out with the toys."

He winked as the parents chuckled.

Krew had to clear his throat as memories of that day, and those leading up to it, washed over him. His father had stormed out on Thanksgiving Day, drunk as usual, screaming insults at all of them. As Christmas had approached, life had been tough, made even more difficult because of his mother's attitude.

"My mother initially refused the items." Krew had been in grade school at the time. He'd been hungry and had worn the same pair of jeans to school all week. "Until it was explained that the Giving Tree isn't a charity. It's simply neighbors helping neighbors who've fallen on hard times."

Krew paused for effect, his gaze scanning the crowd, lingering for half a second on Cassie, who shifted her gaze away. "My mother accepted the offerings, and we had a Merry Christmas. Which is why I'd like to donate three thousand dollars so the Giving Tree reaches its goal. And since my coach always taught me that you don't stop just because you achieve something, I'd like to donate another twenty-five thousand on top of that to make sure that as many families like mine as possible can have a happy holiday."

The cheers that rose from the crowd wrapped around Krew, but he could only wonder why it had taken him so long to pay forward the good that had been done for his family that day.

Though Cassie was seized with the urge to slink to the back of the room, she remained at the front, Axl's hand clasped firmly in hers.

She'd been stunned when she saw Krew was the judge. Cassie thought Mayor Jeremy Rakes was going to do the honors. But she also understood that Krew's name brought a newsworthiness to the event. The problem was, after the way she'd acted at the reception and with him in charge of the final selection, she knew she could kiss any hopes of the prize money good-bye.

Still, the hours she'd spent over the sewing machine last night had been a labor of love. The smile on Axl's face when he put on his costume had made the effort worthwhile.

"...Axl Lohmeier."

Cassie blinked. She wondered how much Axl had won. Maybe it would be enough that she could stop by the bake shop on the way home and pick up treats for the kids.

"Ohmigoodness." Ami rushed over to her and gave her a hug. "I'm so happy for you."

"Thanks."

Ami glanced down at Axl and the table knives sticking out where fingers should be. "Edward Scissorhands. So creative. It's no wonder he won."

"Won?" Cassie's voice pitched an octave higher.

"Go to the front, my dear." Gladys suddenly appeared, putting a hand on her back. "We need pictures of you and the little guy accepting the money."

Cassie's stomach pitched. She was elated that she would have the extra money she so desperately needed. If only she didn't have to accept it from Krew and be photographed with him.

The things we do to survive...

When they reached him, Krew ruffled the boy's spiked dark hair and met Cassie's gaze. "You dyed his hair?"

Although the question held no malice, Cassie stiffened. "Temporary rinse."

Though he had to have caught her terse tone, his smile remained easy. "Congratulations."

"Pick up the boy." Glady's imperious tone rang out. "Then move in close. Krew, pause for a second as you hand Cassie the cash."

Cassie glanced at Katie Ruth Crewes, apparently the official photographer for the event.

Katie Ruth, a perky blonde who'd been in Lindsay's class in high school, was the editor of the Open Door, a weekly online newsletter.

"It will help if you're close together. Having Axl in Krew's arms will add interest to the piece." Katie Ruth's smile wavered when Cassie gave no indication of moving closer to Krew. "Or you can stay where you are."

"He doesn't have cooties." Gladys stepped up to Cassie and gave her a not-so-gentle shove in his direction. "Pick up the boy, Krew. Let's get on with this. The residents are eager for the trick-or-treating to begin."

Krew ignored Gladys's directive. The only indication that he'd heard her was when he lifted a questioning brow in Cassie's direction.

"I wanna trick-or-treat." Axl's whine reminded Cassie that they needed to get this done and over.

"You can pick him up." As she gave the okay, Cassie did as Gladys instructed and stepped close to Krew.

He smelled terrific, a mixture of soap and shampoo and some undoubtedly expensive citrusy scent that was worth every penny he'd paid for it. The scruff on his jawline only made him look more masculine...and dangerous.

Cassie did her best to ignore him.

Axl, who normally didn't like being held by those who weren't family, flashed his claws at Krew and growled like a tiger prepared to swipe. When Krew growled back, the boy's peal of laughter had everyone smiling, including Cassie.

"I got some good ones," Katie Ruth called out. "I'll get more when the kids trick-or-treat."

Cassie pulled back on the bills, relieved when Krew released his hold.

He set Axl down and started to turn away.

The little boy had other ideas. He clamped those scissorhands around Krew's leg and held on tight.

"You come."

The demanding tone had Cassie's brows shooting up.

"Axl. Let go of Mr. Slattery right now." Her attempt to grab her son's arm only ended in him clinging more fiercely to Krew.

"The boy clearly wants the two of you to take him trick-or-treating." Gladys's voice scraped against Cassie's last nerve. "You'll join them, won't you, Krew? It will give Katie Ruth a chance to get more pictures."

No. No. No, the voice in Cassie's head screamed.

Axl had been looking forward to going door-to-door in the Living Center since he'd gotten up that morning.

But to spend this extra time with Krew, well, it wouldn't be worth it.

"While on the surface, having Krew go with us may sound like a good idea, I have concerns." Cassie could have cheered when her voice came out casual and offhand, just as she'd intended.

Gladys arched a dark brow. "What concerns would those be?"

"Krew was the final-round judge." Cassie offered a bright smile. "Axl won the contest. Wouldn't it look odd for the judge to be with the winner and his mother?"

Krew merely continued to stare at Cassie with hooded eyes.

For a second, Gladys appeared nonplussed, as though she'd never considered the ramifications.

Katie Ruth laughed, drawing everyone's eyes.

Cassie was surprised to see her still standing there. She'd been so focused on her son and Krew, and then on Gladys, she hadn't given Katie Ruth a second thought.

"Something funny?" Gladys's tone made it clear she didn't appreciate the levity.

Katie Ruth rolled her eyes. "It's just that no one is going to think that Krew would be interested in Cassie."

Cassie's cheeks burned.

Krew opened his mouth, but Katie Ruth quickly said, "Oh! I-I didn't mean that the way it sounded." The words tumbled out, one after the other, as if she couldn't get them out fast enough. "It's just that Krew is this super-hot, former football player, and—"

Katie Ruth clapped a hand over her mouth as if realizing she was digging herself into a deeper hole.

"I think you best stop right there," Gladys advised Katie Ruth —not unkindly—before refocusing on Cassie. "Your concern is noted, my dear. I appreciate you thinking about the contest. But Katie Ruth will merely say that Krew accompanied the winning child on his search for candy, or something to that effect."

Gladys smiled at Krew. "Let's get started, shall we?"

Protesting any more would be pointless, Cassie realized. When Gladys got something in her head, there was no changing it. Still, she'd had to try. Forcing a smile, Cassie gave a nod. "Time to trick-or-treat, Axl."

On their way to one of the long halls that led to the independent apartments, Katie Ruth touched Cassie's arm.

"I'm sorry, Cassie. It sounded like a slam against you, but it really—"

"I understand." It was a good thing Cassie had years of experience with such comments. The put-down, unintended or otherwise, had barely nicked the armor she'd developed over the years.

"I consider us friends. I don't want you—"

"Drop it, Katie Ruth." Krew's authoritative tone had the blonde glancing at him in surprise. "You offered your apology. Move on."

If it had been anyone else, Cassie would have shot him a grateful smile. Everyone knew that once Katie Ruth got going, it was difficult to shut her up. Cassie had been envisioning having to listen to her apologize for the next fifteen minutes.

Instead, Cassie focused on her son, crouching beside him when they reached the first door. "What do you say?"

"Trick or treat." The boy gave her a sweet smile, and it was all she could do not to pull him into her arms and hold him tight.

"Very good." Conscious of Krew's eyes on her, she kept her gaze fixed on her son. "And what do you say when they put candy in your plastic pumpkin?"

"Thank you."

"Good boy." She stood, startled to see that Gladys was nowhere in sight. "Where's Gladys?"

"She said something about heading to her apartment." Katie Ruth smiled. "I think everyone is excited about having the kids come by."

Cassie wished Gladys had stayed. She would have been one more person between her and Krew.

After several minutes, she realized she needn't have worried. The focus was on Axl.

The boy insisted Krew say "trick or treat" with him.

Katie Ruth stayed in the background, snapping pictures.

For not the first time in her life, Cassie felt as if she was on the outside looking in. Her only reason for being with the group was that she was Axl's mother.

"We're coming up on Gladys's apartment," Katie Ruth announced. "I want to get a picture of all three of you at the door."

"How do you know it's hers?" Cassie asked.

"The elaborate decorations. I especially love the cobwebs at the top of the doorframe with the big spider." Katie Ruth grinned. "Also, her name is on the door."

Cassie hung back until Katie Ruth, her face set in a mulish expression, motioned her forward.

Axl stood between her and Krew. When he smiled up at her, showing a mouthful of baby teeth, Cassie felt herself settle.

"Trick or treat," the three of them said in unison as the door opened.

Gladys, still wearing her witch's garb, cackled. "What do we have here? A little boy? I love to eat little boys."

Instead of cowering, Axl squealed with delight and thrust his plastic pumpkin forward. "Trick or treat."

Gladys's face softened. "Is it candy you want?"

The little boy nodded vigorously.

"You have one or two brothers at home?" she asked Axl.

Axl held up two fingers.

Gladys pulled four large Hershey bars out of her pocket. "I have one here for you and each of your brothers, as well as your mother. You'll share with them."

It was a command, not a question.

The child nodded solemnly as she dropped the chocolate bars into his pumpkin.

"If I'm remembering correctly, Mr. Slattery, the big Snickers bars were always your favorite." Gladys slid her hand into another pocket hidden deep within the folds of her skirt and pulled out a giant Snickers. "Go ahead. Take it. You didn't use to be so shy."

When Krew still hesitated, Gladys pushed it into his hands.

"Thank you."

There was a roughness to his voice, and his eyes seemed to glow with an intensity that Cassie couldn't identify.

Gladys nodded, her eyes seeming to hold their own mystery. "You're very welcome."

Krew waited until Katie Ruth pulled Axl aside to take some additional pictures of the boy in his prize-winning costume. Finding the opportunity to speak with Cassie alone had become increasingly difficult. Seeing the opportunity, he seized it.

"I need to apologize." He kept his tone low.

Cassie arched a brow. "For what?"

"For what happened at the wedding reception. I didn't mean to upset you." He continued, not giving her time to respond, wanting to get it all out before she shut him down. "I have no interest in Dakota. I'd never date a child, and yes, I think nineteen is still a child."

Cassie gave a cautious nod.

"We need to talk." He glanced around. "We're almost through here. We could—"

"No." She shook her head as if wanting to further emphasize the response. "I've told you before. We have nothing to say to each other. Now, if you'll excuse me, it looks like Katie Ruth is done with my son."

Krew clenched his hand as frustration bubbled up inside him. He'd wanted to talk with Cassie before he went to Dakota, but she'd left him no choice.

It was time to speak with Dakota.

CHAPTER FOUR

Krew paced the sidewalk and kept his eye on the entrance to Muddy Boots. He'd discovered Dakota got off work today at three. He hoped she didn't have to work over because this would be his best opportunity to speak with her.

Shortly after three thirty, he spotted her leaving the cafe. Slowing his steps, he managed to have their paths cross in front of Blooms Bake Shop.

"Krew." A smile blossomed on her face. "How are you?"

"Good." He kept his tone casual. "I was hoping I'd run into you. Do you have time for a quick walk?"

Suspicion colored her amber eyes. "Look, Krew, I know you're a famous athlete, but I'm going to tell you straight up that I'm not the kind of girl who cares about stuff like that. I'm flattered by the attention, but you're too old for me. I'm not interested in you like that. I don't want to be rude, but I do want to be clear."

Relief washed over Krew. "I can't tell you how happy that makes me to hear you say that."

Dakota stared, nonplussed. "Then what do you want with me?"

"Please." He held up his hands. "Give me ten minutes."

She gestured with her head. "There's a park not far. We can talk there."

Krew kept the conversation light as they trudged through a light mist to the park and took a seat on one of the benches.

Push forward.

Those two words had been his mantra before any sports trainer or coach had spoken to him about the keys to motivation. Because of his background, he couldn't wait for things to happen, he had to make them happen.

"I don't know if you recall the first time I saw you."

She pulled her dark brows together. "Was it at Muddy Boots?"

He nodded, pleased that she remembered. "I was there with my sister, Tessa, and her husband."

"Owen was with you, too."

"That's right."

"The other waitresses were kidding me. They said you couldn't stop looking at me." Dakota rolled her eyes. "I told them they were crazy."

"Actually, I couldn't." Before she could speak, he continued. "But not for the reason you might be thinking. I mean, you're an attractive young woman, but—"

"I'm way too young for you." Dakota chuckled. "You could be my dad."

Krew couldn't believe it. The perfect segue had just been dropped into his lap. "Yes. And…actually…I think I may be."

Dakota started to laugh, but quickly sobered when she saw he wasn't joining in. Those amber eyes, so like his own, studied him. "Are you serious?"

"I am."

"Wait. What? Why do you think that? I mean, is it even possible that you could be my dad?"

Krew nodded slowly. "Yes."

When she chewed on her bottom lip, she looked even younger. "So, you and my mom—"

"Yes."

She straightened on the bench. "She said she doesn't know who my father is. Now you're telling me it's you?"

"I *believe* it could be me." With fingers that shook slightly, Krew pulled out the DNA test kit from his pocket. He passed it to her. "That's why I want you to give a sample. That way, we can know for sure."

Dakota took the kit, but didn't glance at it.

"Okay, wait a minute. Why now? If you thought I was your daughter, if there was any possibility, why didn't you show up before?" Her chin jutted up, and anger warred with pain in her words. "My life has been hard. Very hard sometimes. Having a father might have made a difference."

"Because I didn't know before." He folded his hands casually in his lap to still their shaking. "But when I saw you at Muddy Boots, well, you could have been my sister's clone at that age. Only her hair was short, and you're much taller. I—"

When Dakota raised her hand, he stopped and watched her visibly fight for control. "Did my mother tell you she thinks you may be my father?"

Score one for the direct question.

Krew didn't want to lie, but he didn't know what Cassie had told Dakota about that night. He certainly didn't want to add to Cassie's burden. Well, more than he already was by talking to Dakota about this before discussing it with Cassie. But if Cassie hadn't kept blowing him off, he'd have told her first.

"It's a complicated situation. That's a question I'd prefer you ask your mother."

Dakota surged to her feet, her hands clenched into fists at her sides, her breath coming in little puffs. "Really? Ask my mother? Did you ask my mother if you could accost me on the street and drop this bomb on me?" Raw anger and pain poured from her.

"The only thing my mother would tell me, the only thing she's ever told me, is she doesn't know."

He hesitated.

"If you had doubts back then, you could have taken a test that would have told you for sure." Dakota's voice shook, but he admired her control. "I needed you back then. I needed a father."

The tears welling in the girl's eyes spilled down her cheeks.

Shame flooded Krew. If he'd followed up to see if the baby Cassie had carried was his—instead of assuming it wasn't because she didn't tell him any different—he could have been there for her and for his daughter.

His heart twisted. He and his sister had never had a father, though the man responsible for their conception had lived under the same roof and had drunk himself into a stupor every night. Tessa still carried the pain of that lack of parental caring with her.

Krew stood, wanting to take Dakota into his arms and comfort her, but not sure he had the right.

He took a step toward her as she silently cried. When she didn't move away, he wrapped his arms around her and pulled her close. Dakota's head dropped to his chest as her body shook with sobs.

Krew didn't say anything, didn't do anything other than hold her. Regret filled him as he thought of all the years they'd missed.

After several long moments, she pushed back, sniffling and swiping at her reddened eyes.

"I'll do the test." She expelled a shaky breath, but her voice was surprisingly strong. "How long will it take to get the results?"

"I'll have them rushed. Two working days is what I was quoted. We can view the results online." He swiped a hand over his own eyes. "We should know for sure by the end of the week."

Dakota blinked back more tears and used the cheek swab he handed her before she headed to the sidewalk.

Krew fell into step beside her. "I know this is a lot to take in. I can give you a ride back to your mom's house."

"I don't live with Mom. I've been staying with my grandmother."

"How come?" If Anita Fishback was the same as she'd been when Krew was in high school, he couldn't imagine anyone choosing to live with her over Cassie.

"Mom's house has bad memories. Axl's father…" She hesitated for only a moment before continuing. "Do you remember Clint Gourley?"

"Clint and Clive," Krew drawled the names, unable to hide his disgust. He remembered the Gourley brothers. They'd lived down the street from him growing up. Punk-ass kids who thought they were hot stuff. Mean SOBs, both of them.

"Clint is Axl's father." Dakota's lips tightened. "He used to live with my mom."

Krew couldn't hide his surprise. It was difficult to imagine Cassie with such a man.

"That is," Dakota continued, "before she kicked him out. He's in prison now."

Owen had mentioned something about Clint serving time. "For burglary?"

She nodded. A hard look filled her eyes, and a shroud of darkness settled over her face. "I hope he rots there."

The guys on his team had always laughed and said he was slow to anger, but when he did get mad, watch out. Krew laid his hands on Dakota's shoulders, not sure he wanted to hear the answer, but unable to stop himself from asking for the truth. "Did he hurt you, Dakota?"

Krew couldn't ask the question any other way. Couldn't bring himself to ask if Clint had touched her or forced himself on her.

"He would have." Her tone was surprisingly matter-of-fact. "I made sure he didn't get the chance."

Krew expelled the breath he hadn't realized he'd been holding. "Thank God."

She'd turned from him for a few seconds. When she looked up again, the pain and hurt in her eyes tore at his heart.

His anger surged. Guys like Clint were everywhere. They preyed on the weak and the vulnerable, or anyone they could physically overpower. With bottom-feeders like him, it was all about control.

Clint Gourley, he thought, should count himself lucky he was behind bars. While Krew wasn't a violent man, he protected his own. If Clint ever got out, Krew would make it clear he'd better keep his distance from Dakota.

If he didn't, Krew would beat the living shit out of him.

Dakota might not have had a dad for the first nineteen years of her life, but if the DNA test confirmed his suspicions, she'd have one now.

CHAPTER FIVE

"Here's your Arnold Palmer." Dakota set the glass of tea mixed with lemonade in front of Gladys. Though the drink wasn't on the Muddy Boots menu, she'd been happy to make it for the older woman.

"You're a dear." Gladys pressed a five-dollar bill into her hand. "For your trouble."

Dakota's eyes widened. "You don't need to give me this. I was happy to help."

When the girl attempted to hand the bill back, Gladys shook her head and forced a firm tone. "I want you to have it."

At ninety-seven, Gladys had no worries about outliving her money. If she could scatter a little joy, so be it.

"You have the prettiest eyes." Gladys effectively stopped the start of the girl's protests with the compliment.

"Thank you." Dakota smiled. "Everyone says I got them from my grandmother."

Gladys nearly rolled her own eyes at that piece of rubbish. She'd looked into Anita's eyes for over half a century. The woman's eyes were hazel, certainly nothing special. Dakota's eyes, on the other hand, were gold, a unique and beautiful color.

The only people who had eyes that color were Krew and his mother. Gladys turned her gaze to a nearby booth that Krew had claimed just as Dakota's shift began. As she studied him, she realized that not only did he share Dakota's unique eye color, but his hair was also the same distinctive walnut shade.

"I know who we're going to match next," Gladys announced to the two women at her table once Dakota stepped away.

Ruby, who was enjoying a cup of her favorite decaffeinated floral tea, turned interested eyes in her direction.

Katherine straightened in her seat. With her suede cloth skirt and cardigan in rust and teal, Eliza's cousin had embraced the Southwestern look today.

Gladys cast an admiring look at the Navajo tiger's-eye earrings. They would look quite nice on her own ears.

"Who do you have in mind?" Katherine kept her voice low, as if wanting to not be overheard by the others in the cafe.

Gladys smiled. "Cassie."

"Cassie Lohmeier." Ruby sighed the name. "That woman deserves some happiness."

Katherine's gaze sharpened. She had a good heart, but was nowhere near as sentimental as Ruby. "With her background and all those children—three of them still at home—Cassie will be tough to match."

That, Gladys thought, was a huge understatement. "I believe we can rise to the challenge."

"Who are you thinking of for her?" Ruby took another sip of the tea that had to be lukewarm by now. Bells over the door sounded, and Ruby's attention shifted to the entrance.

As if simply thinking of her had been enough to conjure her, Cassie strolled into the café. She sidestepped those waiting to be seated and headed straight for the counter.

Her dark pants and white shirt told Gladys that Cassie was working today at the Daily Grind or had just gotten off. The blonde paused behind Pastor Dan Marshall, who appeared to be picking up a to-go order.

Gladys watched Cassie playfully tap the young minister on the shoulder and watched the smile bloom on his lips when he turned and saw who was behind him.

"You're planning on matching her with Dan?" Even Ruby, who could always be counted on to back Gladys's schemes, sounded skeptical.

Katherine simply raised a brow.

"Of course not." Gladys waved a dismissive hand. Did her friends really think she was that crazy? "Dan was once her sister's fiancé. Even if everything else was equal, that has an ick factor I prefer not to touch."

Ruby smiled. "Ick factor. I like it."

A sense of pride washed over Gladys. She liked to think of herself as someone who kept up with the young people's lingo. "I have someone else in mind for Dan."

It hadn't been all that long ago that the three women, bored with dominoes and card-playing, had decided to embrace match-making as a post-retirement hobby. Their success with Lindsay and Owen had buoyed their spirits and made them eager to take on another challenge.

"Don't keep us in suspense." Clearly impatient, Katherine tapped the table with her nails. "Who is it?"

Gladys loved these moments where she had the audience, er, her friends, hanging on her every word. "Krew Slattery."

"You've got to be joking." Katherine laughed, a husky sound that still managed to retain the sultriness of her youth. "You can't fix Krew Slattery up with Pastor Dan."

Ruby's rapidly fluttering eyelids reminded Gladys of a startled hummingbird.

"Oh, for goodness sake." Gladys rolled her eyes. "I was speaking of Cassie and Krew."

Ruby expelled a breath. "Thank God."

"Krew is handsome and rich. He could have his pick of any woman." Katherine spoke pragmatically. "What makes you think he'd be interested in Cassie?"

Gladys lifted one shoulder, the fabric of her purple cashmere sweater caressing her skin. "Cassie is a beautiful woman. She's smart, funny and—"

"—has three boys at home," Katherine pointed out. "Two of them are teenagers, and one is a toddler. I don't know which is worse."

Gladys pointed a finger bejeweled with rings at Katherine. "A wise woman once told me, 'The tougher the challenge, the sweeter the victory.'"

Katherine chuckled and lifted her coffee cup in a mock salute. "If we can pull this off, it'll be one sweet victory indeed."

Cassie wanted to be busy, but she wasn't going to get what she wanted at the Daily Grind. Not at five o'clock. Happy hour, when the drinks were half price, had ended at four.

She had one more hour until the evening crew came in. Though Ryder preferred two employees be in the shop at all times, he'd already left for the day. When he'd hesitated, she'd urged him to go, telling him she could handle whatever happened during this last hour of her shift.

Then Krew walked through the door.

Cassie straightened from where she'd been adjusting the pastries in the bake case. Her heart gave a solid thump against her rib cage.

Cassie told herself it was good he'd shown up. There was something she needed to discuss with Mr. Krew Slattery.

"You were with Dakota at the park yesterday. I heard she was crying and upset. Why are you hanging around my daughter?"

If Krew was startled by the question, he didn't show it.

Instead of responding, he slid his gaze around the shop. He peered around the corner as if making sure all the tables were empty, then glanced at the door leading to the back. "Are you alone?"

"Ryder left early. I'm the only one here until six." She lifted her chin. "Are you going to answer my question?"

He gestured toward a table in sight of the cash register, but not visible by those strolling past the shop. "Let's sit."

"Just answer my question."

As if he'd suddenly gone deaf, Krew crossed to the table.

Fuming, Cassie jerked a chair back and took a seat. "Tell me what's going on between you and Dakota."

He studied her with an intensity that had once had her girlish heart going pitter-patter each time he glanced in her direction. "What has she told you?"

The question caught her off guard and brought a fresh wave of pain. Ever since Dakota's senior year and the situation with Clint, the closeness she and her daughter once shared had disappeared. They were cordial, even friendly at times, but the fact that Dakota was staying with her grandmother while she was back in town said it all.

"Nothing," Cassie admitted. "She hasn't told me anything."

He studied her for a long moment. "Who is Dakota's father?"

Cassie's eyes narrowed. "What? Why would you—"

"I believe Dakota might be my daughter. I asked her to take a DNA test."

It took a second for the words to register. When they did, Cassie reacted with a roar.

"You what?" Slapping her hands on the table, she leaned forward, getting in his space. "You had no right to ask her to take that test. How could you just dump something like that on a child? It's too much. Did you even think about her feelings? You had no right—"

"I have every right, if I'm her father." Krew's calm tone only incited her further.

Her breath came in short puffs. "You should have come to me if you thought—"

"Cassie, I've been trying to talk to you since I've been in Good Hope. You stay as far away from me as possible."

"You're one to talk about staying away."

For a moment, they only stared at each other.

Cassie's anger slid away, replaced by sadness. Why, God, why now?

This past year had been about moving forward, about leaving the past where it belonged. About forging a new life from a position of strength.

Now, this boy, this man, from her past was about to screw all that up. If—when—the DNA test came back negative, as it most surely would, the questions she'd had to deflect all those years ago would return.

Her mother would ask.

Dakota would ask.

And, once again, she would offer no answers.

Cassie wanted to cry, to break down and sob that life wasn't fair. But, she reminded herself as her heart twisted, she'd learned long ago that life wasn't fair.

Her father dying wasn't fair.

Her crush not calling her after they'd made love on the beach wasn't fair.

Her...

She couldn't think anymore. Wouldn't think anymore. Thinking only brought back the pain and the guilt. In her weakness, she'd let her life spiral out of control, seeking comfort in the arms of many men over the years. She wanted to be a good mother, but had failed miserably, especially when it came to Dakota.

"You're not her father." Cassie spoke firmly, despite the inner chaos. "I'm begging you to let this drop."

His intense gaze remained fixed on her. "How can you be sure?"

"Right after you left for college, Mitch and I started…dating." Their former classmate had been a poor substitute for Krew, not a star athlete or ever one of the smart kids, but he'd paid attention to her, something Krew hadn't done after that night on the beach.

Dating sounded so much better than *having sex with a boy who was only out to use me.*

Krew nodded. "My sister told me you and Mitch hooked up. Later, she told me you were pregnant and the baby was his. I had no reason to believe otherwise. Until now."

"Why? Why now, after all these years? Why start wondering?"

"Because I saw her, Cassie. Are you honestly telling me you don't see the resemblance?" Krew took a deep breath to calm himself. "Plus, and I'm not saying my behavior was perfect back then, far from it. But it's not like you were calling me and telling me something different, that you thought there was a chance I was the father. Why shouldn't I believe the baby was your boyfriend's? I swear, if I had thought you were suffering because of me, I would have done the right thing. I never wanted to hurt you, Cassie. I still don't."

Cassie closed her eyes and dug deep for control.

When Krew reached across the table and took her hand, she didn't pull away. She needed the comfort offered in that simple touch.

"If you don't mind my asking, why Mitch? I never thought you liked him."

His voice was so soft and low that Cassie wondered if she'd imagined the question. But there was curiosity in Krew's eyes as he waited for her answer.

"Not long after you left, Mitch approached me at school." Cassie shifted her attention to the clock for a second. "You're right. I was never attracted to him, but after…after what happened with you, I mean, with you ignoring me after we... Well, I was feeling low."

Cassie took a steadying breath and decided there was no need to mince words. "You made me feel cheap and used. Mitch was incredibly sweet. At first. He said nice things, like the characters in the books I liked to read. He was kind and attentive."

"You slept with him." Though there was no judgment in Krew's tone, Cassie felt her cheeks warm.

She lifted her chin. She was done apologizing for that time. She'd been fifteen years old. Yes, she'd been foolish, but she'd been *fifteen*. "At first I said no, but he reminded me I'd already had sex with you, so—"

"You told him about us?"

Cassie blinked. "No. You did."

"I would never." A muscle in Krew's jaw jumped.

Puzzled, Cassie drew her brows together. "How did he know?"

"If I had to say, I'd say he must have guessed."

Cassie considered, then nodded.

"Well, he told me I'd already had sex with you and you weren't even my boyfriend." With great effort, Cassie kept her voice even. "So I did it with him. Six weeks later, he broke up with me. He told me I was worthless and nothing but a slut."

Even twenty years later, recalling the harsh words and the scorn in his voice had her insides trembling. Adding to the damage done by Krew's dismissiveness, that conversation had changed her further, leaving her self-confidence in tatters.

"What did Mitch say when you told him you were pregnant?"

Cassie might have chosen not to answer, but Krew's thumb stroked the top of her hand and his eyes were dark with concern.

"He asked how I knew the baby was his. I'd been with you, so I could have been with any number of guys." Her voice was matter-of-fact, but each word was a shard of glass pricking her heart. "He vowed that if I tried to name him as the father, he'd get a bunch of guys together to say they'd all fu—that they'd all had sex with me."

Krew muttered a curse. "I'm glad he isn't Dakota's father."

"He wouldn't acknowledge her, and I didn't push." Cassie swallowed past the lump trying to form in her throat. "After discovering the kind of guy he was, I was glad he didn't want anything to do with her. I didn't want such a person in my child's life."

"How do you deal with seeing him around town?"

"We mostly ignore each other."

"I'm sorry for that night at the beach."

Hearing the pain in his voice, Cassie looked up.

"You were only fifteen." His golden eyes never left her face. "Beyond the legal issues with the age of consent, I took your innocence. And I took away all those firsts you should have experienced."

As if sensing her confusion, Krew elaborated. "Your first date. Your first dance. The first time you had a real boyfriend. You lost all that because of me."

She shook her head, stubbornly refusing to take the out he offered. "You didn't force me. I wanted you in a way I've never wanted any other man."

Too late, Cassie realized what she'd revealed. She spoke quickly to cover the gaffe. "I was the one who made one bad choice after another. Some of them could have been disastrous."

Cassie thought of Dakota and Clint. She would never forgive herself for not tossing him out of the house the instant Dakota told her of her fears about him.

Tears slipped down her cheeks, and her heart swelled with unbearable pain. What kind of mother didn't put her child first?

"Hey, hey." In one fluid movement, Krew rounded the table. Crouching beside her chair, he pulled her to him.

Even after all these years, the feel of him seemed familiar.

Cassie told herself to pull back. But his arms were so strong and comforting, and her head fit perfectly against his chest.

For a moment, Cassie let herself lean. Let herself forget all the stupid things she'd done and accept the solace his touch offered.

As Krew began stroking her hair, Cassie felt herself steady. Still, she kept her eyes shut for a few seconds more, reluctant to end the closeness.

When she sat back, she swiped at her cheeks. "I need to get back to work."

With obvious reluctance, Krew stood. "We'll talk more later."

"Mitch still might be Dakota's father." Though Cassie had accepted that fact long ago, saying the words aloud made her feel sick inside.

"I don't think so." Krew surprised her by taking her hand for the second time that afternoon. "I'm sorry for going to Dakota. I should have waited until I'd spoken with you."

"I didn't make that easy."

He waved a dismissive hand. "I promise that you and Dakota will never be alone again. I'm going to do my best to make up for the past." His eyes were firmly fixed on hers. Something about those eyes—the shape, or maybe it was the color—struck her.

All these years, she'd been convinced Mitch was Dakota's father. Mitch had dark hair and hazel eyes.

Krew's hair was dark. His eyes weren't hazel. No, they weren't that boring. They were a striking shade of gold.

Just like Dakota's.

"I'll be in touch." Krew's fingers were on the door handle when he turned back. "I never meant to hurt you."

Then he was gone.

Cassie buried her face in her hands.

Her life hadn't been this out of control since the pregnancy test strip showed positive. On that day, her life as she'd known it had ended. She had a feeling she was at a similar turning point now, and this time she had four children counting on her not to lose her way again.

CHAPTER SIX

Friday afternoon, the DNA results still hadn't popped up in Krew's in-box. The walls were closing in, so Krew decided to grab a beer and do some thinking away from the Sweet Dreams motel. As it was barely four o'clock, Krew assumed the Flying Crane would be deserted.

He assumed wrong.

Sounds of laughter and conversation wrapped around him the instant he stepped inside the waterfront bar. He'd forgotten about happy hour.

While the bar's high, tin ceilings were aesthetically pleasing, poor acoustics turned the piped-in rock music shrill and tinny.

Krew was headed for a stool at the bar when he spotted Mitch sitting alone at a table against the far wall.

The thought of how Mitch had used Cassie, of the nasty things he'd said to a frightened young girl, had Krew clenching his hands into fists.

Even back in high school, he hadn't liked Mitch. A second-string ball player at best, the guy was desperate to be a part of what he considered the popular crowd.

He'd also had a thing for Cassie. Krew remembered how he used to leer at the shy freshman.

At that moment, Mitch spotted him and smiled broadly, waving him over.

Krew considered turning on his heel and walking out, but he had a few things to say to this man. He crossed the room in long, purposeful strides. When he reached the table, Mitch jumped up. For one horrifying second, Krew thought Mitch was going to hug him.

At the last second, he clapped Krew on the back. "It's good to see you, man. Sit. Have a beer. Catch me up on what's new with you."

A petite pixie with a mass of curly brown hair and wearing a black shirt with a red Flying Crane logo appeared tableside. She looked familiar. Krew recalled Owen introducing her shortly after Krew had arrived in Good Hope.

"You're Izzie, the artist." Krew had been admiring her artwork on one of the downtown alley walls when the one responsible for such beauty had strolled by. "I don't know if you remember me? Krew Slattery. Owen introduced us."

"It's nice to see you again." Her wide lips curved into a broad smile. "I could say something inane like, 'You're still in Good Hope,' but that'd be ridiculous because you're sitting right in front of me."

He laughed. Though he wasn't interested in dating her, she was beautiful in a boho, artsy kind of way. "I've seen several more examples of your alley art. You're crazy talented."

Her smile widened. "I'd like to take credit for all the wonderful art, but not all of it is mine."

The image of the last mural he'd seen flashed before him. "The screaming faces?"

"Those are amazing." Pride filled Izzie's voice. "That art is actually the work of K.T. Lohmeier. The boy has mad skills."

"Lohmeier? Cassie's son?"

"The very same." Izzie appeared to catch the manager's stink eye at the same time that Krew did. "What can I get you gentlemen?"

"Whatever you have on tap." Krew didn't want to spend any more time with Mitch than necessary, so he chose not to order any food.

"I'll have another pale ale." Mitch shot Krew a pointed glance. "Trust me. You don't want what they have on tap."

Izzie cast Krew a questioning look. He winked.

"Coming right up."

Mitch watched Izzie hurry off, his expression turning sulky. "She doesn't give me the time of day. You walk in, and suddenly she's in no rush."

"I'm new in town." Krew leaned back in the wooden chair. "How've you been?"

One question was all it took to open the floodgates. For the next fifteen minutes, he heard about Mitch's fabulous job as a supervisor with the parks department and his divorce from "Betsy-the-frigid-bitch" two years earlier.

"Any kids?" Krew took a sip of beer before grabbing a chip from the huge mound of complimentary nachos Izzie had set on the table when she dropped off their drinks.

"Thank God, no." Mitch jammed a chip into a mass of beans smothered in cheese. "You?"

One daughter.

"I'm not married, remember?"

Mitch let out a guffaw. "As if that fact stops any of you NFL guys."

Krew clenched his jaw tight. He had yet to bring up Cassie, and he was already ready to leave.

Back in high school, Mitch's parents had given him a generous allowance, and he hadn't been afraid to spend it on friends. That it was the only positive thing about Mitch that Krew could think of said a lot about his priorities back then.

"I ran into Cassie." Krew reached for another chip, more for something to do than out of hunger. "She looks good."

"White trash," Mitch sneered.

"What did you say?" Krew pinned Mitch with the same steely-eyed gaze designed to decimate the opposing team's defensive linemen.

"She's had some hard years." Mitch dropped his gaze and pretended to be immensely interested in loading a chip with guac. "But, yeah, she's looking good."

"I remember her in high school. She was smart and pretty, but serious." Krew had been attracted to the freshman from the moment he'd seen her. Corny as it sounded, their eyes would meet in the hall and sometimes he'd feel this "connection." There was no other way to describe it. "I heard you dated her the beginning of your senior year."

Krew kept his tone casual and his smile one buddy to another.

"Dated is a stretch. We—" Mitch put one index finger and thumb together, then pumped his other index finger through the hole.

It took everything in Krew not to smash his fist into Mitch's face.

"I hadn't had anything to do with her for a couple of months when she tried to pin a baby on me." Mitch rolled his eyes and stuffed another chip into his mouth.

Krew's fingers tightened around the glass of beer. "Really?"

"She came to me, bawling." Mitch leaned back, a smirk on his face. "No sympathy here. I asked her how she knew the kid was mine. God knows how many guys she was screwing. I mean, she'd been with you."

Krew raised a brow.

"Hey, everyone knew, okay, *assumed* you nailed her behind that old house on the beach." Apparently oblivious to the darkness rising like a dark tide inside Krew, the guy continued. "You don't want to admit it. I get it. She was only fifteen. If anyone found out, you could have gone to jail for statutory rape. Bye-bye, scholarship. Hello, jail. But then, I guess your family is used to men being locked up."

At that moment, the tight hold Krew had on his temper began to give way. "You didn't have any problem ignoring the law when it comes to age of consent."

Mitch shrugged. "My dad is an attorney. I warned her, 'You come after me, you'll be sorry.'" Mitch took a long drink of his ale. "No, siree. I wasn't going to let someone like her screw with my life."

Krew remembered how sweet Cassie had been back then, how innocent. He swore she'd been a virgin when they'd been together. That only made him feel guiltier about what had happened that night on the beach.

As Krew's anger surged, he realized he was more pissed off at himself than anyone else. A mirror had been held to his teenage self, and Krew didn't like what he saw. Didn't like it one bit. Despite all his achievements on the football field and the accolades, he'd been the kind of stereotypical teenage boy people assumed a kid from a family like his would be.

Shame swamped him. He'd thought only of himself and *his* plans.

"I bet you've got women throwing themselves at you day and night." Mitch's eyes sparked with interest, but the buzz of his phone had him frowning. After glancing at the readout, he cursed and pushed back his chair.

"Problem?"

"It wouldn't be if my crew didn't have their heads up their asses." Mitch cast him a look of apology. "I've got to handle this myself."

Krew barely stopped a grin. Saved by a park emergency. "The perils of management."

Mitch fairly preened under what he perceived as a compliment. "Exactly. We'll have to get together another time."

Not happening, Krew thought.

Mitch's phone buzzed again. He swore. "Gotta go. Call me."

Krew merely lifted his glass of beer in a gesture of farewell. If Mitch thought they'd be getting together shortly—or ever—he was mistaken.

The picture of what had gone on in Cassie's life in the weeks and months after the beach bonfire came into sharp focus.

One thing was clear.

Krew had a lot to make up for.

~

Cassie liked having her children home in the evening. Tonight, though, she was grateful that Braxton and K.T. had taken Axl to Fun Night at the YMCA.

She hoped Dakota would call. Cassie had tried to reach her several times but her daughter hadn't returned her calls or texts. So, Cassie would study and keep her ears peeled for the phone. One day, the money she'd earn from selling homes and commercial properties would be her ticket off the paycheck-to-paycheck hamster wheel.

There was so much more she wanted for herself and her children than mere survival. While she appreciated Ryder giving her more responsibilities at the Daily Grind, her pay at the coffee shop barely kept her family above the poverty level.

Her sessions with Dr. Gallagher and with Pastor Dan had helped her accept she was a strong, smart and capable woman. More important, she now believed the past didn't have to determine her future.

Feeling hopeful, she booted up the laptop Braxton had "built" for her using parts from a computer one of his friends had scrapped.

As she opened the next module in the course, and prepared to dig in, the doorbell sounded.

Cassie frowned. Her sister was the only one who ever stopped by. With Lindsay still in newlywed mode, it wasn't likely to be her.

She slanted a glance at the baseball bat she kept by the front door. While the neighborhood wasn't horrible, it was on the seedier side of town. Which was why Cassie insisted the boys look through the peephole before opening the door and told them to never open it to strangers.

The doorbell rang again.

"I'm coming." With the lights on and her car in the driveway, anyone with half a brain would know someone was at home. It wasn't as if she was giving out any secrets by responding.

Cassie flipped on the porch light and gazed through the peephole.

Her heart stopped when she saw Krew on the stoop, hands jammed into his pockets.

With trembling fingers, Cassie released the chain, flipped the deadbolt and eased the door open.

A watchful waiting filled his gaze. "Mind if I come in?"

After a momentary hesitation, Cassie stepped aside.

Krew's arm brushed against hers as he passed. His gaze swept the room, lingering on the fraying rug and the sparse furnishings. Cassie flushed, seeing it through his eyes. Though Krew had grown up in a home very similar to this one, that had been a long, long time ago.

For years, the NFL superstar had been living the high life. She bet Krew barely remembered what it was like to share one bathroom with the whole family or to eat meals in the living room because not everyone could fit around a card table.

His focus shifted to the laptop she'd set up in the living room on that ancient table. Reference books and a notepad took up the rest of the space on the peeling checkerboard-patterned top.

"Studying?"

"I hope to take the real estate licensing exam by the end of the year." Cassie couldn't keep the pride from her voice. Not only had she saved enough to purchase the online course, she'd made time to learn and study.

Back on track was what she'd told Dr. Gallagher at their last session.

"My mother's old boyfriend, Tim Vandercoy, has the top real estate firm on the peninsula," Cassie added when Krew sauntered over and picked up the study guide. "I'm hoping there will be a spot for me on his team once I get my license. But first, I have to pass the exam."

He set the guide down. "Sounds like a solid plan."

She shrugged, embarrassed but not sure why. "I don't talk about it much."

"I understand that."

"You do?"

"Getting drafted into the NFL was always my dream." His lips curved in a wry smile. "When I was a kid, nobody asked what I wanted to be when I grew up. They assumed I'd turn out just like my dad."

Cassie pulled her brows together. "But you were such a great ball player."

He glanced away. "Even when I showed promise on the field, most thought I'd flunk out of college and be one of those guys who talked incessantly about my high school glory days."

"You showed 'em."

"Yes. I did." His gaze returned to hers. "So will you."

Though she told herself his opinion didn't matter, Cassie couldn't stop the surge of pleasure. She dropped down on the sofa and motioned to a nearby chair.

"Where is everyone tonight?" He glanced around as he gingerly sat in the recliner with a broken spring.

"It's Fun Night at the Y. The older boys are good at letting me study, but Axl, not so much." She tried for casual, but her laugh reflected her rising nerves. Did he have the results of the DNA test? Was that why he was here? "By the time Axl finally goes to bed, I'm tired and it's hard to concentrate. But I'm making it work."

She was babbling, Cassie realized with sudden horror. "Anyway, what brings you by this evening?"

He cleared his throat. "I have the results."

Cassie's heart slammed against her rib cage. "And?"

"I'm Dakota's father."

She heard the pride in his voice, but there was something else, an emotion Cassie couldn't quite identify.

Cassie fought to find her voice. "No doubt?"

He laced his fingers together, then unlaced them. "None."

"Does she know?"

He shook his head, his gaze searching hers. "I wanted to tell you first."

"I appreciate that." Cassie realized that Krew just might be a nice guy.

"How do you think she'll react?" His voice came out raspy as he studied a strip of peeling wallpaper with keen interest.

Though his tone remained casual, she realized he was as unsure as she was about Dakota's reaction to the news.

"She'll be happy," Cassie said after a long moment. "She's always wanted a father. When she was little, she was always asking about her dad."

Krew flinched, then leaned forward, resting his forearms on his muscular thighs. His gaze never left her face. "What did you tell her?"

"I told her she was a wonderful, kind and smart girl and that I was sure she got some of those characteristics from her father." Cassie licked her lips. "But, unfortunately, I didn't know who he was."

Krew's expression turned skeptical. "She accepted that?"

"For a while." Cassie's heart ached as she recalled the many difficult conversations. "When she was twelve, she dug her birth certificate out of the box where I kept it at the top of my closet. On it, her father is listed as unknown. I found her crying in my room."

Cassie shifted her focus to a fraying thread on the sofa arm. "She never asked again."

"That had to be horrible." Krew scrubbed a hand across his face. "I'm going to make it up to her. And to you."

"Just you being here is enough." Cassie expelled a breath. "Now she'll have an answer."

"It isn't enough. Not by a long shot." His jaw set in a stubborn line. "I'm going to pay for her college."

"Absolutely not." Cassie's voice rose, then broke. Though panic clawed at her throat, she forced herself to steady. "It's not necessary. Once I get my license, I'll be able to help her more."

"Listen, I have more money than I know what to do with." His tone turned persuasive. "There's no reason she needs to wait to save up the money to go back to school. Or for you to take it out of what you need to support yourself and the boys."

"You can't just come here like Santa Claus and make everything right."

"I would think you'd be happy that her college costs are going to be covered." Instead of anger, confusion clouded his amber eyes.

"I don't know how to explain it." Cassie surged to her feet. She thrust her hands out in frustration. How could she explain a feeling she didn't understand herself? "Please, just don't say anything to Dakota about the college money. Not yet."

He moved to her, standing so close she could feel the warmth of his body. "If that's how you want it, I'll go along. For now."

"Thank you."

He placed his hands on her shoulders, looked her straight in the eyes. "I want to make it up to you, Cass. Not just to Dakota."

"You don't owe me anything." Cassie tried to smile, but her lips refused to cooperate.

"I do."

Cassie didn't have the energy to argue with him. "Telling Dakota is the first step. I'll let you know how she reacts, and we'll go from there."

A determined gleam filled his golden eyes. "We should tell her together."

"I think it's better—"

"It's best if I'm there, too." Apparently sensing her distress, he softened his tone. "I want to be in the room when you tell her, as much for your support as for hers."

Bone-weary, Cassie dropped back down on the sofa.

She didn't know what to think when he sat beside her.

"You don't have to go through this alone." His gaze met hers. "There's no need. I'm here now."

"For how long?" She glanced around the room, the bare-bones ugliness oddly reflective of her life for so many years. "When you leave, it'll be me who'll be left to pick up the pieces."

A muscle in his jaw jumped. "I promise I'll be here for Dakota. And for you."

He hadn't answered her question, but then, she hadn't expected he would.

"Dakota will be angry with me." Despite her resolve not to break down, tears filled her eyes. "She's going to think I somehow knew and that I kept you from her."

"We'll make sure—"

"How?" Her voice pitched high. Too high. "I don't want her knowing about Mitch. About all that drama."

"Don't worry." His arms slid around her, and he pressed a kiss against her temple. "It will be okay. I'll make it okay."

Cassie wanted to believe him. Dear God, she wanted to believe him.

But she couldn't let herself. There had been too many disappointments over the years for her to believe any man's promises.

CHAPTER SEVEN

"I'm so happy you called." Lindsay looked up from her salad and smiled at Cassie. "It's been too long since we had lunch together."

Cassie absently stabbed a piece of endive with her fork. As soon as Krew left last night, she'd reached out to her sister and made plans to meet her at Muddy Boots.

"There's something I want to discuss with you." Cassie set down her fork, no longer able to pretend interest in food. "I hope you can help me."

Concern furrowed Lindsay's brow. "Absolutely. Tell me what you need."

"First, I want to thank you."

A startled look crossed Lindsay's face. "For what?"

"For not writing me off despite all the stupid stuff I've done." Cassie felt her cheeks warm. "Despite my many mistakes, you've always been there for me and my kids."

"I love you, Cass." Lindsay reached across the table and squeezed her hand. "And I love my niece and nephews. Tell me what's troubling you. I want to help."

Cassie licked her suddenly dry lips. "You know how I said I didn't know the identity of Dakota's father?"

Surprise flickered in her sister's eyes. This conversation was obviously headed down a path Lindsay hadn't foreseen. She nodded.

Cassie took a deep breath and began by explaining everything that had happened between her and Mitch.

Lindsay winced. "The rumors back then were that her dad was Mitch Peskin. Please tell me he's not."

"No. I thought he was, but…" Cassie squared her shoulders. "Her father is Krew Slattery."

Lindsay's mouth dropped open. "You're kidding me."

"Nope." Cassie picked up her fork, needing something to do with her hands. "A DNA test confirmed it."

"Wow." Lindsay sat back in the Muddy Boots booth. "I didn't know you'd ever, ah, been with him. I mean, Mom heard rumors you'd kissed him. I thought that's as far as it went."

Cassie's lips lifted in a wry smile. "It started with a kiss. It went a whole lot further."

"Obviously." Lindsay's quick burst of laughter eased the tension. "What does Dakota think of all this?"

Cassie's heart began to flutter. "Dakota knows it's a possibility but not that the results are back."

Lindsay's gaze remained fixed on Cassie. "How do you feel about Krew being her father?"

"I'm glad it's him and not Mitch."

"I agree. I can see why you never said anything about Mitch. I never liked the man. After hearing how he treated you, I really can't stand him." Lindsay's soft pink lips curled in a sneer. "Low-life scum."

"Slopsucker," Cassie added.

"I like that one." Lindsay grinned. "A lot."

The sisters exchanged a smile.

Cassie cleared her throat. "What do you think about having Krew there when I tell Dakota?"

Lindsay took a sip of iced tea. Her brows pulled together in thought. "I think that'd be a good idea. If she has questions of how this will look going forward, both of you will be there."

Cassie fought an urge to sigh. That's what she thought her sister would say.

"Krew wants to pay for her college."

Lindsay's eyes went wide. "Why, Cass, that's wonderful. Dakota will be able to—" Her sister paused as if sensing something amiss. "It...isn't wonderful?"

This time, Cassie did sigh. "What if Dakota sees his money and how easy life would be with him and it makes her turn away from me even more?"

"I don't think that will happen."

The fact that her sister didn't sound completely convinced only fueled Cassie's insecurities.

"I've been really trying, Lin, trying to be a better role model, trying to get my life together to help the kids, and I feel like I'm so close. But Krew, he can come in and take away everything just like that. And if he does, then what's the point of all my work? How am I any different from the fifteen-year-old girl he used and left? From the girl Mitch called stupid and worthless? From the woman who let Clint, a predator, get dangerously close to her child."

Simply voicing her deepest fears brought a hollow feeling to Cassie's gut.

"Speak of the devil." Lindsay's gaze flickered to the door, then back to her sister. "If you don't want to talk to Krew now, I'll tell him we're having a meeting."

Cassie didn't have the opportunity to respond. She barely had time to breathe before Krew was beside the table, the citrusy scent of his cologne teasing her nostrils.

She looked up, and her traitorous lips curved automatically. "Hey."

"Hi." Looking more gorgeous than a man had a right to look in a green sweater and jeans, he shifted his gaze and widened that heart-stopping smile to include Lindsay. "How are you, Lindsay?"

"I'm good. Just discussing some flower business with my sister." Lindsay gestured to her barely touched plate. "And enjoying some lunch."

"I don't want to interrupt…"

When he looked at her, Cassie knew she had only to echo Lindsay's words to have him walk away. But chatting with Lindsay had solidified her next step in Cassie's mind.

Cassie scooted over, making room beside her in the booth. "Lindsay and I are just finishing up. Why don't you join us?"

His gaze shifted to Lindsay.

"I promise. We don't bite." Her sister flashed him a saucy smile. "At least, I don't. I can't speak for Cassie."

Krew laughed and slid in beside Cassie. By the time Krew's food was delivered, Lindsay had even come up with a few floral-related questions for her. Then she made her exit. But only after meeting Cassie's gaze in a steady one that said, *You got this. You can do it.*

"I hope I didn't cut your meeting short." Krew took a big bite of burger, his gaze searching hers.

"I was planning to call you."

He cocked his head.

"You were right. We should tell Dakota together." Cassie took a breath and let it out. "I also think we need to tell the boys together."

Krew took a long drink of soda. His dark brows pulled slightly together, as if he were dissecting a playbook. "You're right. It's a family thing. I should have thought of that."

"Sometimes, parenting takes two heads." The words came so easily, but were so unfamiliar that they gave Cassie pause.

The quick flash of his smile warmed Cassie's heart.

"We should do it soon."

Krew nodded as he skimmed a fry across a mound of ketchup.

"Dakota texted me three times this morning, asking about the results."

Cassie tapped the table in thought. "I work from one to five. I know Dakota was helping her grandmother earlier this morning, but she isn't working today. We could meet with her now, then tell the boys tonight."

"I'll bring pizza tonight. But do you have time to speak with Dakota before work? It's almost noon now." He gestured to her nearly full plate. "You've barely touched your lunch."

Cassie pushed the salad aside. "I'm not hungry."

"What if Dakota wants to spend time with you after she finds out?"

"If there's anyone she'll want to spend time with afterwards, it'll be you." Cassie chewed on her bottom lip. "If she does need me, I'll call in."

Krew pulled out his phone. "Where and when?"

Cassie thought quickly. Someplace private. Someplace close. Somewhere they wouldn't be disturbed. "Your place?"

Minutes later, she and Krew strode down the block to the Sweet Dreams motel to meet Dakota.

Feeling conspicuous, Cassie stood off to the side of the door while Krew pulled out his key. Before he could open the door, Mavis Rosekranz stepped out of a unit several doors down.

The proprietress was a portly woman, almost as wide as she was tall, with tightly permed gray hair and a ready smile. She offered that smile now, but Cassie saw the speculation in her gaze.

Cassie waved, grateful when Krew opened the door and she could step inside.

The room, spacious with a homey, country décor, had been completely renovated just last year. This unit even had a fireplace.

Krew turned on the lights, started a fire then opened the curtains. Sunlight streamed in through the windowpane, but it didn't do much to warm the chill that wrapped around Cassie like a straitjacket.

How would Dakota respond? Would she be angry? Would she understand that her mom had never meant to hurt her?

"Hey." Krew moved to her, his hands sliding up and down her arms. "Don't worry. She'll understand."

Before Cassie could respond, a knock sounded.

Here we go, Cassie thought.

"This is a crazy place to meet." Dakota unwound the scarf from her neck. "You should have seen the look Mavis gave me—"

Only then did Dakota notice Cassie. Her gaze darted from Krew to her mother. The look in her daughter's eyes when they met hers tore at Cassie's heart.

"Well, you're here, so it's true, then." Dakota took her time hanging her jacket and scarf on the metal coat stand. "Krew is my father. All this time, and you never told me—"

"No. I mean, yes. Krew is your father, but I didn't tell you—or him—because I didn't know." When Dakota clasped her hands together to still their trembling, Cassie's heart lurched.

"How could you not know? What kind of woman doesn't know which guy got her pregnant?" Dakota stalked to the window, then whirled. "All I know is I've had to suffer all my life because my mother was some kind of slu—"

"Enough." Krew's voice slashed the air, startling Dakota into silence. "This is your mom. She did her best, and you owe her respect."

Cassie inhaled sharply at Krew's defense of her. She'd never had that before.

Dakota's gold eyes, so much like her father's—Cassie could see that clearly now—pierced the air between them. She cocked her head. "Oh, and did you respect her when you slept with her and left?"

A muscle in Krew's jaw jumped. "I would have been there for you both if I'd known."

"Then why weren't you? Did you even check to see if she'd gotten pregnant?" Dakota's laugh contained no humor. "Or did you just have your fun and never look back?"

It was so close to the truth that there was nothing Krew could say.

Dakota crossed to the fireplace as if the tumult of emotions wouldn't allow her to remain still for long. Placing a hand on the mantel, she heaved a sigh. "That's what I thought."

"We were kids, Dakota." Cassie took a step toward her daughter. "Both of us were younger than you are now. Krew and I, well, we made mistakes."

Tears filled Dakota's eyes. "I wanted a dad so much."

"I know you did, and I'm sorry." Cassie took another step forward, wanting to comfort her.

"Don't." Dakota held up a hand even as tears slipped down her cheeks.

"What's important isn't what we didn't know then, but what we do know now." Krew cleared his throat. He appeared calm, but the way the fingers of his right hand clenched and released told a different story. "I'm here now, and I'd like to get to know both of you better."

"Oh, so we're just going to pretend to be a family now?" Dakota asked sarcastically. She gestured with one hand, encompassing the beautiful room. "Pretend we're normal?"

"I don't know about you, but none of the families I know are normal." Krew's joking expression turned serious. "Besides, we won't be pretending. We *are* a family."

For a long moment, the only sound came from the wood crackling in the fireplace. When Dakota's gaze narrowed on her, Cassie managed a tiny smile.

"Is that what you want?" Dakota asked.

Cassie decided that was a question best sidestepped. "I want you to get to know your father. And for him to get to know all of us better. Not just you and me, but the boys, too. We're a unit."

Indecision skittered across Dakota's face.

Cassie knew how much her daughter had wanted to know her dad. Now that Krew was here, she was scared. Scared to love. Afraid of being hurt.

"Where we go from here is up to you, Dakota." Cassie kept her tone even. "Just tell us what you want."

CHAPTER EIGHT

Cassie was driving home shortly before six, tired and frustrated. When she'd left work, snow was falling and it had taken her three times to get the car started. When the engine finally had turned over, it had wheezed and coughed like a smoker who'd just run a 5K.

It wasn't the car or the crazy afternoon that had her on edge. She was worried about Dakota. Her daughter had a tough outer shell but a gooey center. Finding out that Krew was her father had rocked her world.

Cassie wished she could have done more to comfort her, to reassure Dakota that she and her brothers would continue to be there for her.

As Axl continued to throw brightly colored foam cars at the back of her head, Cassie pulled to a stop in their driveway. She shut off the ignition, and the car belched before it shuddered, then stilled.

"I wanna get out," Axl called out as he rocked up and down in his seat like a caged gorilla.

"In a minute." Cassie needed just a few seconds to steady herself for the ordeal ahead.

"Want out." Axl called from the backseat before a blue car sailed by her ear.

"No more cars for you." With a sigh, Cassie pushed open the door. She released Axl from the binds of his car seat and watched him race toward the front door.

The driveway ran alongside the house. Neither it nor the walkway had been cleared of the recent snowfall, so her feet—and his—were soaked by the time she pushed open the slightly ajar front door.

"The door was open," she called out, grabbing Axl so she could remove his shoes.

"What's the problem?" Braxton stepped out from the bedroom and stifled a yawn.

"You left the door open. Not just unlocked. Open." When he continued to stare blankly at her, she continued. "Anyone could have walked in."

"Oh, sorry." He yawned again.

"Were you sleeping?"

At his nod, she narrowed her gaze. What teenage boy took a nap in the afternoon? "Are you feeling okay?"

"I feel fine." He swung Axl high into the air, and the boy who'd been whining and sour-faced seconds before dissolved in giggles. "I stayed up late building a website for one of the teachers last night."

"Why would a teacher need a website?"

"She has a side business selling some kind of oils." Braxton shrugged. "Easy money. I'm happy. She's happy."

Familiar guilt sluiced through her. She'd never had to work in high school. Her boys had started mowing lawns at twelve. They'd had to work if they wanted anything beyond the basics. "Where's your brother?"

Braxton plopped down on the sofa and flipped on the television. "Which one?"

Cassie rolled her eyes. "Well, since two are right in my field of vision, who is it you think I mean?"

"K.T. is at school. He's working on another art project. Don't ask me which one or what for, they all mash together." Braxton's gaze remained riveted on the television. "He should be home any time."

"I want you to turn off the TV and pick up this room. We're having company tonight." When he didn't immediately comply, Cassie used her "mom voice." "Now, Braxton."

Her eldest son hit the off button on the remote and slowly turned his head. "Who's the company?"

"Krew Slattery."

Braxton frowned. "I thought you were swearing off guys for a while."

"It's not like that between Krew and me." Despite the protest, Cassie felt heat rise up her neck.

Not for the first time, she cursed her tendency to blush.

"What is it like, then?" His eyes were filled with a familiar watchful waiting.

"He's not my boyfriend, Brax. He's—"

The door flew open and K.T. burst in, snow dusting the top of his dark head. He dropped his book bag to the floor. "Someone left the door unlocked."

"Mom was last inside." Braxton turned to his brother. "We're having company for dinner. Krew Slattery."

"Your sister will be here, too."

"I thought you were done with men." K.T. strode past her to the refrigerator and peered inside, assessing the meager contents. "I hope he's bringing food."

"I *am* still off men," Cassie insisted. "And we're having pizza. Krew is bringing it."

A knock coming at that particular moment seemed fitting, considering the way her day was going.

Even though the door was unlocked and any criminal could

just push their way inside, Cassie made a show of looking through the peep before opening the door.

"I'll be back." Krew shoved two large pizza boxes into her hands. "I've got soda in the car."

At the enticing aroma emanating from the boxes, K.T. shut the refrigerator door. Like a hound that caught a scent, he made a beeline for his mother.

Before Krew even made it to his car, each boy had a box in his hands.

"I want." Axl jumped in the air, but Braxton lifted the box he held just out of reach.

"Here." K.T. stacked his box on top of Braxton's, then made quick work of clearing off the rickety card table.

"Bayside Pizza." Braxton read the logo on the top box as he set the pizzas on the table.

"Their pies are the best." K.T. blocked Axl's grabbing hands. "You need to wait."

Braxton must have felt no such compunction, because he opened the top box and was reaching inside when Cassie slapped *his* hand away. "I need you to get plates, glasses and napkins. Enough for everyone, including your sister."

K.T. shifted his gaze from Axl. "Dakota is coming?"

"I said she was." Sometimes Cassie had the feeling only fifty percent of what she said got through.

"We don't eat pizza off plates," Braxton protested.

"We do tonight." Cassie's hard-eyed stare had both boys muttering on the short distance to the kitchen.

Krew returned with a two-liter bottle of Dr Pepper in one hand and Coke in the other. "I don't know what everyone likes, so I got one of each."

Cassie took the bottles from him. "You didn't have to bring dinner."

"Yeah, he did. There wouldn't have been anything to eat

otherwise." Braxton dumped a fistful of mismatched silverware on the table.

"Someone left the door unlocked," Dakota called out as she stepped into the craziness.

She looked better, Cassie saw with relief. Though her daughter's eyes were red-rimmed, Dakota had applied fresh makeup and even curled her hair.

Minutes later, the plates sat unused on the table—well, other than by Axl—while the rest of them used paper towels and ate with their hands instead of silverware.

"Mom told us she wasn't going to bring any more guys around." K.T. reached for his third slice. "But you can come around anytime you want."

"*If* you bring pizza." Braxton was on his fourth slice. "But ditch the hamburger."

"Yeah," K.T. piped up. "We like pepperoni best."

"Boys." Cassie's voice was sharper than it needed to be. But, darn it, she didn't like the feeling she'd just been sold out for a couple of pizzas. "I told you that isn't why Krew is here."

"Is he *your* boyfriend?" K.T. asked his sister.

"Yeah, are you dating old guys now?" As he spoke, Braxton wiped sauce from Axl's face with a crumpled paper towel.

Dakota, who'd been quiet all through dinner, lowered her slice of pizza, her gaze focused on her brothers. "He's not my date. He's my dad."

Braxton's fingers opened, and the soiled paper towel fluttered to the floor.

K.T. choked on a bite of pizza.

Cassie slapped him on the back and handed him the bottle of Coke.

Her middle son drank straight from the bottle, sputtering when he was finally able to catch his breath.

Only Axl remained oblivious. The child was too focused on

pulling the pepperoni from the top of his slice to notice the sudden tension in the room.

Braxton's gaze shifted from Krew to Dakota. "Seriously?"

Dakota nodded. "DNA confirmed it."

"You didn't say anything to me about doing any test." Braxton turned to K.T. "Did she say anything to you?"

K.T. slowly lowered the bottle of Coke he held now in a death grip and slowly shook his head.

Braxton leveled his blue-green eyes on Cassie. "You said you didn't know who Dakota's father was. That's what you told us. That's what you told Grandma."

Though his voice remained calm and controlled, Cassie heard the accusation...and the hurt.

"I didn't know," she told her sons, but saw they didn't believe her.

Braxton turned to Krew. "You knew she was your daughter and you're only now coming around?"

The controlled anger that had been leveled at her only seconds before was now directed at Krew.

"Lay off him, Braxton," Dakota said.

"I didn't know." Krew held up his hands. "I'd like to think if I had known, I'd have been there for her. I hope I would have been."

The honesty in his response must have hit a chord with Braxton, because those eyes, so like her own, returned to her.

Braxton jerked a thumb in Krew's direction. "Is he our dad, too? Are you guys a couple now?"

Cassie knew he was referring to him and K.T., because they were all too aware that Clint was the father of Axl. "No, to both questions."

Braxton's face remained expressionless as he nodded.

K.T. shrugged. "Good. Having an old man around to boss us sucks."

In that moment, Cassie's heart shattered. She knew her sons

well enough to see through their tough-guy facades. They wanted a dad, too.

Not one like Clint, but one like Krew.

Dakota had hit the jackpot, while they were left behind with just Cassie and the memory of too many men who didn't care about them or about her.

"I want Krew to be a part of my life," Dakota told her brothers. "You know, holidays and all that stuff. Having him be a part of my life means he'll be a part of yours, too. I need to know if that's cool with you guys."

The boys exchanged glances.

"I know this is a shock," Cassie said to them. "It was for me, and for Krew and your sister, too. I want you to know that I meant what I said. I'm focused on our family now, not on men." She cast a quick glance at Krew, who gave a slight nod as if to reassure her he understood. "Like Dakota said, Krew is part of our family now. It's important for me to know if you're okay with that. You don't have to decide right now—"

"We get it, Mom." Braxton responded without looking at either Cassie or Krew.

"Are you planning to move back to Good Hope?" K.T. asked Krew, his expression curious.

"No, but I plan to visit often." Krew cleared his throat. "Would you guys be okay with me coming around, maybe spending holidays with all of you?"

Cassie held her breath. Though Krew had kept his tone light, she sensed their response mattered to him.

She wished she could reassure him that her sons would be fine with him being around for those events, but the truth was she didn't know.

Would they be happy for their sister and open to getting to know Krew? Or would he simply be a reminder of all they lacked in their own lives?

"I'm okay with it." Braxton lifted a shoulder.

"Fine with me." K.T. glanced at Dakota. "If it's what you want."

Dakota slanted a glance at Krew and smiled shyly. "It's what I want."

"Anyone want more Coke?" K.T. lifted the bottle.

"Not after you slobbered into it," Braxton said with such aplomb, they all laughed.

Too restless to sit any longer, Cassie pushed up from the chair.

"I need to get Axl ready for bed." Cassie pointed to her sons. "You two are on cleanup duty. I expect everything to be put away."

Cassie glanced at Dakota. "Your only chore is to relax and keep Krew company."

But when Cassie returned from the bedroom she shared with Axl's crib, her daughter was gone.

"Where's Dakota?"

"She's working the early shift at Muddy Boots tomorrow." Krew's tone was a little too casual. "She wanted to stay and say good-bye, but—"

"I understand," Cassie said quickly. "It's been an emotional day for her."

"We're done." K.T. tossed the dish towel on top of the rack of plates in the drainer.

"Before you ask, I took out the garbage," Braxton told her.

"Thank you." Cassie let her gaze slide from Braxton to K.T. "Both of you. For everything."

"C'mon, K.T." Braxton started toward the bedroom they shared. "You've got to see this cool new game I downloaded."

"Don't you have something to say to Krew?" Cassie asked.

For a second, both boys looked puzzled.

Then Braxton grinned. "Thanks for the pizza."

"Yeah," K.T. added. "Thanks. Just next time ditch the hamburger."

"K.T." Cassie slapped a hand against her forehead.

Krew only grinned and pushed to his feet. "Time for me to leave."

Cassie walked him to the door, not sure whether she felt relieved or disappointed. It had to be relief. This had been a long, emotional day for everyone.

"Thanks for letting me come tonight."

"Thank you for the pizza."

He waved away the thanks and rubbed his jaw. "It's been a long time since I felt a part of a family. The fact that you and Dakota want to share yours with me means a lot."

"Despite what they said, I think the boys were disappointed you aren't their father."

"They're great kids, Cass. You've done a good job."

She shrugged.

"Hey." He tipped her chin up. "Take the credit. You earned it."

She gazed into the liquid blue depths of his eyes, and the warmth and the admiration reflected there took her by surprise. Cassie couldn't remember the last time any man had looked at her that way. If ever.

Their eyes locked, and she couldn't look away.

When Krew lowered his head and kissed her softly on the mouth, it felt so natural that the thought of pulling away didn't occur to her.

His lips lingered an extra beat before he gave her arm a squeeze, then stepped outside, leaving her wondering what had just happened.

With a quiet laugh and a disbelieving shake of her head, Cassie shut the door and locked it.

CHAPTER NINE

The following Friday, Krew found himself once again on Cassie's front stoop. When she unlocked the door and pushed it open, he lifted his hands. "No pizza. I hope I'm still welcome."

"We have something even better on the menu this evening." Cassie stepped aside to let him enter.

Was it only his imagination, or did her gaze linger on his mouth for an extra beat?

Over the years, Krew had kissed a lot of women, but feeling Cassie's lips move beneath his last Saturday had been a heady experience. He told himself it'd be best if he didn't kiss her again. Not only because of their history, but because he wouldn't be staying in Good Hope.

Still, there was something about her…

"Krew." Dakota surged up from the sofa, a broad smile lifting her lips. "You came."

"Hey, Dakota." Krew crossed the room, unsure how to interact with a grown-up daughter. Should he give her a hug? He decided to push it.

When Dakota had invited him over for dinner and family game night, he'd jumped at the chance. He wouldn't be in Good

Hope long, and he wanted to take advantage of any opportunity to get to know Dakota and her siblings better.

"It's ready to be strained, bro." Exasperation filled K.T.'s tone as it filtered into the living room.

"I set the timer on my phone." Braxton's voice remained calm. "It needs to boil another minute."

"Just taste it," K.T. urged.

"Get away. I'm making dinner, not you."

Krew glanced at Cassie, who was setting out silverware and mismatched bowls on the card table. She must have felt him looking, because she looked up and smiled.

Tonight, her blond hair was pulled back in a low ponytail and secured by a sparkly clip. Black leggings hugged her slender thighs, and the tunic top, with a bold geometric pattern, accentuated her willowy frame.

He'd spotted her boots and socks on the rug just inside the front door. Despite the cold outside, she was barefoot. Her feet were as long and slender as the rest of her, with brightly painted red nails that matched the color on her lips.

"We'll eat in the living room." Dakota's voice came from beside him. "I hope you don't mind."

Krew heard the hesitation in his daughter's voice, and he realized she was as unsure as he was about how to navigate this new relationship.

"Fine with me." Krew pulled his attention from Cassie. "I eat most of my meals on the sofa."

The relieved look that crossed Dakota's face had him relaxing.

Axl tugged on his hand. "I picked tonight."

Krew studied the small boy, who wore carpenter jeans with a plastic hammer hanging from one loop and a Spider-Man shirt. "What did you pick?"

"I picked tonight," the boy shouted, as if saying the words louder would make what he said clearer.

REUNITED IN GOOD HOPE | 85

"Axl chose tonight's meal." Cassie scooped the boy up in the air, making him giggle. "It's something we all like."

"What are we having?" Krew asked. Based on the argument he'd overheard, it sounded like some sort of pasta.

That was okay with him. He'd rarely encountered a pasta dish he didn't love.

"Mac and cheese," Axl answered from his perch in his mother's arms.

"Not just mac and cheese." Dakota's eyes twinkled. "What else?"

"Fish." The boy hissed the word as if he were snake.

Krew frowned, not sure he'd heard correctly. "Fish?"

"Food is ready." Braxton sauntered into the room, a stainless-steel pot in one hand, a serving spoon in the other. He began dishing pasta straight out of the pan into the bowls.

"It's milk for all." K.T. filled the glasses from a plastic gallon container.

"Sit down. I'll get yours," Dakota said to Krew, then hurried to the table.

"Having you here means a lot to her." Cassie spoke in a low tone obviously meant for his ears only.

"How often do you do this?"

"Eat?" A dimple Krew had never seen before flashed in Cassie's left cheek. "Every night. But family, food and fun happens once a month. We take turns picking our favorite food for dinner, and then we play a game or two."

Krew was surprised the older boys and even Dakota still wanted to participate, especially on a Friday night. As a teenager, he'd made it a point to stay away from home as much as possible.

"Here you go." Dakota handed him a bowl of what he recognized as the macaroni he'd loved as a kid. Heck, still loved.

As Krew glanced down, he noticed something else in the bowl. "What's in here?"

"Tuna fish," Dakota said.

"Cream of mushroom soup," Cassie added. "It's delicious."

Krew's stomach did a slow roll. He hated everything about tuna...and mushrooms.

"If you don't like it, we might have something else in the refrigerator." The distress on Dakota's face was reflected in her eyes.

"It looks good." Krew offered a reassuring smile. "I've just never heard of that combination before."

K.T. shoved a plastic tumbler of milk into Krew's hand. "Mac and tuna is a family favorite. Welcome to the family, bro."

A half hour later, Krew gave thanks that the family favorite wasn't as horrible as he'd imagined. He'd been able to eat it, thanks to milk chasers. The day-old cookies Cassie had brought home from the Grind helped get rid of the lingering tuna taste.

Despite the food, these were his kind of people. He was at home sitting on a sofa with his food on a metal TV tray in front of him. He always felt out of his element in houses with silver and china and three different kinds of forks.

The conversation flowed easily, and by the time Cassie and Dakota cleared the dishes, Krew had completely relaxed.

They played a quick game of Sneaky, Snacky Squirrel with Axl before Cassie put her youngest to bed.

Krew assumed that was the end of game night, but he was wrong.

"Are you familiar with The Game of Things?" Braxton asked.

"I haven't played many board games."

"This is more like a card game. We didn't want to buy it, so we made up one that has similar rules, but with our own questions." Braxton went on to explain how the game worked.

Krew listened intently, his competitive spirit never far from the surface. "Let me see if I understand. The person who is 'it' makes a statement. Everyone writes their response on a piece of paper. The person who is 'it' reads the answers, then we go around and guess who gave each answer. I get one point if I guess correctly. The person whose answer was guessed—"

"It's easy. You'll pick it up as we go." Clearly ready to get started, K.T. began passing out scraps of paper.

"He's never played before, K.T. Give the guy a break." Dakota shot him a reassuring smile.

Though Krew had no trouble standing up for himself, he realized Cassie had raised a compassionate daughter.

The game began. They went through several questions, laughing over the ridiculous answers, razzing each other when an answer was easily matched to the person.

"My turn." Dakota tapped a finger against her lips. "I've got one. Things Mom shouldn't show to my prom date."

"Awww, Dakota." Braxton rolled his eyes. "You know K.T. and I aren't into prom."

"I've never gone, either, Braxton." Cassie offered her sons an encouraging smile. "But I can still imagine what I wouldn't want my mom to show my date."

Krew had gone to prom both his junior and senior years. Though the dances had never been a big deal to him, attending seemed almost a rite of passage.

He glanced at Cassie, who was busily writing on her scrap of paper. An unaccustomed lump formed in his throat. Learning she hadn't gone to prom was another reminder of how his careless actions had changed her life forever.

Beside him, Dakota was busily writing something down. Her life, too, was far different than it could have been.

As Krew scribbled an answer on his paper, he vowed to redouble his efforts to make it up to his daughter and to Cassie.

By the time the game ended, it was close to eleven. The boys headed to the room they shared, leaving Krew alone with Cassie and Dakota.

"This was fun." Dakota glanced from her mother to Krew. "It was how I always imagined it would be if I had a dad."

Krew thought about mentioning that family game night was something her mother had thought up and instituted. But he stopped himself just in time, not wanting to spoil the moment.

Dakota gazed down at her hands for a second before looking up. "I wonder what you two would think about maybe doing this again. You know, getting all of us together. Having dinner together most nights and do things."

Krew exchanged a glance with Cassie. "Sounds good to me."

Cassie inclined her head. "What exactly are you asking?"

Two bright swaths of color stained Dakota's cheeks. "I just think it'd be nice to experience what it's like to be part of a family —a real family—with both a mom and a dad, for just a little while."

"I won't be returning to Green Bay until after the first of the year. We've got a couple months." Krew kept his tone easy and conversational.

Dakota's smile faded.

"You'll probably be back in college by then, anyway." Krew stopped himself from saying more when he caught Cassie's sharp glance.

"Maybe." Dakota looked doubtful. "I'm not sure I can get enough money together by second semester."

Dakota's eyes shifted to her mother. "I realize the two of you aren't close, but I'd like it if you could both set aside your feelings and do this for me."

Krew glanced at Cassie. "I'm game."

As if realizing the ball was in her court, Cassie smiled. "When do you want to start?"

A week later, Cassie was still coming to terms with the fact that Krew was Dakota's father. For so many years she'd been convinced it was Mitch who fathered her firstborn. Mitch, who'd refused to take any responsibility, who'd threatened to trash her reputation even further if she "tried to pin the baby on him."

Her only worry now was her attraction to Krew.

A session earlier this week with Dr. Gallagher had Cassie voicing her fears. What if spending time around Krew awakened old feelings? She'd worked so hard to finally feel independent, but one brief kiss had made her yearn for more. How could she risk falling for a man—even a potentially good one—again?

Dr. Gallagher reminded her of the gains she'd made in the last year. She was strong. Being aware of potential pitfalls would make it easier to avoid them.

Though she wasn't a coward, Cassie was thankful she was scheduled to work tomorrow when Krew invited her and the boys to go snowmobiling with him and Dakota. Earlier in the week, Krew and all her children had put on snowshoes and gone hiking at Peninsula State Park. She'd been working that day, too.

As she wasn't on the schedule and had already turned down two invitations, Cassie accepted Krew's request to meet to establish some ground rules for what their lives would look like going forward.

Her hands were steady as she rapped on the heavy wooden door of the home Krew had rented for the next two months on Millionaire's Row. A gust of wind off the bay cut through the thin fabric of her coat. She knocked again, wrapping her arms tightly around her body as she turned to block the frigid air.

The door swung open, and Krew motioned to her. "Come in. It's freezing out there."

Blessed warmth wrapped around Cassie like a towel fresh out of the dryer the instant she stepped over the threshold. The first thing Cassie noticed was that this home was as beautiful on the inside as it was from the road.

Gleaming hardwood floors. A gorgeous staircase with balusters and newel posts in white and the handrail in gleaming walnut.

A fire burned in the hearth. A delicious scent she recognized as applewood filled the air.

Krew held out a hand. "May I take your coat?"

His easy tone belied his watchful eyes.

Cassie shrugged out of the simple tan coat. When she was hurrying to make her early shift at the coffee shop, she'd noticed a button was loose. Now the button was gone, only a few threads marking the spot where it had been.

"You look nice."

She knew he offered the compliment to fill the awkward silence. The leggings were old, but they fit her slender frame like a glove. The ski sweater was relatively new, a birthday gift from her mother.

Cassie cleared her throat. "Thank you."

He looked amazing in a brown sweater that made his eyes look like polished amber.

"I made coffee." He gestured to a tray with mugs and a carafe sitting on a table between the sofa and an oversized chair.

She hesitated for a second, oddly touched by the gesture.

As if misunderstanding her silence, he quickly added, "Unless, after working all day at the Grind, you're sick of the stuff."

"Actually, we're so busy I don't often get a chance to sit down and enjoy a cup." She offered a tentative smile. "I'd love some."

This wasn't a date, Cassie reminded herself. There was no reason to feel jittery.

She sat on the sofa and took a long drink of coffee, noticing the muscle jumping in Krew's jaw. She realized with a kind of startled amazement that he was equally uncomfortable.

"I agree with Dakota. It'd be nice if we could be friends." His gaze searched hers. "But I get the feeling that isn't what you want."

Cassie set down her mug. "It isn't that I don't want that. It's just my feelings for you are complicated. I tell myself to move on. Leave the past in the past, but—"

"You can't." His voice was flat, and she saw disappointment in the golden depths of his eyes.

"I wouldn't say I can't." Cassie fumbled for words. "Maybe it's just because I have questions that keep me from moving forward."

She expelled a frustrated breath. None of this was coming out the way she wanted.

"The questions." He studied her face. "Are they ones I can answer?"

She nodded.

"Ask, then, whatever you want."

He'd given her the opening, and she would take it. Cassie twined her hands together in her lap. "After...after we made—" She stopped herself. "After we had sex on the beach, why did you ignore me?"

Even now, remembering how he'd turned his back on her brought an ache to her heart. She'd been young and innocent. He'd been the first guy she'd ever kissed. That had been as far as she'd intended to let him go. But she and her mother had fought that night, and her emotions had been in a tangle. Then his hands and his lips had ignited a fire in her and...

"I regret how I acted that night. More than you'll ever know."

Cassie winced, but Krew didn't appear to notice.

He surged to his feet, moving to the front window, a large expanse of glass that afforded a perfect view of the bay.

Cassie joined him, keeping a couple of feet between them. She stared at water that was as gray as the sky. The night they'd made love, the sky had been clear. The gentlest of breezes had kept the bugs away.

For years, Cassie had considered what she'd say to Krew if she had the chance. He'd taken her virginity, then cast her aside as if she were a piece of trash.

"If you regret it so much, why did you kiss me in the first place, much less have sex with me?"

She braced herself for the words *because you were there.* Or maybe a variation, like *the girl I really wanted wasn't there that night, so I thought you would do.*

Instead, he surprised her.

"All during my senior year, there was something about you." He shoved his hands into his pockets. "I'd see you in the halls, or in the bleachers, and I couldn't look away."

Krew gave a harsh bark of a laugh. "This will probably sound crazy, but I felt this connection between us."

"I felt it, too," Cassie admitted, almost to herself.

When his head jerked up, she realized he'd heard.

"That summer after graduation, I was on the verge of starting a new life. I was going to college. Me. The son of the town drunk. Because of my skill on the football field, I'd been given a chance to succeed in life." He turned and faced her. "I couldn't let anything—or anyone—get in my way."

"You could have said that to me." Cassie cursed the crack in her voice. She took a breath to steady her rioting nerves, and when she spoke again, the tremor was gone. "I'd have understood."

"I wanted you even more after that night." Krew spread his hands, palms down, and simply gazed at them. When he looked up, she saw the regret. "I liked you so much. But I was leaving in a few weeks. It seemed smart to keep my distance and ignore your calls and emails. I'm sorry. I realize now that the only one I was thinking of was myself."

Cassie found surprising comfort in the explanation. She returned to the sofa and poured more coffee into a mug that was nearly full.

His gaze searched her face as he took a seat in a nearby chair. "Are we cool?"

Cassie lifted the mug to her lips and took a sip. "We're cool. I appreciate you being honest."

Nodding, Krew dropped into a nearby chair.

"Dakota has enjoyed our outings this week, but she said she wants to experience what it's like having both a mother and father...together. I'm trying to make that happen." He flashed a smile. "Your job is making that difficult."

"I can't stop working—"

"Hey, just kidding. I understand you have to work." His expression softened. "I only wish you could have been with us. We had a great time. The boys are smart and fun to be around. I like watching Dakota with them."

"She's a wonderful big sister." Cassie let the heat from the cup warm her hands. "They—*we* really missed her when she went off to college."

He drank more coffee, but his gaze remained on her face. "Does the boys' dad come around much?"

"Not at all. Eugene left when I was pregnant with K.T. I found out later he was married and had another family back East. He pays child support, but wants nothing to do with his sons." Shame rose inside her as if this man's shortcomings were her own. Well, in a way they were, Cassie supposed.

She'd fallen for his lies and his promises. Yet, she'd come out of that dark period with two amazing sons. "Gene was older—in his late thirties at the time—and incredibly intelligent. He was in the area working on a habitat restoration project that dealt with reconstructing some islands in the lower bay. I lived with him for over two years."

"Did you love him?"

She had to think about that for a minute. "I thought I did at the time, but looking back, I'd say no. I wasn't even twenty. Gene offered stability, and he was kind to me. He made enough money that I could stay home with Dakota and then with Braxton. Then the project ended, and he left even though I was pregnant with his second son. All he told me was I wasn't what he wanted. I found out later he was married the whole time."

She waited for Krew to ask how she couldn't have known that

someone she was living with had had another life. Quite simply, she'd trusted him. "I think his leaving was, for me, the beginning of a self-destructive downward slide that lasted way too long."

"You had so much potential." The second the words left his mouth, he started to backpedal. "I'm sorry, I—"

"Don't apologize. It's what everyone thinks, but doesn't say."

"Dakota mentioned Axl's dad is Clint Gourley."

Cassie froze. It took her a moment to find her voice. "What else did she say about Clint?"

"She doesn't like the guy."

"Trust me. There isn't much to like." Cassie relaxed, just a little. "Hooking up with Clint was the worst mistake I ever made. The former men in my life are just that...former. You won't have to deal with them. Though being a part of Dakota's life means you *will* have to deal with Lindsay and Owen. And my mother."

"Owen and I are buds. We go way back. And I like Lindsay." Krew leaned back in the chair. "Your mother, well, she's a wild card."

"That's being kind." Cassie chuckled. "Mom is better since she started dating Len, but she can still be challenging."

"Did you ever meet my folks?"

Cassie shook her head.

"Consider yourself lucky. My mom...don't get me wrong, I love her for everything she did for me and my sister, but the woman had no filter and no desire to have one." Krew's laugh rang hollow. "Living with her and my dad taught me a lot about dealing with difficult people. Trust me. Your mother won't be a problem."

Cassie cocked her head. "I'm confused. At the costume judging, you made it sound like your mom was your hero."

Krew blew out a breath. "Being the better parent of two bad parents isn't saying a lot. I'm sure my mom would say she did her best, but she didn't protect us. Her best still had me and Tessa suffering."

"I'm sure people would say the same things about me."

"The situations are totally different. You may have struggled financially, but you'd never knowingly put your child in the path of abuse."

A hard knot formed in the pit of her stomach as the image of Clint flashed before her. She struggled to calm her breathing and waved an airy hand. "Enough about family."

"I'll drink to that." Krew lifted his mug of coffee.

"You'll be in Good Hope through the holidays?"

"I can't go back on the field until the doctors release me." A shadow passed over his handsome face. "My injury is a season-ender. It may even be a career-ending one."

"But you were MVP last year."

That quick smile that lit up his entire face flashed again. "Following my career?"

"We have television. Not to mention the *Gazette* has published a few articles about you." She stiffened, feeling embarrassed despite there being no reason.

"Hey, I'm just teasing." Without warning, he reached over and gave her hand a squeeze.

The simple touch had desire surging.

For a second, Cassie felt like a hormone-riddled fifteen-year-old again. She concentrated on the conversation, ignoring the intoxicating scent of his cologne. "Are you saying you might not be able to play ever again?"

Doing something you loved for so many years, then not being able to continue had to be difficult. Not that she had any experience in such matters. At thirty-five. she was still looking to launch her first "career."

"The team's number one pick last year was a wide receiver, Javin Wilcox. They planned to groom him to eventually replace me. Since moving up to starter, he's exceeded all their expectations." Krew's expression turned distant. "From all reports, Javin has a great rapport with the QB. It's as if they've played together forever."

"And the team is winning."

"And the team is winning." Krew blew out a breath. "I'm guessing they'll decide to keep him in that position."

Cassie's anger spiked. "What about you?"

"My agent can find me another team, if that's what I want."

"Is that what you want?"

"I'm thirty-seven. Football is all I know."

"I bet you're selling yourself short. They probably can't wait to have you back."

"They want me to consider a position as an assistant coach to the wide receivers."

"Oh." She cocked her head. "What does an assistant coach do?"

"I've heard the job described as handling the nuts and bolts of the daily football operations." Krew shrugged. "The focus is on developing players. The team I played for has what you could call a complex system. As a wide receiver coach, I'd be responsible for making sure the players understand the intertwined route combinations and option patterns."

Cassie nodded, but he might as well have been speaking in Greek. Still, she appreciated that he wasn't dumbing it down for her. Or dismissing her questions.

"You've been a successful player," she reminded him. "It sounds to me as if you'd be a perfect fit for such a job."

"You think so, do you?"

That grin, well, it made her want to smile or kiss him. Cassie decided a smile was safer. "I do. Have you interviewed for the position? Do you even need to interview?"

"I still need to meet with the front-office people and speak with the head coach."

"You think it's a slam dunk."

He chuckled. "Wrong sport, but yeah, I think it'd be a slam dunk."

Cassie sensed Krew's drive to succeed. Lazy people didn't start where he had and rise to the levels that he'd already reached. Being an "assistant anything" didn't seem his style, at least not for the long run. "Would you ever want to be a head coach?"

"You're full of questions."

Despite the words, he didn't seem to mind. In fact, if his willingness to answer her questions was any indication, he appreciated her interest.

Of course he does, Cassie thought. She understood what it was like to have people dismiss you. Even though Krew had been wildly successful in his pro career, one devastating injury had changed his trajectory.

Her life-altering hit had come when the pregnancy test turned positive. Even though it had taken her nearly two decades to find her feet again, she was determined to make a good life for herself and her children.

She couldn't undo the past, and there was one specific thing that she would give anything to change, but because she couldn't, Cassie had vowed to forgive herself and look forward.

She would be successful moving forward.

So would Krew.

She slanted another glance at him, found him staring and impulsively shot him a wink.

Yep, they were both on the path to success.

Slam dunk.

CHAPTER TEN

Krew had no doubt that in the next five minutes Cassie would come up with a reason to leave. He didn't want her to go. Not yet. He enjoyed her company, and each time they were together, it seemed to him that the wall she'd erected around her heart lowered just a little.

Krew hoped in time it would lower enough for her to let him in.

"Have you ever thought about getting married?"

The question snapped him back to the present. He found Cassie's curious blue-green eyes focused on him.

"Pardon me?" He had to have misunderstood the question.

"I asked if you've ever thought about marriage." She shrugged. "You and I aren't young anymore. You've likely dated a lot of women. I'm surprised you've never settled down."

In some ways, Krew was surprised, too. His closest friends in the league were married.

There were, of course, plenty of young guys, like Javin, who were more into partying than settling down.

"I never found the right woman." It might sound cliché, but it was the truth. "My parents, I don't know why they ever got together, much less stayed together. I never wanted that kind of relationship, so it made me cautious. What about you?"

A look of startled surprise crossed her face. "Me?"

Her voice rose, then cracked.

"You never married." At least, he didn't think she'd ever walked down the aisle. "Why?"

"Same reason as you, I suppose. My parents' marriage was happy, but once my dad died and my mother remarried Bernie… That marriage was a disaster from the start." Cassie's fingers picked at the hem of her sweater.

"Yet, you lived with different guys."

Cassie's gaze sharpened, but the lack of judgment she must have seen in his eyes had the tight set to her shoulders relaxing.

"Yes," was all she said.

"Raising four kids alone has to be hard."

The doorbell rang before she could respond. Cassie pushed at her hair with her fingers. "Are you expecting someone?"

"No." Krew shrugged. "Probably someone wanting to sell something."

"I doubt it."

Actually, Krew doubted it, too. This area was too remote for door-to-door sales.

He opened the door to find David, Hadley and Brynn Chapin smiling at him. Hadley held a plant, and the child had her arms wrapped around a white baker's box.

"I hope we're not intruding." David's hand rested on his wife's shoulder. "We wanted to stop by and welcome you to the neighborhood."

"Come in. Please." Krew stepped back. "I heard you lived nearby. We didn't have much of a chance to talk at the wedding."

Krew glanced down at Brynn. Nine or ten, she had long blond hair and blue eyes, just like her mother.

Brynn thrust the box into his hands. "There are lots of

different kinds of cookies in here. They're all superduper good. My mom and I made them. She says everyone likes cookies."

Hadley chuckled. "I hope you enjoy them."

"Come in and sit down."

"Well, just for a minute." David cast a glance at his wife and received a nod of agreement. "Brynn's bedtime is coming up, but we have a little time before—"

The architect's voice faltered when he noticed Cassie rising slowly from the sofa. "Cassie."

David's gaze shifted to Krew. "I didn't realize you had company."

"Actually, I was just leaving." Cassie's smile was bright, but Krew saw the strain around the edges.

"Please, stay." Hadley stepped forward. "I haven't seen much of you in the last few months. I understand you've been busy studying for the real estate licensing exam."

"At least stay and have a cookie." Krew held out the box. "I have it on good authority," he winked at Brynn, "that they're superduper good."

Krew expected Cassie to make up an excuse and rabbit. Instead, she made a great show of peeking in the box. "I suppose I could stay for a cookie."

Krew brought out more coffee, and they ate the cookies straight out of the box.

"Where's Axl?" Brynn glanced around as if expecting the little boy to pop up from behind the sofa.

Cassie broke a cookie in half. "My mother is watching him this evening."

Hadley's eyes widened. "Anita is babysitting?"

"Len is with her." Cassie laughed. "He loves kids, and he's amazing with Axl."

"It's unfortunate Len and his first wife weren't able to have children," Hadley said. "Lindsay told me he wanted a whole houseful."

"We're going to have a whole houseful," Brynn declared, lifting her gaze from the box of cookies. "I'm the first, and the baby will be—"

Brynn clapped a hand over her mouth and glanced at her parents. "I'm sorry. I forgot it was a secret."

Krew remembered back to his childhood. Whenever he or Tessa had divulged information his parents hadn't wanted shared, they'd gotten a hard slap.

David only smiled and ruffled his daughter's hair. "It's okay, sweet pea. Everyone will know tomorrow night."

"Your secret is safe with us," Krew assured the Chapins.

The *us* had Hadley and David exchanging a glance.

Krew pretended not to notice. He'd misspoken and would make things only more awkward if he tried to explain.

"Congratulations." Cassie gave Hadley a hug. "I'm happy for you."

"We were going to wait, but..." Hadley lifted her hands, let them fall. "God had other ideas."

Krew glanced at Brynn. If the couple wanted their children to be close in age, it appeared they'd already waited too long. But it was none of his business. And frankly, the talk of babies made him twitchy.

While he'd been away at college, studying and being lauded for his prowess on the field, Cassie had given birth to his child. A daughter he was only now getting to know. He'd missed so much...

"It seems like everyone is having babies this spring." Cassie raised a hand and counted off. "There's Lindsay, Ami and Eliza. Now—"

"Don't forget my mommy," Brynn piped up, and everyone smiled.

Krew glanced at Cassie. He wondered what Dakota had been like at that age. Had she been as talkative as Brynn? Or more on the quiet side, like her mother?

He could tell at a glance that Brynn was all girl, from her pink high-tops to her hot pink dress covered in flowers and dragonflies. Had Dakota liked to dress up?

Had there even been money for Dakota to have pretty clothes? He'd been in his fifth year with the NFL when Dakota was Brynn's age. He'd had a luxury condo, a sports car and more money than he could spend. Dakota had had to share space with two younger brothers.

He clenched his jaw tight. There had been so much he could have done for her, done for them, if only he'd known.

Cassie didn't appear to notice his scrutiny. She was too busy talking with Hadley about her pregnancy.

David noticed.

When Krew shifted his focus, he found the architect studying him.

"We're having a little party at our house tomorrow at seven." David smiled at Cassie. "We'd love for both of you to come."

"It's when we're telling everybody about the baby," Brynn added.

"Thank you so much, but—"

Krew wasn't sure what got into him, but he closed his hand over Cassie's, stilling her words. "Sounds like fun. We'll be there."

Cassie waited until the Chapin family left before she exploded. She jerked her hand from Krew's. Her chest rose and fell as if she'd just finished a long race. "What were you thinking?"

"You don't want to attend their party?" His gaze was curious, his easy tone at odds with her agitated one.

"You made it sound like we're a couple." God, she hated it when her voice trembled. She took a deep breath. This time when she spoke, her voice was firm and steady. "We're not a couple."

"I know."

Though the agreement was exactly the response she wanted, there was a momentary pinch in the area of her heart. She might have stopped there, perhaps should have stopped there, but Cassie had made great strides in the past few months, and she refused to get pulled off track.

"I'm going to be straight with you, Krew. From what you already know of my history, none of this should be a surprise. But I want you to hear it from me." She settled her gaze on his handsome face.

He gave a nod, his expression turning serious. "Why don't we sit down?"

She shot a glance at the cozy living area and shook her head.

"Then let's talk in the kitchen while I put this stuff away." Without waiting for her reply, Krew picked up the now empty carafe of coffee and the cups, then started toward the kitchen.

Cassie scooped up the bakery box and everything else and followed him. She'd never been around a man who picked up after himself. Her father would have helped, but her mother had insisted on doing everything herself.

Every man Cassie had lived with had been lazy, insisting that picking up or cleaning was woman's work. Her sons helped, but only when prodded.

Krew put the cups and carafe in the dishwasher, then found a container in the cupboard.

Cassie stood back and watched.

When he finished, he gave her a puzzled look. "Why are you staring at me like that?"

"I'm impressed. It appears your mother taught you right."

"Our house was a pigsty." His eyes turned opaque. "I hated living in filth and clutter."

Krew gestured to a round table positioned near floor-to-ceiling windows that overlooked the wooded yard.

For some reason, Cassie found herself calmed by the beautiful scene with the blanket of white and the thick evergreens. She took a seat and focused on the view.

He sat across from her, and she felt his assessing gaze on her. But he didn't rush her or try to take control of the conversation. Instead, he waited.

"When I was young, my father was my knight in shining armor, my champion. I always had his love and support. Even though he had high standards, I did everything I could to make him proud of me." Cassie had thought that after so many years, she might quit missing her dad, but the pain remained. "One day, when I was in middle school, he had a massive heart attack. He didn't survive. I never got to say good-bye or tell him one last time how much I loved him."

"You were lucky."

"Lucky?" Her voice rose and cracked.

"You had a parent you looked up to, one you loved."

Krew didn't elaborate. He didn't need to say more. She understood.

"My mother and I have never gotten along. Lindsay says it's because we're so much alike." Cassie pushed back from the table and stood.

She paced, conscious of Krew's scrutiny.

"After my dad died, my mom and I argued constantly. I see now that we were both grieving and feeling very alone. Lindsay tried to bring us together, but between teenage hormones and my mom's sharp tongue, it didn't work."

Cassie sensed Krew's confusion. If she didn't already know the end of this story, she'd be urging herself to get to the point.

"The night of the bonfire, my mom and I had a huge argument. I'd taken a summer school course, and grades had just come out. I got my first B." Cassie gave a laugh that sounded harsh even to her own ears. "She was furious. She told me my life was on a downward course. When I went to the beach, her words kept circling in my head."

"You had sex with the son of the town drunk to spite her." Krew's voice was hard, flat.

"No." Cassie felt her cheeks warm. "I was going to make out with a boy I'd liked and fantasized about all year. That is, assuming he would even want to kiss me. I never intended to have sex with you. Heck, I'd never even been kissed before."

His eyes widened, but before he could say a word, she continued.

"I liked you so much and I was over the moon when you noticed me and asked me to take a walk with you. Just holding your hand was a thrill." She cleared her throat, avoiding his gaze as she continued. "When you kissed me, I was a goner. As the kisses continued, my body felt as if it was on fire. I never knew you could want something as badly as I wanted you."

She stopped pacing. "It was beautiful. You made it beautiful. You were a kind lover. I've learned since that not every guy is like that."

The thought of all the men she'd been with since that night brought on the self-loathing she'd been fighting. She'd made great strides in forgiving herself, but she wasn't there yet.

"In the past, I've made the men in my life my priority, to the detriment of everything else. No more. My children are my focus, and until I can trust myself to make good choices, my life will remain free of men."

Dropping down into the chair, she expelled a breath, feeling proud of herself.

"I'll make it clear to David and Hadley that you and I are simply friends. Even joking, I shouldn't have made it seem otherwise."

There was apology in his words, but the look in his eyes had her heart fluttering. His expression looked, well, it looked like respect.

"Dakota," Cassie paused, wanting to be completely honest, "has always wanted a father. I, at least, had mine for all those years. While some people say you can't miss what you never had, I don't think that's true. Not for her. She missed you."

He flinched as if she'd struck him. Then it was his turn to take a deep breath. "I'm not trying to make Dakota, or you, or your boys, feel like yours was any less of a family because there wasn't a dad in the house. You were there for your kids, and your kids were there for each other. That's what family is about."

She hadn't been there for Dakota while Clint was around, but Cassie shoved the thought aside.

"You were wrong in what you said earlier," she surprised herself by saying. "I really would like to be your friend."

"Same here."

She extended her hand to him. "Friends?"

His large fingers closed around hers, and his smile arrowed straight to her heart. "Friends."

CHAPTER ELEVEN

"Don't use the car unless it's an emergency." Cassie let the keys dangle from her finger as Braxton's eyes followed the swinging movement. "Understand?"

Braxton nodded and reached for the keys.

She pulled back. "Not so fast. No one comes over tonight. Is that understood?"

Brax rolled his eyes. "Sheesh. Who would come over? I don't really like anyone at school, and K.T. only cares about his art."

"You don't have any friends at school?" She handed him the keys, but was realizing she had more to worry about than a party.

Braxton was a computer whiz, a smart boy who'd always been a little too serious. Part of the problem, she knew, was he spent a lot of time watching over his younger brothers. And there had never been enough money for him to be involved in any extracurricular activities that required cash.

She'd let him down, just like she'd let down his siblings.

"Hey, I was just jokin'." Braxton's smile teased one from her own lips. "I got friends. Lots of 'em. More than I want. They're coming out of the woodwork, like roaches."

She laughed and would have reached down to ruffle his hair.

But he was already taller than she was and no longer a little boy. "I won't be out late."

"Why are you going with him?" Braxton asked.

K.T. cocked his head.

"He's Dakota's dad."

"But Dakota isn't going to the party." Braxton aimed those assessing blue eyes at her.

When put that way, her decision to attend this party with Krew didn't make sense. She'd told Krew she wanted to be friends, and she meant it. Dakota deserved two parents who could get along.

But getting along wasn't the problem. Cassie couldn't have a man in her life when she was trying to be a better mother.

The party tonight would be full of couples, not "friends," and the last thing she needed was to be with Krew in a room full of happily married people.

Picking up her purse, Cassie pulled out her phone.

"What are you doing?" K.T. asked, his dark brows pulling together.

"I'm texting Krew and telling him to go without me." She expelled a shaky breath. "It isn't as if any of these people are my friends, anyway."

Braxton lifted the phone from her hand, his eyes dark and serious on hers. "You said Aunt Lindsay and Owen would be there."

"They're part of this group. These are their friends, not mine." What had she been thinking? Hadley had invited her only because she was with Krew at the time.

Krew was their new neighbor and a sports star.

"Give me my phone back, Brax. I have to send the text before he comes to pick me up."

Her temper flared when Braxton held the phone out of reach, just as she'd done only moments before with the keys.

"Braxton." Her voice was a warning growl.

"You dressed up." Her eldest son gestured with the hand holding the phone to the cranberry-colored sweater dress she'd picked up at a consignment shop in Sturgeon Bay.

"You even put on the boots Grandma gave you." K.T. studied the heeled boots, his artist's eye in full force. "Black or tan would have been a better choice, but brown works, too."

"I-"

Before she could protest further and insist Braxton give her the phone, a knock sounded at the door.

Axl, who'd been sitting on the floor building towers out of blocks, only to knock them down and rebuild them, jumped up. "I answer."

"I'll get it, brat," Braxton told his brother while tossing the phone to Cassie. "I need to make sure it's not the boogeyman."

On his way to the door, Braxton lunged at Axl, making the little boy squeal.

Since she was watching, Braxton glanced through the peephole before opening the door. He yelled back at her, though Cassie stood only a few feet away, "Your ride is here."

Cassie pushed aside her son as a cold wind swept inside the house. "Would you like to come in for a minute?"

"Sure." Krew stepped inside, and her breath caught in her throat.

His coat was black cashmere. Though his dark pants and gray sweater weren't flashy, they screamed wealth.

He cocked his head as if sensing her unease. "Is something wrong?"

"Mom is thinking about skipping the party." K.T. spoke without looking up from his drawing. "She doesn't think they want her there."

The eyes Krew fixed on her were definitely puzzled. "Why would you think that? You look great, by the way."

The simple compliment had the blood sliding through her veins like warm honey. But whether she looked acceptable or not didn't change the fact that she didn't belong with those people.

"Why don't you want to go?" Krew asked when she remained silent.

"David and Hadley are your neighbors." Cassie kept her tone light. "I simply happened to be there when they stopped over. They almost had to invite me."

"I tried to tell her Aunt Lindsay would be there, but..." Braxton shrugged.

"These are people you grew up around, people you've known your whole life." Krew displayed a surprising unwillingness to let the subject drop. "If anyone is the outsider, it's me."

"You're right. Most are people I grew up around." Cassie wasn't sure he'd understand the distinction, but there definitely was one. "They haven't been my friends in years."

"Because you were busy raising your kids and trying to survive." Krew studied her for a long moment, then his voice softened. "Let them get to know you as you are now, the woman who is working and studying hard to make a better life for her family."

"I don't know—" Cassie hesitated.

"Or we could stay here and all get better acquainted." The barest hint of a smile tugged at Krew's lips as he shifted his gaze to Braxton. "Let's talk more about prom. Who do you think you'll be taking?"

Moments later, Krew slid behind the wheel of his expensive sports car. Cassie turned to him. "Did you see the look of terror on Braxton's face when you mentioned prom?"

"K.T. was equally worried." The cheery quality to Krew's voice had Cassie turning suspicious eyes on him.

"You didn't really want to talk to the boys about girls and prom, did you?"

Krew laughed. "I knew they'd push you out of the house if they thought me staying was the other option."

"You manipulated the situation." While it was amusing, she wasn't sure how she felt about the tactic.

"If you don't want to go, that's fine." Krew made no move to back the car out of the driveway. "Since David and Hadley made the effort to welcome me to the neighborhood, I feel obligated to make an appearance."

"It's been a long time since anyone invited me to a party." Cassie gazed down at her hands. "At least, one that doesn't involve my sister or mother and an obligatory invite."

"You're making changes to your life, good changes. Let everyone see those changes. That's the only way they'll begin to look at you differently."

"Okay." As he pulled the car onto the street and drove down the road, she studied his handsome profile. "I didn't think football players were so astute."

A muscle in his jaw jumped. "Contrary to popular belief, we aren't a bunch of over-muscled Cro-Magnons out on the field. It takes intelligence as well as strength to make it in professional sports."

"I'm sorry." She found herself reaching over, lightly touching the soft sleeve of his coat. "That was unfair. I apologize."

"Apology accepted." He slanted a glance in her direction. "I meant what I said earlier. You look amazing."

"I believe the word you used before was great." She kept her tone light. "But I like amazing, too."

Whether it was the heated seats or the comfortable ride, Cassie felt herself relax.

"Do you have any idea who will be there tonight?" he asked.

Cassie had already given that matter some consideration. "Steve Bloom recently married Lynn Chapin, David's mother. That means his sister and brother, as well as all of the Bloom sisters and their spouses, will likely be there. Of course, Eliza and Kyle are on everyone's invitation list."

"What about your sister?"

"Yes, of course. Lindsay and Owen are also part of that social circle." Cassie lifted her shoulders in a shrug. "There's probably more that I'm not even thinking of."

Krew only nodded, his gaze focused on the increasing traffic. "I ran into Izzie Deshler. She had nice things to say about K.T."

He'd deliberately changed the subject.

Cassie understood. You could only talk so much about being an outsider. "What did Izzie say about him?"

"She raved about how talented he is for someone so young." His hands relaxed on the steering wheel. "I didn't realize those screaming faces in the alley were his work."

"He was the youngest artist chosen to participate in the alley art project last year." Cassie couldn't believe she'd been blessed with such talented kids.

"I know he's got several years before he graduates, but I was wondering if he has an art school picked out."

Silence filled the car for several long seconds.

"He's continuing to build his portfolio." Cassie knew K.T. had big dreams, and she didn't want to squash them. But all the schools he was looking at were expensive. Grants and scholarships wouldn't begin to cover the costs.

"What about Braxton? What does he want to do when he graduates?"

Cassie wondered if Krew was actually interested. If this was his attempt to ease her nerves about the upcoming party, it wasn't working.

"Brax is big into computer stuff. He's talked about computer engineering. I'm not sure exactly what that involves, but it sounds impressive."

It also, Cassie thought, sounded expensive. Like a program that could last far beyond the four years she already couldn't afford. Unless she sold dozens of houses on the road they'd just turned down.

"Any chance their father will help with college expenses?" Krew's tone seemed overly casual.

Hadn't Krew listened to a word she'd said about Eugene? Cassie shook her head. "I had to take him to court to get him to pay child support. So having him suddenly appear with a check for college is highly unlikely. Then again, you showed up."

She regretted the flippant remark the second she uttered it.

A muscle in his jaw jumped. "I didn't know I had a daughter."

The edge to his voice was one she'd put there with her thoughtless response. "You're right. I'm sorry. The situations are totally different."

"I care about Dakota. I want the best for her."

"I know you do."

"That's why I want to pay for her college."

"No." Panic surged. "We've talked about this before, Krew."

"Now we're talking about it again." There was more puzzlement than irritation in his voice. "Help me understand why you're refusing to let me help our daughter."

Our daughter.

Her heart lurched.

"Dakota is a bright girl. I don't want to see her struggle to get an education when I have the means to help. Heck, if I had known about Dakota, I would have been paying child-support all this time, so all that money would probably add up to college tuition."

Cassie shut her eyes for a second. How could she tell him she worried if he started tossing money her daughter's way, Dakota would prefer him over her without appearing childish? There was no way, because her reason for refusing was all about her feelings and fears. Not about what was best for Dakota.

She expelled a breath. "Okay."

"Okay?"

Cassie nodded.

"You're agreeing to let me pay for her education?" Shock had his voice rising.

"Yes."

"That's wonderful. We'll tell Dakota the good news together."

"No. You tell her. It's your gift to her." Cassie forced a smile. "She'll be thrilled."

As Krew turned off the road onto the long lane, the house came into view.

Instead of having a modern look with lots of glass, like the one where Krew was living, David and Hadley's home had been designed to look as if it was constructed in the 1920s. She gazed admiringly at the multi-gabled roof through her realtor's lens and knew that if this home ever went on the market, it'd be snatched up the same day.

Krew parked behind a truck that Cassie recognized as her brother-in-law's. By the number of vehicles in the driveway, it appeared they were late arrivals.

As if sensing her hesitation, Krew made no effort to get out of the car.

"Whenever you step outside your normal, whatever that normal is, it can be frightening." His tone was conversational as he leaned back against the leather seat as if getting out of the car had yet to cross his mind. "But when your normal isn't where you want to be, you have two choices. Stay mired where you're at, or tough it out and forge a new path."

Cassie thought of the life she'd lived since high school. She knew people talked about her, gossiped about the mess she'd made of her life. She'd catch bits of it, usually accompanied with some variation of the statement, *Such a shame, she had so much potential.*

What Krew was saying wasn't anything she hadn't said to herself when she'd sought out the job at the Daily Grind. When she'd scraped together the money and signed up for the real estate licensing class. When she'd squared her shoulders and swallowed her fear and made an appointment to see a psychologist.

Coming to this party, stepping out as the woman she wanted to be, rather than the woman who'd disappointed so many people, including herself, was scary.

One step. Dr. Gallagher had told her change began with a single step in the direction you want to go.

Despite her racing heart, Cassie fluffed her hair with her fingers, checked her makeup in the car's vanity mirror and turned to Krew. "What are we doing sitting out here? We've got a party to attend."

CHAPTER TWELVE

Krew didn't know what to think when Gladys opened the door. Her hair was upswept in a style that reminded him of a place where a bird would build a nest. Her flowing, robe-like dress was mostly black and white with splashes of orange.

Her pale blue eyes glittered when they shifted to Cassie. "Don't you look lovely this evening. Come in. Come in. As my mother used to say, we're not heating the outside."

Once inside, Gladys motioned to a young boy to take their coats. The kid was big, but his pudgy face told Krew he wasn't as old as he looked.

"Can you accept tips?" Krew pulled several bills from his pocket. Though he was more on the conservative side with his money, he hadn't forgotten those years when tips tossed his way had made a huge difference.

"I-I think so." The boy's eyes darted to Gladys.

"If someone offers, you may accept." The older woman smiled at the child. "But you do not ask."

The boy nodded. "Gotcha."

Krew handed him his coat and then Cassie's, along with two five-dollar bills.

The boy's eyes widened. "Gee, thanks."

Cassie's gaze remained thoughtful as she watched the child leave the room. "He looks familiar, but I can't place where I know him from."

"The coffee shop?" To Krew, it seemed to make the most sense.

"He and his mom have the apartment next to where your sister used to live." Gladys kept her gaze on Cassie.

"Cody Treacher. The monster next door." Cassie shook her head. "He isn't old enough to have a job."

"He's twelve. You're correct. He isn't old enough for a real job. But his mother struggles to make ends meet. In exchange for Cody's help this evening, he and his mother will receive vouchers for free meals at Muddy Boots."

"How did David and Hadley find out about this kid?" Cassie found the puzzle pieces to this story intriguing.

"I mentioned his situation to David when I received the party invitation." Gladys's sharp eyes shifted their focus to Krew. "His mother, Sissy Treacher—her maiden name is Janek--used to help me with my lines at the Playhouse. I believe if you mention her to Tessa, she'll remember her."

For as long as Krew could remember, Gladys had been a star performer at the Community Playhouse. Back when there hadn't been enough money for clothes and other things girls love, Gladys had "paid" Tessa to help her with her lines.

It sounded as if she'd done the same for Cody's mother. Now, she was helping the woman's son.

Neighbors helping neighbors.

It wasn't simply words in this community on the Door County peninsula, it was a way of life.

Cassie cleared her throat. "That's nice of you to help."

"Pshaw." Gladys swept the air with a hand on which each finger sported a ring of some kind. "I'm not doing anything."

The older woman's gaze narrowed as it went from Cassie to

Krew. She lifted her hands, positioning them as if framing a picture. "Yes. Perfect."

Krew exchanged a glance with Cassie. "We should say hello to David and Hadley."

The *we* came out before he could stop it and rephrase, but Cassie didn't appear to notice. Either that or she was as eager as he was to get away from Gladys.

Thankfully, the doorbell rang and they were spared any further conversation.

"Go. Enjoy yourself." Gladys made a shooing gesture before moving to open the door.

They'd taken only a few steps down the hall to the living room when Cassie leaned close to Krew. "Was it just me, or was there some weird gleam in her eye when she looked at us?"

"I noticed it, too." He kept his voice low. "What was that picture-frame thing she did with her hands?"

"Not a clue. But what she's doing for Cody and his mom is sweet."

"She's a good person. That's something I didn't realize until after I'd left Good Hope."

Cassie cocked her head.

"This community is full of good people. People who truly care about each other."

The second they walked into the large open living room with the massive stone fireplace, they were engulfed by those good people.

Owen was one of the first to welcome him with a manly half hug and a slap on the back.

"Marriage agrees with you," Krew told him.

While there had been some happy times between his sister and Owen, they'd never been a good fit. Lindsay made him happy, and God knew Owen needed it after what he'd endured.

Sweet Mindy.

No one should ever have to lose a child.

"We're very happy." Owen's arm remained around his wife's shoulders, as if he found it difficult to keep from touching his bride.

"You're starting to pooch out." Cassie's comment had her sister's hand moving to the swell of her belly. "March will be here before you know it."

Lindsay glanced down. "Ami's due around the same time, and she looks much more pregnant than me."

"It's also her second baby," Cassie reminded her. "With Dakota, I barely showed at all. With Braxton, I looked like I was ready to pop months before I was due."

Cassie stopped suddenly, two bright spots of pink dotting her cheeks. "Anyway, you look terrific."

"You look nice this evening, too." Lindsay smiled. "Red is definitely your color."

"I got this in Sturgeon Bay at the consignment store," Cassie admitted.

"I love that place." Hadley stepped forward and gave Cassie a hug. "I'm happy you came tonight."

She extended her smile to Krew, but her focus quickly returned to Cassie. "Did you get this dress at the Christmas in July markdown?"

As the three women talked about sales, Krew watched Cassie relax.

David wandered over to join them and held out his hand to Krew. "Thanks for coming."

"Thanks for inviting me."

The conversation was interrupted by Brynn and a huge dog nearly as large as she was.

"Brynn Chapin." David's voice turned stern as his gaze settled on the animal. "What did your mother and I tell you about keeping Ruckus upstairs?"

"He just came down to hear the announcement." Brynn offered her father a sweet smile. "Ruckus is part of the family. As soon as you tell everybody that Mommy is going to have a baby, I'll take him upstairs. I promise."

With the leash held firmly in one hand, Brynn crossed her heart with the fingers of her free hand.

"Okay." David expelled a breath. "If your mother is okay with making the announcement now, he can stay for a few more minutes. Then right back to your room."

For a second, it looked as if the child was going to argue. She must have thought better of it, because she only nodded.

Moments later, David and Hadley had positioned themselves in front of the windows with Brynn beside them.

Krew found himself standing beside Cade Rallis, who'd replaced Len as sheriff, and his wife, Marigold.

"It looks like they're ready to make some kind of announcement." Cade glanced at his wife.

The sheriff was taller than Krew, with broad shoulders and an athletic build. Krew wondered if he'd ever played any ball.

"What would they have to announce?" Despite the light words, a watchful wariness had filled the pretty blonde's eyes.

"Maybe they're moving away from Good Hope?" Cade rubbed his chin. "I don't know what else it could be."

"Shhh." Ami moved to stand beside her younger sister. "I want to hear this."

Lindsay had been right, Krew saw. The size of her baby bump didn't begin to compare to Ami's.

His gaze slid to Cassie, whose gaze was focused on their hosts. He wondered how much of her not showing her pregnancy with Dakota had been first-baby stuff and how much had been hiding the fact she was pregnant at fifteen.

Fifteen.

If Anita had found out about him and come after him with both barrels loaded, he'd have deserved it. The fact that he'd been a kid himself didn't excuse his actions.

"Hadley and I are happy that you could join us this evening."

"I'm glad, too," Brynn piped up, her voice carrying easily. "So is Ruckus."

Laughter rippled through the room.

Krew wished he could have known Dakota at that age.

"When Hadley and I married, the plans were to wait a little while to start a family." David paused and glanced at his wife.

Their eyes locked for several seconds.

"God, however, had other plans." David chuckled as he glanced at Pastor Dan, then refocused on the rest of his guests.

"What David is trying to say is, we're pregnant." Hadley lifted her hands. "Surprise."

Ami gave a squeal.

"We're extremely happy about this." David grinned. "We wanted you here to share our joy."

"To answer your question, baby Chapin is due to arrive at the beginning of May." Hadley glanced in Eliza's direction. "The same time as Eliza and Kyle's little one."

Beside Krew, Marigold stiffened and blinked rapidly. "They haven't even been married a month."

At her low whisper, Cade pulled her close and placed a kiss on the top of her head. "Our time will come."

There was a story there, Krew thought. He shifted his gaze, having no desire to intrude on what looked like a private moment.

Krew wasn't eager to battle the crowd who milled around David and Hadley, but he suddenly wanted to be somewhere else.

He took Cassie's arm. "Time to do some exploring."

Interest flickered in the blue-green depths of her eyes. "Where to?"

Krew gestured toward the hallway. "The kitchen."

Several of his married friends on the team had recently built new homes. They were impressive, but he didn't believe any of their kitchens were as fine as this one.

"I'm not much of a cook." Cassie moved to the island and ran her hand along the white marble countertop. "But if this were my kitchen, I think I'd learn."

He watched her gaze take in the double electric ovens, the gas range that was bigger and better than any range he'd seen and the cabinets that went all the way to the ceiling.

Krew chuckled. "I think I might learn, too, if this was mine."

Cassie turned and rested her back against the countertop, the red of her dress a bright splash of color against the white. He didn't know too many women who'd be content hanging out in a kitchen talking to only one person during a party, but Cassie appeared in no hurry to get back to the festivities.

"I never asked where you live." She gave him what he interpreted as an encouraging smile. "I mean, normally, when you're not visiting here. I know you live in Green Bay, but do you have a condo or a house?"

"Until recently, I shared a loft with three teammates."

"Three roommates." She widened her eyes. "Didn't that get crowded?"

"It was a big loft." Krew smiled, remembering. "We each had our own bedroom and bathroom. The kitchen was big, though nowhere near as nice as this one."

"Surely you could have afforded your own place."

"Of course." He shrugged. "But these guys are friends, and none of us spent much time at home."

"Real estate is a good investment."

He smiled. No doubt, that fact was repeatedly emphasized in the courses she was taking. "True. But you never know from year to year where you'll be. I didn't want to be stuck with a house to sell."

"One day I'm going to buy a house."

Her words sounded like a solemn vow.

"There's a lot of upkeep involved in being a homeowner."

She flushed and pushed away from the counter. "I know the house I live in looks pretty bad. The landlord won't do anything.

I've called him, but he'll only do the bare minimum. Most of the time, not even that."

Krew's parents had always rented. With his dad's sporadic work history, there was no way they could save enough money for a down payment, much less qualify for a loan.

Their rental house had been a dump. He and his sister had avoided being at home as much as possible. Krew realized now that he could have at least mowed the yard.

"Do you or your boys know how to do basic home repairs?" Krew had barely known the proper way to swing a hammer when he'd left Good Hope. But a couple of summers of working construction during his college years had taught him a lot.

The pink in her cheeks deepened as she shook her head. "I've been thinking about seeing if Len could teach us. Nothing big, but one of the shutters is coming off, and the screen is out on the door."

Krew started to nod, was about to agree with her that getting her mother's boyfriend involved was a good idea. But he stopped and considered that perhaps this was one way he could help Cassie and get better acquainted with Dakota's brothers.

Teaching her and the boys rudimentary construction skills could never make up for leaving her to fend for herself all these years, but it would make her life in the future easier.

"I could teach you and the boys how to do some basic repairs."

"That's nice of you to offer." She smiled. "But I'm afraid you'd be wasting your time. We don't even have tools."

"I've got some."

"You do?"

"Yes." Or rather, he would by the time he stopped over. "Let's plan to get together once I'm back. I've got some things I need to take care of in Green Bay first."

Things like see the team doctor and speak with the coach. Things like figure out what was going to happen once he was off the disabled list.

"Sure." Cassie shrugged. "If you want to—"

"I wondered where you were."

Krew turned, and there was Gladys, beaming at the two of them as if she'd found a pot of gold, instead of two people having a conversation in a kitchen.

"Are you having a nice time this evening?" Cassie asked with a warmth that told Krew she was fond of the eccentric older woman.

"Oh my dear, I'm very encouraged by this turn of events."

Krew exchanged a glance with Cassie. *Encouraged?*

"You mean Hadley being pregnant." Cassie spoke gingerly, as if not certain of the direction Gladys was headed.

"Of course I'm happy for her and David. But I was referring to another couple in love." Gladys cackled. "Though they don't yet know it."

Cassie's lips quirked. "Who are you matchmaking this time?"

"Matchmaking?" Krew asked.

"Gladys, Ruby and Katherine conspired to help Lindsay and Owen's romance make the leap from friendship to love." Cassie chuckled. "Lindsay didn't realize it at the time, but looking back, she saw signs of their meddl—er, interventions."

"Hadley and David were actually our first foray into bringing young lovers together." Gladys sighed melodramatically. "Now a baby. I couldn't be happier."

"Who is it you have your eye on now?" Krew repeated the question Cassie had voiced but Gladys hadn't answered.

"No. No. No." Gladys wagged a finger at him. "That's a secret. The only hint I'll give you is they're both at this party. I'll leave it to you to figure out the rest."

CHAPTER THIRTEEN

The second they returned to the living room, Cassie found herself glancing around the room, trying to see who Gladys had her eye on. She caught Krew doing the same thing.

"I think I know," she told Krew in a low voice, taking a sip of the club soda someone had handed her.

"Who?"

"Over by the fireplace." Cassie nodded. "In fact, I'm sure of it."

Krew lifted a bottle of beer to his lips and cast a casual glance in that direction. "The minister and Katie Ruth?"

"Katie Ruth does a lot of volunteering at the church." Cassie lowered her voice even further. "I always thought she'd be a better match for him than my sister."

As they watched, Gladys strolled over to the couple.

"Why do I get the feeling they aren't going to know what hit 'em?"

Cassie laughed, a silvery tinkle that rose from deep inside. "Maybe we should warn them."

Krew took a swig of beer. "It'll be more fun to sit back and watch. Besides, we don't know for sure it's them."

"Sure we do."

"I like your confidence, Ms. Lohmeier."

"I call 'em like I see 'em."

"Cassie." Lindsay, Owen at her side, looked mildly astonished. "I thought you'd left."

"We've been mingling." The moment the *we* left her lips, Cassie wished she could pull it back. Now *she* was making it sound as if she and Krew were a couple.

"Us, too." Lindsay slipped an arm through Owen's. "But I'm exhausted, so we're heading home. It's fabulous news about Hadley and David."

"I'm happy for them," Cassie said. "And for Brynn."

"Brynn told me she'd love to have a sister." Lindsay smiled. "I told her I understood, because I have a sister and they're great."

Cassie felt a warmth rise up inside her.

Krew chuckled. "Mine was a pain in the ass most of the time."

"Mine were, too." Owen sipped his drink.

"Men." Lindsay shook her head, but her eyes were dancing. "Take me home, husband?"

"Gladly." Owen brushed a kiss across her cheek, then shifted his gaze back to Cassie and Krew. "Enjoy the rest of your evening."

They'd taken only a step or two away when Cassie remembered the prize money. "Owen."

When he turned, she felt foolish. This certainly wasn't something that needed to be discussed at this moment. Still, now that she had his attention, she continued. "I finally have the money to pay for the repairs my car needs. I'll give you a call, and hopefully you have times open so I can bring it in."

"You don't need to pay me for repairs, Cassie." Owen's tone held more than a hint of exasperation. "We're family now."

"I won't mooch off you and Lindsay." Cassie spoke firmly. "I pay my own way."

"We'll talk about this when you bring in the car." Owen took his wife's hand. "Just call. I'll fit you in."

"I'll bring my checkbook."

Owen chuckled and shook his head.

Krew didn't speak until they were out of earshot. "He's right, you know."

Cassie frowned. "Right about what?"

"He's family. He wants to help. You should let him."

"I pay my own way." Cassie knew it appeared she was being foolish and stubborn, but she'd taken advantage of friends, family and the system for too long. Being independent was a heady feeling.

"But—"

Cassie held up a hand.

"Not long ago, I couldn't have said that." Cassie heard the pride in her voice. "I want my boys to see…heck, I want *everyone* to see a new Cassie. A woman who is strong and pulls her own weight."

"But Owen is a successful mechanic who wants to do something nice for his new sister-in-law."

Hadn't he heard a word she'd said? "I'm going to pay him. I have the money."

"There's probably a lot of other places where that money could go." Krew's gaze turned brooding. "I wish I'd done more to help my sister. Looking back, I've spent most of my life thinking only about myself."

"Your gift to the Giving Tree was very generous."

"I like the philosophy of neighbors helping neighbors." His gaze met hers. "Everyone needs help sometimes. But I also understand the need to stand on your own two feet. You'll do the right thing. For you. And for your family."

Would she ever understand this man? When Cassie had heard he'd been a first-round draft pick the year he got out of college, she'd pegged him as an arrogant jock only out for himself.

Now Cassie wondered if she'd been wrong.

About him.

About a whole lot of other things.

~

Krew returned to Good Hope midweek in a pisser of a mood. The team doctor had examined him, said his healing was par for the course after a ruptured spleen, but refused to release him to play the rest of this season.

It didn't take a genius to know that returning to the field next year might be too late. Heck, it was probably already too late for him. His replacement, Javin, was playing the best football of his life.

Lunch with his agent had been equally depressing. When his agent suggested he should seriously consider the offer from the front office to be an assistant coach for the wide receivers, Krew knew his starting position was history.

He'd texted Dakota, but she was busy helping her grand-mother at her shop. His refrigerator was empty. Which did little to improve his mood. It appeared he had two choices—either do some grocery shopping or go grab a bite somewhere.

The Seat Yourself sign at Muddy Boots had Krew heading to an empty booth by the window. Nearly there, he stifled a groan when he heard his name.

Izzie sat at a table with high school principal Clay Chapin on one side of her and K.T. on the other. Instead of food, there were papers scattered across the Formica tabletop and Clay had his laptop open.

Krew covered the short distance to the table in one stride. "Good to see you again, Izzie. Clay. K.T."

"My mom said you were out of town," K.T. said in lieu of a greeting.

"Just got back." Krew noticed the new blue streak in K.T.'s hair. "I was in Green Bay on business."

"I heard the team doesn't want you back."

REUNITED IN GOOD HOPE | 129

The worry in the kid's eyes didn't stop the words from drawing blood.

"I thought you didn't follow sports." With great effort, Krew kept his tone even.

The boy lifted one skinny shoulder and let it drop. "I like to keep up with what's going on."

"Won't you join us?" Clay gestured to the empty chair between him and K.T.

"I don't want to interrupt." Krew let his gaze settle over the table. "It appears you're working rather than eating."

"We were just getting ready for dessert." Izzie smiled. "We'd love to have you join us."

"That'd be cool." K.T. started shoving some papers into his messenger bag.

Clay closed the lid of his laptop and dropped it into his briefcase.

It spoke to how pathetic his outlook was for the evening that Krew found himself actually considering the offer.

"I don't—" That's when he saw them.

Gladys.

Katherine.

Ruby.

The three were seated at a table on the other side of the dining room, their piercing gazes focused on him.

When his gaze met Gladys's, she lifted one bony hand and wiggled her fingers. The gemstones on her fingers caught the light, sending sparks of multicolored flames.

Krew knew as well as he knew his own name that if he moved from the spot where he was currently standing, he'd be done for. The three would be on him like flies on sh—

"Sure. I can sit for a few."

He'd barely pulled out a chair when an orange-haired waitress, an older woman he didn't recognize, took the others' dessert orders. Instead of the burgers and fries Krew had come for, he ordered the special of the day, a meatloaf dinner.

"What are the three of you working on?" Krew knew if he didn't go on the offense, he'd be the one answering questions. And he wasn't in the mood to talk about the state of his football career.

"Izzie and K.T. are helping me revamp a local program for at-risk teens." Clay smiled up at the waitress when she brought pie for him and the other two. "Thank you, Helen."

The high school principal was as blond as his brother, David, was dark. Both Chapin boys possessed a quiet confidence that came from knowing their place in the world. Krew found it interesting that David and Clay had forged their own career paths. Their sister, Greer, was the one poised to take over the family's banking empire.

"The program isn't technically part of the school system, but it's one I fully support," Clay continued.

"It's being relocated from the YMCA building. Because of the explosive growth of the Y's fitness and youth programs, they don't have the room we need," Izzie added. "We looked at the churches. While they could help, they're pinched for space as well."

Helen returned and set a heaping plate of food in front of Krew.

All he could do was stare. Instead of coupling meatloaf with traditional mashed potatoes and gravy, the cook had taken a baked potato out of its skin, mashed it up, added butter and covered the potato with cream corn. The bacon, onions and peppers that had topped the meatloaf while it cooked were added to the corn.

It looked strange, but the first bite Krew took was mouthwateringly good. The toasted homemade sourdough bread on the side would add a nice crunch.

"That's my favorite of the daily specials," Izzie confided.

Clay grinned. "It's a heart attack on a plate, but you can't beat the taste."

"It's good," K.T. agreed.

Krew chewed, swallowed, nodded. "What alternate locations are you considering?"

"We really have only one option." Izzie ignored the pie in front of her, her expression intense. "The—"

"I'm telling you," K.T. didn't even wait for Izzie to finish, "no kid will want to hang out at a nursing home."

"It's a senior living center." Gladys appeared tableside just in time to correct the boy in a tone that dared K.T. to disagree. "The Good Hope Senior Living Center is primarily independent living, though there is a wing devoted to assisted and full care."

"It's a lovely facility. It even has a community day care. Teen mothers receive free childcare so they can continue their education," Clay added.

Krew couldn't help wondering what would have happened if those services had been available when Cassie was pregnant with Dakota. She'd have been able to continue her education. Instead, her only option had been to drop out of school and get her GED later.

"Look," K.T. said, "Brax and I aren't really part of the kids you're labeling at risk, but I'm telling you, no matter how nice it is, if it isn't cool to go there, the place will sit empty."

Krew admired the boy's tenacity and willingness to state his opinion. Especially since it was obvious the adults at the table didn't agree.

While the debate continued, Krew ate and let his thoughts drift back to his own high school years. There were plenty of times that he'd have loved to have had an alternative to being at home, especially in the summer and between sports seasons.

For some reason, the face of Earl D'Angelo, popped into his head. "There was a program in Green Bay that one of my teammates started. I don't remember the name, but it recruited at-risk youth and taught them building trades. They were paid through some sort of grant while doing repairs for those in the community who needed help."

Krew wished he'd paid more attention when Earl had extolled the program's virtues. "The organization was very hands-on and gave the kids marketable skills."

"I bet Kyle Kendrick would be interested in helping with something like that." Clay tapped the table with one finger.

Krew went back to eating while the others at the table, as well as Gladys, who pulled up a chair and sat down, discussed the possibilities.

"Would you be willing?"

Krew's last bite of meatloaf was poised only inches from his mouth. He slowly lowered the fork. "To do what?"

"Reach out to your friend." Gladys waved a hand in the air. "Ask him to send information to Izzie or Clay regarding the program he launched."

Krew started to say he didn't have time. For years, that had been his go-to response when anyone asked him to do anything that didn't involve football.

But he had the time now.

Krew set down his fork. "When do you need the information?"

The next morning, after getting the information from Earl and relaying Clay's contact information, Krew drove out to Cassie's neighborhood. She was right. Her house was in need of repair.

The screen in the combination storm door was half in and half out, and a shutter on one of the windows looked as if a gentle breeze would send it crashing to the ground. The yard… well, it was impossible to tell what kind of shape it was in because of the snow, but it was apparent that no one had shoveled the walk or the sidewalk.

Just like home.

The thought made Krew half sick.

Cassie hadn't grown up like this. She'd had a nice home and family.

Hooking up with him that night on the beach had been the start of a downward spiral for her. Though she was doing better now and working hard to give her children a better life, she needed help.

She needed *his* help.

Casting one last glance at the ramshackle house, Krew put the car in gear and decided it was time to shop for some basic tools. He returned five hours later, pulling up as Cassie arrived home from work.

She'd just gotten Axl out of the car when Krew handed over a sack bulging with hoagie buns and assorted meats and cheeses. Though chips weren't exactly healthy, he'd grabbed a couple of bags of those as well.

Cassie peered into the bag. "What am I supposed to do with this?"

"I'm surprised you don't know food when you see it." His teasing tone had her chuckling as he followed her inside, Axl now on his shoulders. "I thought the older boys and I could clear the walk and the driveway while you make sandwiches. They'll probably be ready to eat once they're done."

K.T. and Braxton exchanged a look.

Braxton lifted both hands, palms up. "The handle on our snow shovel broke last week."

Krew smiled. "Good thing I brought a couple of extras."

Cassie touched his arm, and concern blanketed her face. "Should you be doing such strenuous activity? I mean, so soon after your ruptured spleen? It hasn't even been two months since your surgery."

"As long as your sons don't tackle me," he offered the boys a grin, "or whack me with a shovel, I'll be fine."

Braxton gestured vaguely with one hand in the direction of the bedroom he shared with his brother. "Ah, I have homework."

Not to be outmaneuvered by his older brother's quick response, K.T. was ready with his own excuse. "I'm working on an art project that's due next week."

Krew clapped both boys on the back. "Good thing shoveling doesn't take long. Especially with three men on the job."

Axl was already chowing down on his sandwich by the time the three stomped back in. Their cheeks were flushed, but they were all smiling.

Cassie took that as a positive sign. "Done so soon?"

"The hardest part was getting your car to start so we could move it to clear the driveway," Braxton declared, shooting her a look like it was her fault the vehicle was struggling.

"We got it started," Krew said in answer to her questioning look.

"Krew let me back out his car," Braxton announced. "Man, that is one sweet ride."

Cassie didn't know what to say. Before this moment, she'd had no idea cars were even on the radar of her computer-focused son. "Next time, I get to back it out." K.T. glanced at Krew as if seeking confirmation.

"Absolutely." Krew placed a hand on the boy's shoulder. "These two guys can really shovel snow. For the most part, I supervised."

"Our sidewalk is the cleanest on the entire block." K.T.'s voice held more than a little pride.

"You won't get your feet wet getting out of the car anymore." Braxton glanced at her shoes, sitting on a rug by the door.

"Good job, guys." Krew's voice was matter-of-fact. "I'll leave two of the shovels for you. I'm taking the third one to my place."

Cassie met Krew's gaze. "Thank you."

"Don't thank me. Your sons did all the work."

Cassie nodded, but knew differently. She'd tried to get the boys to shovel before, but like they did with Krew this evening, they'd had all sorts of excuses. The difference was, he hadn't let them get away with it. Somehow, he'd even made it fun.

"Krew has tools. Lots of them," K.T. informed her. "He told us the house he grew up in was worse than this one. He's going to show us how to make repairs since Old Man Winkle won't do anything."

"Yeah," Braxton echoed. "Just because Winkle won't do anything doesn't mean we can't."

"Working with tools is a skill you can always use," K.T. told her.

"Yes, it is." Cassie's heart swelled. She resisted the urge to ruffle K.T.'s hair, knowing he wouldn't appreciate the gesture. Not in front of Krew. "Sandwiches are on the counter, along with mayo and mustard. You can eat in here or in your room. Your choice."

"See ya later, man." Braxton lifted a hand.

"Thanks for the food," K.T. called over his shoulder, already on his way to the counter. "Even if we did have to work for it."

The two boys grabbed the sandwiches and a bag of chips and disappeared into their bedroom.

"Thank you. Sincerely." Cassie gestured toward the kitchen. "Let me make you a sandwich. A kind gentleman brought enough food to feed an army."

Krew grinned, but shook his head. "I should get home. I'm guessing you have some studying to do."

She pointed at Axl. "Once I get him to bed."

"When is your test?"

"I can take it anytime I feel ready." Cassie couldn't stop the shiver of anticipation. "I'm aiming for the week after Thanksgiving."

"You'll pass."

"If I don't, I'll try again."

"You've done a good job with the boys." Krew met her gaze. "They're amazing kids."

The compliment had tears welling in Cassie's eyes. She hurriedly brushed them away. In the past few years, compliments about her parenting skills had been few and far between. "Are you really going to teach them how to do home repairs?"

"Absolutely." Krew flashed her that heart-stopping smile, then hesitated. "Cass…"

"What is it?" Cassie furrowed her brow at his suddenly serious expression. "Did one of the boys say something? Or do something you didn't want to mention in front of them?"

"No. Nothing like that." Krew swallowed. "I just want to say thank you."

"It's me who should be thanking you." She smiled. "For the shovels and the clean driveway. Not to mention all the food. You brought enough to feed us for a week."

"I wasn't referring to any of that." He cleared his throat. "Thanks for letting me be here, for allowing me to spend time with you and your children. It's been a long time since I felt I was part of a family."

Cassie saw he meant every word. If he could be honest and take a risk, so could she. "I like having you around."

Krew studied her for a long moment before stepping to her and resting his hands on her shoulders.

An ache of longing filled her. Not since she was fifteen had anyone touched her heart like Krew. She wanted him to kiss her.

Her body quivered with anticipation. Just when she thought she couldn't wait a second longer, he tugged her to him.

Finally, blessedly, his mouth closed over hers. Krew's lips were warm and sweet. He kissed her with a slow thoroughness that left her yearning for more.

Cassie stroked the back of his neck, twining her fingers in his thick, soft hair.

When he stepped back, they stood there gazing at each other until he moved her arm so her hand slid down to his and he gently locked their fingers together.

He smiled at her.

She smiled back.

Then, as if he couldn't help himself, he brushed another kiss across her lips before strolling out the door.

CHAPTER FOURTEEN

Cassie was still basking in the warm glow of the previous evening when her mother and Len walked through the door of the Daily Grind. It wasn't unusual for the two to stop by, but they usually waited until happy hour, which was still several hours away.

Ryder was busy in the back room.

"Cassie." Her mother rushed to the bake case. "We were hoping you were working today."

There was no denying that Anita Fishback was an attractive woman. Layered auburn hair waved gently around her angular face. For a woman in her late fifties, her skin was remarkably free from wrinkles. Partly because of good genes, mostly thanks to regular Botox treatments.

Anita was as slender as her willow-thin daughters, but with bigger breasts. Though Cassie considered her mother's hazel eyes her best feature, she had no doubt her mother would declare her favorite asset to be her sexy figure.

"Good to see you again, Cass." Len offered her a gap-toothed smile, then dropped his gaze to the case. "I have a hankering for something sweet. What do you recommend?"

"The coffeecake this week is caramel apple." Cassie didn't mention that the variation was a huge hit. It still didn't sit well with her mother that Blooms Bake Shop had the exclusive contract to provide pastries to the Daily Grind. "It's really good. While the cake is moist and buttery, the caramel-streusel topping adds that extra bit of delicious."

"I have a caramel apple coffeecake that I make in my bakery." Anita sniffed. "People tell me it's the best in town."

"I'm sure it's delicious," Cassie said. While her mother wasn't much of a cook, she was an excellent baker. "I can't wait to taste it."

Len glanced at Anita. "You should make some for the kids. Maybe have some on hand so they can take it home after Thanksgiving dinner."

"Wow. Thanksgiving. It seemed so far away, and now it's almost here." Cassie shifted from one foot to the other. She had a sinking feeling her mother was going to offer to make Thanksgiving dinner.

Please, no.

"That's why we're here." Len put a hand on Anita's shoulder. "Lindsay wants to host Thanksgiving this year, but to take some of the burden off her, your mother is handling the coordination."

"Oh." Cassie wondered if that meant her mother would be cooking, too. If that was the case, she knew the boys would rather eat hot dogs at home.

"She's already invited me," Len added, "and I said yes. I can't imagine not spending the holidays with my Muffy."

The pet name he had for her mother had always struck Cassie as silly. Today, it seemed, well, sweet.

"Your sister has offered to make the bird, the stuffing and the mashed potatoes," Anita informed her. "I thought you could bring that green bean casserole the boys love and cranberry relish."

"Sure." Relief washed through Cassie. "I can do that."

"Dakota and I will handle the rolls and the pies."

"It sounds like a good plan." Cassie thought of Krew. "Has Dakota said anything about wanting to invite someone else to dinner this year?"

Anita's gaze sharpened.

Len inclined his head. "Does Dakota have a boyfriend?"

"I hope not," Anita huffed. "The girl doesn't need the distraction."

Len laughed. "Most girls that age seem to like that kind of distraction."

Anita's lips pursed. "Dakota needs to stay focused on her education. One mistake can start a snowball of changes, all downhill."

Len's brow furrowed. "I'm not sure I follow."

"She means Dakota could have sex, get pregnant and end up unmarried with four kids and working in a job for little more than minimum wage." Cassie gestured to herself. "Like me."

"Oh, honey, I'm sure that wasn't what she was thinking," Len said in an obvious attempt to soothe her.

Cassie met her mother's eyes.

To her surprise, Anita looked away and her voice softened. "I want the best for Dakota. Just like I want the best for you."

"I let you down."

"You let yourself down." Anita cleared her throat. "And I let you down."

Her mother's admission had Cassie blinking back tears.

"Mistakes are a part of life." Cassie finally managed to find her voice. "I've learned from mine."

"You've made great strides." Anita glanced at Len. "I don't know if I told you, but Cassie has taken a sabbatical from men. She's going to concentrate on herself and her boys. I couldn't be prouder."

Cassie found it interesting that this was what made her mother proud, rather than her efforts to get her real estate license. She thought of Krew and the kisses they'd shared.

It meant nothing, she told herself. Just some friendly kisses between two people who shared a daughter.

But why, then, did she find herself thinking about last night's kiss and wondering when she could kiss him again?

∼

Krew paused at the door leading into the day care center at the Good Hope Living Center. When Cassie had called and asked if he'd mind picking Axl up at day care and walking him over to the Daily Grind, he hadn't hesitated.

He liked Cassie. They were friends. While he was in Good Hope, he would do what he could to make her life easier.

The bells over the door jingled as Krew stepped inside and strode to the reception desk. The brightly colored clock on the wall read five fifty-eight. Krew smiled. He'd made it with two minutes to spare.

An older woman, her salt-and-pepper hair pulled back in a stylish twist, was on the phone. "Roy was lucky the fire department arrived when they did. If he'd been in there much longer…"

She met Krew's gaze and held up a finger. "Angie, I'll need to call you back."

The women set the receiver back on its base and smiled up at Krew. "How can I help?"

"I didn't mean to overhear, but were you by any chance talking about Roy Davis?"

"Yes." Surprise skittered across her face. "Do you know him?"

"I think everyone in Good Hope knows him." Krew smiled. "A field trip to Cherry Acres has been a grade-school tradition for as far back as I can remember."

"Yes, well." The older woman sighed. "I'm afraid there was a fire at his place last night. His house burned to the ground."

"But he's okay?" Krew recalled Roy as being a kind, if rather intimidating, man.

"My friend said they took him to Sturgeon Bay with smoke inhalation. It sounds like he'll be fine."

"That's good news."

The clock on the wall began to chime. Krew looked up in alarm.

"Don't worry. You're not late." The woman glanced at her computer screen. "Who are you here for?"

"I'm Krew Slattery. I'm here to pick up Axl Lohmeier. I believe his mother called and gave her okay."

The woman's smile faded. "Our normal protocol is to have something written on file before releasing a child to someone other than a parent."

"I believe Cassie spoke with the director and got her okay."

"Let me call her quick." Holding up one finger the woman made a quick call then smiled and pointed to an arched doorway. "Axl will be in there with the other two children waiting for their parents."

The money clock was ticking for those parents. According to Cassie, if Axl wasn't picked up by six, she'd be charged twenty dollars for each fifteen minutes after six, whether she was late by a minute or fifteen.

A young woman with curly brown hair, who couldn't be much older than Dakota, sat on the rug with the three children. They were tossing a ball back and forth between them.

Krew cleared his throat. "I'm here for Axl."

She looked up, smiled, then turned her attention to Axl, who'd already scrambled to his feet.

"Don't forget your picture." The teacher pointed to a table, then turned to Krew. "Each child drew pictures of their family today. Axl's is quite detailed. You may have a budding little artist there."

"One of his older brothers is very artistic."

Axl scooped up his picture, then lowered his head and ran full speed toward Krew. Just before he got tackled, Krew grabbed the boy and swung him up in the air, making him giggle.

The sound was so infectious, Krew smiled.

"Is that your dad, Axl?" a small red-headed boy, who appeared to be a year older than Axl, called out.

Axl studied Krew for several seconds, then nodded.

"Cool." The boy snatched the ball from the smaller child while the teacher's attention was on Krew.

"Axl's coat is over there, on the hook beneath his name." The teacher gestured to a row of mostly empty hooks and three remaining coats.

"Get your coat," Krew told Axl. "We're going to walk to where Mommy works."

Axl grabbed the coat with one hand and shoved the picture at Krew with the other. "For you."

Krew shook his head. "It's a picture of your family, Axl. Your mom will want it."

"It's for you." Axl's chin jutted out. He spread open the paper and pointed to a man standing beside a tall woman with yellow hair. "That's you."

The teacher had been right. It was a detailed picture and depicted him and Cassie as well as the three boys and Dakota, each of them easily identifiable.

For a second, Krew found it difficult to breathe. He put the paper in the inside pocket of his coat. When he spoke, his voice was raspy, as if he'd just consumed several shots of whiskey in rapid succession. "That's really good, bud. Thanks. Now put on your coat, please."

Axl struggled with the zipper, frowning.

"Can I help?"

"I do it." Axl's blond brows remained pulled together in concentration. He grinned broadly when the zipper caught and he pulled it up. "See?"

"Good job." Unlike Cassie's coat, which was totally unsuitable for winter weather, Axl's coat appeared well insulated. Krew narrowed his gaze, spotting a hat and gloves peeking out of his pockets. "Put on your gloves and hat. It's cold outside."

To his surprise, the boy obliged.

Before they left, Krew pulled out two twenties and held them out to the teacher. "I'd like to leave this to cover the extra cost for those two."

He gestured with his head toward the two boys playing with the ball on the rug.

The woman hesitated. "Well, I don't—"

"Spirit of the season and all that." Krew offered her a persuasive smile.

Her fingers curved around the bills. "Thank you. I'm sure they'll appreciate it."

As soon as Krew stepped out the door, Axl placed his small hand in his. Though it was likely something he'd been conditioned to do while crossing streets, Krew felt his heart lurch.

It was as if Axl was putting his trust in him, counting on Krew to take care of him and keep him safe.

Krew tightened his grip around the little fingers. There was an ache in the area of his heart, and he knew he would protect this child with his life.

Despite Axl wanting to jump on every crack in the sidewalk, they made good progress until the entrance to the downtown park came into view. It wasn't a large park by any standards—a few swings, an old-fashioned metal slide and a merry-go-round. The bushes shaped like animals and the ornate streetlights illuminating the area made it unique.

Axl tugged on his hand. "I want to go on the merry-go-round."

"I need to call your mom first to make sure it's okay." When Krew released Axl's hand to pull out his phone, the boy started through the black wrought-iron gate gilded with gold. "Stop right there."

Reacting to Krew's forceful tone, Axl froze as if playing a game of statue. The boy turned, his eyes large and very blue. He didn't move a muscle.

Krew held up a finger as he brought the phone to his ear. "Cassie. I've got Axl, and we're nearly to the Grind. Did your coworker show up yet?"

Cassie exhaled an audible breath. "Not yet. But I reached her. She says she's on her way."

"Do you mind if we stop at the park for a few minutes? I know you said Axl could wait in the shop until your replacement arrives, but this might give him a chance to run off some energy."

"Is it too cold?"

Instead of tossing off an answer, he considered. "It's chilly, but he's got his hat and gloves on, and we won't stay long. After a couple turns on the merry-go-round, I bet he'll be ready to leave."

"Okay." Cassie hesitated. "Thanks for picking him up, Krew. If I'd had any other options, I wouldn't have bothered—"

"It's not a bother." He cleared his throat. "I'm here to help. You can count on me. Remember that."

By the time Krew and Axl arrived, it was feeling like a party inside the Daily Grind. Shortly before Cassie's replacement arrived, Dakota walked through the door with K.T. and Braxton.

"I'm sorry," Cassie said to Krew. "Dakota and the boys weren't supposed to get back until seven. If I'd known they'd get back early, I could have had them pick up Axl."

His eyes met hers. "It wasn't a problem. Axl and I enjoyed ourselves at the park. Your youngest has an abundance of energy."

Cassie chuckled. "Tell me about it."

Krew turned to his daughter. "Do kids in grade school still go out to Cherry Acres?"

"They did when I was in third grade," Dakota said.

K.T. and Braxton both nodded.

Krew slanted a glance at Cassie. "Did you hear about the fire?"

"I heard Roy's house was a total loss." Cassie sighed. "At least he made it out safely."

Dakota and the boys exchanged glances.

"The lady at the day care said he was in the hospital in Sturgeon Bay, for smoke inhalation," Krew said.

"He was." Dakota glanced at her little brother, who was busy putting handprints all over the glass-fronted bake case. She lowered her voice. "I saw a local news alert on my phone on the way here. Roy died at the hospital."

"Cardiac arrest," Braxton added.

"Oh no." Sadness washed over Cassie's face. "Roy ran a tight ship on those tours, but he was always nice when he came into the Grind."

"Does he have family?" Dakota asked.

Cassie's gaze turned thoughtful. "A daughter, but I think they may have been estranged. I know she doesn't live around here."

"Well," Krew rocked back on his heels, "it was great seeing all of you—"

Dakota's hand curved around his muscular biceps. "You're not going anywhere, mister."

His lips curved at her teasing tone. "I'm not?"

"Not unless it's bowling with all of us."

Krew's gaze shot to Cassie, but she only shrugged.

"They're doing bowling bingo at Pin Chasers in Sister Bay tonight." Dakota glanced pointedly at her brothers as if enlisting their support. "We called on the way back into town and signed up. We got the last five spots."

Cassie's brows pulled together in puzzlement. "I didn't think you boys liked to bowl."

"We do when there are prizes," K.T. told her.

"The grand prize is a new MacBook," Braxton said.

"You guys go." Cassie tugged her youngest away from the bakery case glass. "I've been away from Axl all day. I don't want to leave him with a sitter."

"The brat can come along." Braxton lifted the boy and flipped him upside down, making him squeal with joy. "They've got a concession area with real food. Since we're running late, we can just eat there."

Cassie thought of the small amount of money she had in her checking account. Money that would have to last her—them—until her next payday.

"Tonight is my treat." Krew spoke before she could shut down the idea. "Food, bowling, shoe rental…all of it."

"That's nice of you," Dakota said with a smile.

"Yeah, thanks," Braxton told him.

K.T. gave him a thumbs-up.

Cassie thought about protesting, very nearly did, but then she caught his gaze. He flicked a glance toward Dakota, and suddenly Cassie understood. This was an activity they could do as a family.

"What do you think, Mom?" Dakota asked, two lines of worry between her dark brows at her mother's silence.

Cassie placed a hand on her daughter's shoulder. "I think it sounds like a lot of fun."

CHAPTER FIFTEEN

"C'mon, Mom," Braxton called out. "You can do it. Straight down the middle."

"Whatever you do, don't put it in the gutter." K.T. chewed on the edge of his nail.

If Cassie could avoid sending her ball into the gutter and knock down at least one pin, their bingo card would be filled and eligible to be entered into the big drawing.

Krew watched Cassie's shoulders tense. She wasn't much of a bowler. All evening, the gutters had been her ball's best friends.

Even though bowling wasn't his game, either, Krew's innate athleticism had proven to be key to his success.

Cassie stood there for several seconds, black ball in hand. He sensed just how much she wanted to pull this off. Her boys and Dakota continued to shout words of encouragement, but Krew remained silent, not wanting to add to her stress.

He would be here to support her, regardless of the outcome. Krew was mentally preparing what he'd say to her disappointed sons, and then she gave a heave and released the ball.

It made a thudding sound as it hit the shiny lane.

Cassie didn't turn around, but stood and watched her ball's

progress from a front-and-center position just shy of the foul line.

For Krew, it was as if the world had flipped into slow motion. The ball chugged its way down the far right of the alley at the speed of a tortoise, precariously close to the gutter.

Like a sideline run, where one misstep would put you out of bounds.

Five feet to go.

Three feet to go.

Krew held his breath.

The ball reached the pins and toppled two.

The boys cheered and pumped their fists in the air.

"Way to go, Mom." Dakota curved her thumb and finger, put it between her lips and whistled.

Cassie whirled, a look of stunned disbelief on her face. Then her lips parted, and the broadest, brightest smile Krew had ever seen flashed.

He wasn't thinking about anyone but her as he reached her, lifted her in his arms and spun around. "You did it."

She looked at him, and suddenly she was that young girl on the beach, joy radiating from every pore.

His lips closed over hers in a kiss that had everyone hooting.

The hands she'd wrapped around his neck fell to her sides. Her rosy cheeks turned dark. She gave a little laugh. "I think you got caught up in the moment."

"Wow," K.T. said. "I'm glad I didn't throw the winning ball."

The comment had them all laughing, but Krew caught Dakota's assessing look.

"How long until they draw for the MacBook?" Cassie asked.

"It'll be at least another thirty minutes." Braxton glanced at Axl, asleep on the rounded plastic seating. "We don't have to wait."

Cassie looked confused. "But they told us you have to be present if your card is called in order to win."

"We probably won't win, anyway," Dakota said, her eyes dark and unreadable.

"I had a coach who told me that to win, you have to believe you're going to win." Krew slung an arm around Dakota's shoulders. "I say we get some ice cream at the snack bar and wait. What do you say, oh daughter of mine?"

The tension on Dakota's face eased in a smile. "I say that sounds like a stellar idea, Daddy-o."

They ordered hot fudge sundaes, the bowling alley's evening special. While they devoured the ice cream, Dakota told Cassie and Krew about her trip to Green Bay with her brothers earlier in the day.

"We picked up the art supplies K.T. needed, and Braxton got his computer stuff."

"What did you get?" Cassie asked.

"A sweater to wear on Thanksgiving." Dakota turned to Krew. "You're going to join us, right?"

"If I'm invited." Krew wanted to spend the day with Dakota and her family, but he hadn't wanted to assume.

"Consider this your formal invitation." Dakota's smile faded as she shifted her gaze to her mother. "Before dinner, we need to get together and tell Grandma that Krew is my dad."

Krew heard the tension in Dakota's voice. From what he recalled about Anita Fishback, this might be a difficult conversation. "If it's going to be a problem, I can skip Thanks—"

"No. I want you there," Dakota cut him off. "We should have told Grandma before now."

"I can tell her," Cassie began.

Dakota shook her head. "My dad. My conversation."

"I want to be there," Cassie said.

"Me, too." Krew didn't want either of them having to deal with Anita's sharp tongue alone.

"Can't wait to watch the blowup," Braxton said.

"It'll be better than the Fourth." K.T. grinned. "I love Grandma, but she has a short fuse."

"She'll understand," Cassie said, but Krew saw the doubt in her eyes.

"We'll do it tomorrow." Dakota gave a decisive nod. "I'll set up—"

"Shhh," Braxton said. "They're drawing the winning bingo card."

They'd chosen this table specifically because they could hear all the winning announcements.

"—Lohmeier. Is Cassie Lohmeier present?"

"Yes." Braxton shot a fist into the air. .

Cassie frowned. "Why did they call *my* name?"

"You have to be over eighteen to win. I put your name on the card." Braxton motioned for her to go, then called out, "Over here. She's right here."

Cassie hurried forward, and the bald-headed man at the microphone beamed. "Congratulations, Ms. Lohmeier."

"Wow." Dakota leaned back in her seat. "We never win anything."

"Axl won the Halloween costume contest," K.T. reminded her.

"You won the lottery," Braxton told his sister.

She rolled her eyes. "You're crazy."

"You did," K.T. agreed.

"When?" Dakota's tone challenged her brothers.

Braxton jerked a thumb in Krew's direction.

Dakota's smile lit up her whole face. "You're right. I did win the lottery."

Cassie expected Krew to leave once they got back to the house. Instead, he lifted a sleeping Axl from his car seat and carried him inside. The little boy didn't even wake when she washed his face and hands and put on his pajamas.

"He sleeps in here with you?" Krew kept his voice low as he studied the twin beds in the room.

"There's only two bedrooms, and the older boys share the other one." Cassie lifted a shoulder. "You know how it is. You make do with what you have."

She tucked the blanket around Axl and brushed a kiss across his cheek. "Sleep well, little man."

When Cassie straightened, she felt Krew's eyes on her. She squared her shoulders. "It's not an ideal setup, but once I get my real estate license, I'll look for something bigger."

"It isn't that." Krew waved a dismissive hand. "I slept on the sofa in the living room for most of my life."

"What, then?"

"You. You're amazing."

"I am not—"

He stepped forward and took her hand. "Don't put yourself down."

"Are you two about—?"

Cassie turned, her hand still in Krew's. Dakota stood in the doorway.

"I'm sorry. I didn't mean to interrupt." Dakota appeared flustered. "I was getting ready to leave and—"

"Don't go just yet." Krew smiled. "I have something I want to tell you."

Dakota's gaze shifted between her parents. "About the two of you?"

Cassie gave a nervous laugh and pulled her hand from Krew's warm grasp. Though they hadn't discussed when exactly to tell Dakota about her college tuition, she knew Krew was eager to ease Dakota's mind. "This is all about you, and it's all good."

"All about me? I like the sound of that." A tiny smile hovered at the corners of Dakota's lips. "What is it?"

"Let's talk in the living room. We don't want to wake Axl." It took Krew until he reached the doorway to realize Cassie hadn't followed him. "Aren't you coming?"

"It's for you to tell." Despite her casual tone, she felt her heart thunder against her ribs.

She didn't know what to think when he returned to her side, took her hand and tugged her to the door. "It's for *us* to tell."

Cassie let herself be maneuvered onto the sofa, surprised when Krew sat beside her.

She could hear Braxton and K.T. rummaging through the cupboards in search of a late-night snack.

Dakota took a seat in the recliner with the broken spring. Knowing the chair as she did, she perched on the edge and offered them a tentative smile. "Now tell me before I go insane with curiosity."

"Dakota, you and I both know how hard your mom works." Krew paused and waited for his daughter's slow nod. "She's in the position many parents are in nowadays, wanting to do more for their children, but the money just isn't there."

"If this is about paying for school, I understand there's no money." Puzzlement furrowed Dakota's brow. "That's why I'm working, to save enough money so I can return to La Crosse."

Dakota met Cassie's gaze. "I know you're doing the best you can. I'll get the funds together eventually. Like you, I'm not a quitter. I don't give up."

There was no way for Dakota to know just how much those words meant to her.

Krew winked at Cassie before focusing on their daughter. "The thing is, your mom and I talked, and I'm going to pay for your education. Tuition, books, room and board. All of it."

Dakota's eyes went wide. She swallowed convulsively. "You don't have to do that."

"I want to." He leaned forward, his forearms resting on his

thighs. "Your mom has been your sole support all these years. It's only fair I do my part."

Did he realize, Cassie wondered, that he'd made it sound as if this was a team effort? He wasn't giving himself proper credit.

"It's very generous of your father—" That was as much as Cassie got out.

Dakota launched herself at them, laughing and crying.

"Thank you so much." Her words tumbled out, her voice thick with emotion. "I won't let either of you down. I promise."

Overcome with emotion, Krew closed his eyes for a second as Dakota gave him a fierce hug. "I love you, Dad."

"I love you, too."

Wiping her eyes, Cassie looked back and saw Braxton and K.T. in the kitchen doorway, watching the scene with inscrutable expressions.

K.T. shoved his hand into a bag of chips, then stuffed a bunch in his mouth.

For just an instant, Cassie saw the longing in Braxton's eyes. Then her oldest son shrugged and said to no one in particular, "Told you she won the lottery."

As the Lohmeier family appeared to be riding a winning wave, Cassie hoped that good fortune extended to the upcoming talk with her mother.

"Grandma and I are baking pies later today." Dakota paced Cassie's small living room. "I could have told her then. It wouldn't have seemed so orchestrated."

"I know." Cassie blew out a breath. "But your dad insists on being there."

Dakota grinned. "He's stubborn."

"Like someone else I know." Cassie pointed to Dakota, and her daughter's smile widened.

"Actually, I think it's sweet," Dakota said.

They both started at the sharp rap on the front door.

"I'll get it." Braxton was out of his room and opening the door before either Cassie or Dakota could even think about moving.

"I'm still not sure it's a good idea for your brothers to be here." Cassie spoke in a low tone to Dakota.

"We're family." Dakota's voice softened. "Families stick."

"Woo-hoo. Look what Krew brought." Braxton held up a white bakery sack. "Doughnuts from Blooms Bake Shop."

"Dibs on the frosted chocolate," K.T. called from the bedroom, where he was entertaining Axl with a drawing program on the new laptop.

"Don't let your grandmother see that sack," Cassie warned. "We don't want her feelings to be hurt the minute she walks in."

For today's meeting, Krew wore dark pants and a gray cashmere sweater instead of jeans. He looked handsome, successful and good enough to eat.

The thought had warmth spreading across Cassie's cheeks.

"Are we ready to do this?" he asked.

"You better be ready." Braxton munched on a doughnut and pulled the curtain back from the window. "Because she and Len just drove up."

"Len is with her?" Cassie wasn't sure how she felt about one more person. Then she reminded herself that Len was important to her mother. Not only was he a nice guy, he was a stabilizing force in Anita's life.

"Show time." Dakota moved to the door and opened it before her grandmother had a chance to knock. "You're looking pretty this morning."

Knowing how important appearances were to her grandmother, Cassie wondered if Dakota might have offered the compliment to put Anita at ease. But when her mother stepped inside, Cassie realized it was the truth.

Anita's sage-green sweater dress brought out the green in her hazel eyes, which widened when she saw Krew. "I didn't realize he would be here."

Cassie smiled. "I didn't realize you were bringing Len. I'm glad you did."

She crossed the room and gave the retired sheriff a hug.

The boys brought in folding chairs from the kitchen, providing just enough seats for everyone. After a few minutes of talking about the weather and the clean driveway, they all sat down.

"I'm not sure why I'm here." Anita had chosen a spot beside Len on one of the folding chairs. "It's a busy time of year, and I—"

"This won't take long," Cassie assured her. "There's something we want to tell you."

Anita's sharp-eyed gaze shifted between Cassie and Krew. "You're moving in with him."

"No. I'm not moving in with anyone." Cassie kept her voice even. For Dakota's sake, she would not let her mother goad her into losing her temper.

"Thank God for that." Anita heaved an audible sigh.

"I'm Dakota's father." Krew spoke in a calm, matter-of-fact tone, apparently deciding there was no reason to delay the announcement.

"What?" Anita's gaze whipped to his. "What did you say?"

"He's my dad." Dakota, who was seated between Cassie and Krew on the sofa, smiled. "We did the DNA thing, and the test confirmed it."

Silence filled the room for several long seconds.

"Well." Anita huffed out a breath. "Thank goodness it's you and not that bastard Mitch."

Cassie and Dakota exchanged startled glances.

"Mitch?" Dakota mouthed.

"Not important," Cassie mouthed back, then turned her attention to her mom. "You—you don't seem upset."

"What did you expect me to do, rant and rave?" Anita looked at Len and gave a little laugh.

"Yes," Cassie and Dakota said in unison.

"I even thought you might throw something." K.T. looked around the room. "Not that there's much to throw."

Anita waved a hand and chuckled as if she thought the boy was joking. But her expression sobered when she turned to Cassie. "That was a difficult time for you. I wasn't there for you, not the way I should have been. I'm sorry. I hope when you're ready, we can talk about it. I'd like to hear everything you went through, when you're ready to share."

Tears stung the backs of Cassie's eyes. "I'd like that."

Anita nodded, then the softness faded, and she was a fierce mama bear who pinned Krew with her gaze. "As for you, if you think you can treat my daughter like she's disposable and spend nineteen years hiding from your responsibilities, you have another thing coming. You have a lot of atoning to do to prove you were worthy of Cassie then and worthy of Dakota now."

"I agree." Krew's gaze locked with Anita's, and whatever the older woman saw there had the tightness around her mouth easing.

"Well, then." Anita's searching hand found Len's, and when his strong fingers closed around hers, she appeared to steady. "Will you be in Good Hope long?"

"Until after the holidays," Krew said.

Though the words brought a pang to Cassie's heart, it was a good reminder that his stay was only temporary. She couldn't let herself get too attached.

Cassie would have to keep an eye on Dakota after he left to make sure she was coping okay. She knew it was going to be hard for her daughter to let him go.

"We're having our family Thanksgiving dinner this year at Lindsay's home." Anita glanced at Dakota briefly before her gaze resettled on Krew. "I hope you'll join us."

"You're inviting me to Thanksgiving dinner," Krew repeated.

"You're Dakota's father. That makes you family."

After firming up the time and place—Lindsay's house at one p.m. Thursday, Anita and Len left.

"Did that really happen?" Cassie tapped her lips with a finger. "Or was it a dream?"

K.T. shook his head. "Not a single firework."

"You got off easy, man," Braxton told Krew. "Trust me. Grandma is a barracuda with sharp teeth."

"In the past, Brax. But I've spent a lot of time with her lately. Grandma is more mellow. She's definitely not a marshmallow, but she's not a barracuda anymore." Dakota met Cassie's gaze. "I hope the two of you can find a way past your differences and be close again. I know she feels bad about letting you down. Hopefully, like she said, you two can talk and work things out. I think a mom and daughter should be close. Sometimes that isn't possible, I know."

Her mother's heartfelt apology had touched Cassie's heart. Anita had extended the olive branch. "She and I will talk."

"Will you forgive her?"

Will you forgive me? Cassie wondered.

But this wasn't about the rift between her and Dakota. This was about her and her mother.

"Dr. Gallagher once told me that if we live long enough, someone we love will disappoint us." Cassie expelled a breath. "I can't hope for forgiveness for myself if I can't forgive others who've hurt or disappointed me. So, yes, I will forgive your grandmother. In fact, I already have."

CHAPTER SIXTEEN

Though not as large or modern as the house Krew rented, Owen and Lindsay's single-story Craftsman home, with its gray exterior and red door, exuded charm. Each time Cassie walked through her sister's front door, a feeling of warmth wrapped around her.

Maybe it was the comfortable mission-style furniture or the beamed ceiling. It could be the fireplace, with its decorative tiles and cheery blaze in the hearth. In her heart, Cassie knew at the core it was the love found between these walls.

"I wonder when Krew will get here." Dakota pushed back the lace curtains to gaze out the front window. "I can't wait to see what he thinks of my pie."

Tradition in the Lohmeier family dictated there be two pies at Thanksgiving. The first was homemade pumpkin—no store-bought or frozen variety for this family. The second was the one Dakota had been in charge of baking.

"He probably doesn't like golden-raisin pie." Dakota glanced back at her mother, and Cassie saw the request for reassurance in her daughter's eyes.

"What's not to like?" Cassie moved to stand beside her, realizing they were now the same height. "I caught a glimpse when you were taking it out of the oven, and that lattice crust is a work of art."

Dakota flushed. "Grandma said it was top-notch."

"That's high praise."

"What did I say?" Anita strolled into the living room, looking chic in navy pants, a silk shirt and heels.

Cassie glanced down at her leggings and turkey tunic. At least Axl loved her shirt. "Mommy, pretty," he'd said over and over, stroking the red velvety wattle beneath the turkey's beak.

The never-worn sweater had been another of her consignment shop finds, undoubtedly a gag gift someone had gotten for Christmas the previous year. The sweater might not be haute couture, but it was quirky, fun and today *was* Thanksgiving. "We were discussing Dakota's awesome pie-making skills."

Anita bestowed an approving smile on her eldest grandchild. "You could have a successful career as a baker."

"Thanks, Grandma." Dakota shot another quick look out the window. "I love baking, but I'm not sure I'd like to do it full time."

"You have lots of time to decide." Anita shifted her gaze to Cassie. "Dakota mentioned Krew will be covering her college expenses."

Before Cassie could speak, Dakota piped up. "He said Mom had to handle all the expense of raising me, now it's his turn to help."

"Sounds like a smart man." Len strolled into the room and looped an arm around Anita's shoulders. "Everything smells delicious."

"We should be ready to eat within the hour." Anita frowned. "I hope we'll be able to tear Owen and the boys away from the foosball table."

Lindsay came up from the basement. "I gave them the thirty-minute warning."

"Is Axl behaving himself?" Cassie knew the boys had

promised to watch their brother, but it would be easy to forget about him while they were engaged in a game.

"He's fine." Lindsay grinned. "Owen set out some of Mindy's old toys. They're new to him, so he's in hog heaven."

Cassie frowned. "Are you sure Owen doesn't mind Axl playing with her things?"

Losing his daughter to cancer had knocked Owen to his knees. Her death had been hard on everyone in the community. Mindy's irresistible smile and personality had won her hearts all over town.

"Owen says watching Axl play with the toys brings happy memories of Mindy, so it's all good." Lindsay shifted her attention to the dining room, visible through an archway, as if reassuring herself the table was ready.

"I love the centerpiece." Cassie wondered where her sister had gotten her creative bent. As far as Cassie was concerned, Lindsay had outdone herself this year. She'd piled fruits, flowers and foliage into one arrangement.

"I went for unique. It's designed to reflect the bounties of the season." Lindsay studied the arrangement thoughtfully. "Next year I think I'll do baby pumpkins on candlestick holders."

"That sounds...interesting." Though Cassie couldn't quite picture it, she had no doubt it would be both stylish and striking. She cocked her head. "Are the colored markers on the table?"

"Ohmigoodness." Lindsay started toward the kitchen. "Mom and I put down the butcher paper, but I forgot all about the markers."

"You stay right here. You've been running around all morning." Len put a hand on Lindsay's shoulder. "Tell me where I can find these markers. I'll put them out."

"They're in a plastic box in the drawer under the Keurig." Lindsay gestured as she spoke. "There needs to be one at each place setting."

"What are we doing with them?" Len asked.

Lindsay shot him a wink. "You'll see."

"I can't wait." Len headed to the kitchen.

"He's such a nice man, and it's obvious he's crazy about you." Lindsay studied her mother. "When's the wedding?"

Anita's eyes widened. It wasn't the kind of direct question one would expect from Lindsay.

"Don't tell me he hasn't asked, because I won't believe you," Lindsay added.

"Len asked you to marry him?" Dakota's voice grew loud.

"Shh. Keep your voice down." Anita took a breath. "Yes, he asked. I declined."

Cassie told herself to stay out of this conversation, but she couldn't stop herself. "Why would you do that?"

"Len and I have a perfectly nice relationship just the way it is." Apparently seeing the skepticism on her daughters' and grand-daughter's faces, Anita added in a low tone, "I don't want to be hurt again."

"You can't think that Len is like Bernie." Cassie had never given much thought to her mother's love life, but now she worried her mom could miss out on something truly special with Len. She didn't understand how the woman dubbed I-Need-a-Man by the Bloom sisters, who'd finally found The One, would want to keep the relationship at friendship.

"Of course I don't think—"

The doorbell rang, and relief crossed Anita's face. "I'll get it."

It had to be Krew, or at least Cassie hoped it was him. Dakota had been worried he wouldn't show, though he hadn't disappointed her yet.

"Krew, we wondered when you'd get here."

"I thought we were eating at one."

"We are," Lindsay, the hostess, slipped in front of her mother to give him a hug. "Welcome."

Krew handed her a bottle of red wine. "For you."

Lindsay inspected the label. "Ooh, I love Pinot. Too bad I can't have a glass, but I'm sure everyone else will enjoy it. Thank you, Krew."

"Thanks for inviting me."

"Happy Thanksgiving, Dakota." Krew gave his daughter a hug, then studied Cassie's sweater. "I'd give you a hug, but that turkey looks like it might bite."

Cassie laughed, relieved when he only gave her arm a squeeze. She wanted to hug him, but with everyone around, it might be apparent to those with eagle eyes—namely, her mother and Dakota—that she enjoyed his arms around her a little too much.

"Krew, good to see you." Len strode over and gave his hand a shake. "Your team isn't playing today, but we plan to watch some football later this afternoon."

"Sounds good to me." Krew glanced around. "Where's Owen and the boys?"

"Downstairs playing foosball." Lindsay smiled sweetly. "Would you mind terribly going down and telling them they need to get washed up? We're going to start putting the food on the table."

Krew did as she asked, but instead of staying downstairs as Cassie expected, he returned to help carry food to the table.

"Would you mind carving, Krew?" Lindsay asked. "It's not Owen's or Len's strength."

Cassie didn't like seeing Krew put on the spot. He hadn't grown up in a home where carving a turkey was part of his education. "Krew's a guest and—"

Krew's hand closed over the one she'd raised, and when he lowered their hands, he kept hold of hers as he talked. "I admit I'd have declined the offer five years ago. But my friend Earl is one mean turkey carver. I spent the last few holidays with him, his family and a mammoth bird. Not to brag, but I have mad skills with a carving knife."

"Fabulous news. Let me show you the way to the turkey." Lindsay grabbed his arm.

Krew reluctantly released Cassie's hand, but only after giving it a squeeze.

"I'll fill the water glasses." Cassie lifted the crystal pitcher, and when she turned, she found Dakota studying her with a curious expression. "Something wrong?"

"No." Dakota's eyes were hooded. "I better see what's left to do."

Soon, they were all seated, platters of food filling every square inch of the table.

"Before we begin passing around this amazing food, I need to remind everyone of our family traditions." Lindsay lifted the marker next to her plate. "Everyone must write one thing—though we encourage you to write more—for which you are grateful. You can write these anywhere on the butcher paper."

K.T., who'd been drawing a scene, put down his marker.

"If any of you want to draw, that's fine. Just make sure you write one gratitude." Lindsay smiled at K.T. "At the end of the meal, we'll go around the table, and everyone can share one thing. The next tradition—"

"Sweetheart," Owen's fingers curved around Lindsay's hand, "I don't mean to interrupt, but I'd like to say one thing about the power of gratitude."

"Certainly." Lindsay ceded center stage to her husband.

"Mindy kept a gratitude jar. Every night, she'd write down one thing she was grateful for." Owen's voice wobbled, but he quickly steadied it. "I read some of them after she passed away. She always found something to be grateful for, even during her darkest days. So if you're having trouble thinking of something, remember it doesn't have to be big. A sunny day. A hug from someone you love. A good night's sleep, which for Lindsay and me, will probably be in short supply once our baby arrives."

Laughter rippled around the table.

Lindsay laughed along with the rest of her family and resumed her instructions. "The next tradition is, if you get the turkey wishbone in your serving of meat, you get to choose who you crack it with. That's all."

Cassie lifted her fork, ready to dig in when Len cleared his throat.

"Lindsay and Owen asked me to say grace. If you could join hands and bow your head, I'll begin."

Krew had settled himself between Dakota and Axl, with Cassie on the other side of Axl.

Apparently realizing Axl wasn't big on holding hands, Krew reached around him to take Cassie's hand. He caressed her palm with his thumb as he lowered his head, a tiny smile playing at the corners of his mouth.

Cassie fought to steady her breath as Len began.

"In a country where so many go hungry, we give thanks for the bounty you have bestowed on this family. In a time where loneliness is prevalent, we thank you for the gift of family and friends. May you impress upon our hearts the desire to bless others as we have been blessed. Amen."

"I'm hungry," Axl called out.

"Bon appétit." Lindsay waved a hand as if she held a starting flag, and the passing of food began.

Dakota had Krew engaged in conversation during most of the meal, but Cassie noticed Krew kept his eye on Axl.

He cut up the child's turkey before Cassie had a chance and stopped the boy from slinging a bun at Anita.

Every so often, Krew's gaze would flick to her, and their eyes would lock. Each time that happened, Cassie's heart skipped a beat.

"Cassie, I just noticed you got the wishbone." Lindsay couldn't have sounded more pleased if it had turned up in her own turkey.

"Who are you going to crack it with?" Braxton asked. "Just so you know, I'm available."

"Me, too." K.T. pointed to her, then back to himself.

"I'm considering my options." Cassie had set the bone aside to let it dry. "I need to pick a weakling, so I get the big piece and can make a wish."

Cassie let her gaze deliberately settle on Axl, who was contentedly gnawing on a turkey leg.

"I wouldn't choose him," K.T. told her. "He'll jerk the entire wishbone out of your hand and then start screaming when you try to take it back."

The fact that Cassie could so easily visualize the scene told her that was exactly what would happen. Thankfully she didn't have to decide right now.

Cassie forgot about the wishbone as she dove into her food. She'd had made a serious dent in whipped potatoes made delicious by the addition of sour cream and real butter and was working on her turkey and dressing when she saw Krew pick up his marker and write something near his plate on the paper.

Dinner was nearly over, and Cassie still hadn't written anything on the butcher paper. Some years she'd had difficulty thinking of something to be grateful for, but Owen's comments had put things in perspective. If his little girl, fighting for her life because of an inoperable brain tumor, had been able to find things to be grateful for, so could she.

Picking up her marker, Cassie began to write, vowing to never again take the blessings in her life for granted.

Braxton and K.T. were assigned the task of clearing the table to ready it for dessert. Cassie was in charge of pouring the coffee, while Len took pie orders. It would be up to Dakota and Anita to deliver the slices.

"We have two selections," Owen advised. "Pumpkin with real whipped cream or, what I understand is a family favorite, golden raisin."

Instead of relying on his memory, Len went from person to person, writing down each selection on a small notepad.

Cassie was about to refill Krew's coffee cup when Len paused beside him.

There was no doubt in Krew's mind what he was going to order. Pumpkin pie was a personal favorite, and the real whipped cream was a special bonus. His taste buds were ready.

"What would you like, Krew?"

At that moment, Cassie bent close on the pretext of filling his cup. "Raisin."

Her voice was low, for his ears only.

Startled, he looked up.

Cassie only smiled and moved to the next cup.

"What'll it be?" Len asked. "Pumpkin or raisin?"

"Raisin," Krew found himself saying.

In less than a minute, Dakota set a piece of raisin pie, topped with a dollop of whipped cream, in front of him.

At least, Krew thought, eyeing the pie, he'd like the topping.

"I was excited when Len told me you'd picked the raisin pie." Dakota gazed down at the dessert in front of him.

"I got a piece, too." Cassie slid into her seat and smiled at the two of them. "Dakota made the raisin pie, Krew. Prepare to be wowed. Our daughter is an amazing baker."

"You can take a bite now." Dakota kept her voice low. "You're not supposed to, but you can if you want a taste."

Cassie's eyes urged him to do so.

Thank you, he wanted to say to her. Without her intervention, he'd have chosen the pumpkin.

Krew forked off a small bite, determined to rave. The taste was intriguing. He discovered it wasn't just the whipped topping he liked. "This is good. I taste more than raisins. There are apples and some kind of nuts."

Dakota smiled. "Walnuts."

Cassie's eyes widened. "You altered the recipe."

"It's not set in stone." Dakota tossed her head. "I also added apple cider and lemon zest."

"Let me taste it."

Before Krew could react, Cassie had forked off a large bite of *his* pie.

"Umm, this is incredible."

When her fork moved in for a second bite, Krew shielded his plate with his arms. "Hey, you've got your own piece."

Dakota laughed. "I can get you another piece if you're still hungry once you finish. It makes me so happy that you like it."

"It's delicious." Krew was glad he could answer honestly. "I'll definitely need a second—"

The clinking of a fork against a crystal glass had all conversation ceasing.

"It's come to my attention that the wishbone has yet to be cracked." Owen's gaze settled on Cassie. "Have you chosen who will crack it with you?"

Krew didn't know what to think when Cassie held the wishbone out to him. He took one end and pulled. Though he gave it his best effort, he could have cheered when the bigger half remained in Cassie's hand.

"Make a wish, Mom," K.T. said.

"Make it a big one," Braxton urged.

Cassie closed her eyes for half a second, then smiled. "Time for pie."

Krew ended up eating another piece of raisin pie and half a piece of pumpkin before he pushed back from the table. "I am so full."

When he started to rise, Dakota pulled him back down. "It's not over yet."

He glanced over to Cassie. She gestured to her sister, who'd just stood.

"It's now time for us to go around the table and share one gratitude." Lindsay smiled at her husband, then back at everyone else. "I'll start. I'm grateful for all of you and thankful we could gather together today."

Krew felt himself tense as his turn to speak got closer. He told himself to keep it generic. After all, he *was* thankful for the wonderful food.

But when it finally came to him, Krew couldn't take the easy route. That had never been his way. "I'm grateful to be part of this family. And thankful you invited me to share this wonderful meal and your company."

He smiled at Dakota then shifted his gaze to Cassie. The emotion storming in her eyes matched his own.

Krew knew this was one Thanksgiving he wouldn't soon forget.

CHAPTER SEVENTEEN

"What's on tap for the rest of the day?" Krew asked.

"Football at three on the tube." Owen moved the centerpiece off the table to the mantel.

"I brought a puzzle, if anyone's interested." Len gestured with one hand. "Anita is getting a card table set up in the family room."

"I love puzzles." Cassie slanted a glance at her sister. "We used to put them together as a family all the time when we were kids. Do you remember, Lindsay?"

"I remember," her sister said with a wistful smile.

"Muffy and I do several puzzles a week." Len's lips curved. "We finish one, and the next night we move on to another."

"You and Mom see each other every night?" Cassie kept her tone casual and offhand.

Len thought for a moment, stroking his mustache. "Pretty much."

"That's quite a drive for you," Lindsay observed.

"Not that far. Seeing my Muffy is worth it."

"Where is it you live, Len?" Krew asked.

When the man described the location, Krew cocked his head. "You and Roy Davis were neighbors."

The light in Len's eyes dimmed. "He lived down the road from me for nearly forty years. My wife and his were friends until Paula ran off."

Cassie's brows pulled together. "A customer at the Grind said he had a daughter. If he did, I don't recall ever meeting her."

"She was a lot older than you and Lindsay." Sadness filled Len's eyes. "From the time she was a little girl, Shannon and Roy butted heads. They were so much alike, both stubborn and hard-headed. That summer after she graduated from high school, they had a huge fight. She stormed out of the house and left town. As far as I know, Roy never heard from her again."

"That's a long time to stay angry with someone you love." Cassie's gaze shifted to where Anita now stood in the doorway.

"Roy could be stubborn. He was waiting for Shannon to make the first move." Len spotted Anita and motioned her over. "It should be a lesson to us all."

"It can be difficult making that first move," Cassie said.

"But it's worth it," Anita answered.

Cassie thought of all the holidays they'd spent apart. She smiled at her mother. "Yes, it's definitely worth it."

Krew shot the ball. When it bounced off the rim and into Braxton's hands, the boy hooted.

"That's HORSE." Braxton glanced at Krew. "One more game?"

They were tied now, one game each. Though Krew had never professed to be a great basketball player, his competitive spirit wouldn't let anything end in a tie.

"Let's do it."

Braxton shot the ball to Krew in a quick move that made Krew grin. They'd scrimmaged some with Dakota and K.T. before the two, complaining of the cold, went inside.

Krew was lining up to shoot when Braxton spoke.

"That's a good thing you're doing for my sister."

Pausing, Krew turned to Braxton, rotating the ball in his hands.

"You know, paying for her college. Spending time with her."

"I'm her dad."

"Mine doesn't want anything to do with me. Or with K.T." While Braxton's tone said that was of no consequence, his eyes told a different story. "The guy had another family. Mom didn't know. He told her he was single."

Braxton hurriedly added that last part, as if wanting to make sure Krew didn't blame Cassie.

"That's low." There was more Krew wanted to say about a man who would deliberately take advantage of a young woman's trust, but he reminded himself this jerk was Braxton's father.

"I know his name. I even know where he lives." Braxton's voice grew thick, and he cleared his throat. "I've seen pictures of him and his kids. He's got a son a little older than me and a couple of girls younger than K.T."

Krew knew finding out all this information would be child's play for someone with Braxton's computer skills.

"K.T. doesn't say much, but I know it bothers him."

Krew bounced the ball and caught it, never taking his gaze off Braxton.

"It doesn't bother me."

Lie, Krew thought, but only nodded.

"I understand K.T.'s confusion. I mean, you'd think the guy would want to see him. My brother is an incredible artist. But he doesn't." Braxton's shoulders slumped, even as his jaw tightened. "Want to see us, that is."

"Have I ever told you about my old man?"

Braxton shook his head.

"He was a drunk, a mean one." Krew's fingers tightened on the ball. "He didn't care about me or my sister. The happiest day of my life was when I left home. We haven't spoken since."

"Yeah, that's what I try to tell K.T. We don't need a dad."

"My father was never a dad. There's a distinction. Everyone has a father, but not all of us have someone who cares about us, who mentors us, who has our back."

Braxton considered the comment, then nodded. "Didn't hurt you. You turned out good."

"My college football coach was as close to a dad as I ever got. He cared about his players, cared about me. Not just how I handled the ball, but me. He served as an example of what a good man is like." Krew bounced the ball, caught it. "There'll be men who'll come into your life, guys you can look up to and feel that connection. It may be Owen. Or Len. Or someone else."

"Like I said, it's K.T. who feels like he's missing out." Braxton gave a humorless laugh. "I tell him, be thankful. Just think if Clint Gourley was our father. Talk about a miserable excuse for a human being."

"That's right. He lived with you guys."

"Worst years of our lives." Braxton's hands clenched into fists at his sides. "He pretty much stayed out of my face. But what he did to Mom—"

Everything in Krew went cold. It took all his self-control to keep his tone even. "What did he do?"

"Beat her down." Braxton must have seen the anger that filled Krew, because he added, "Not physically. He didn't hit her. In a way, what he did was worse."

Krew waited for his pulse to return to normal. Before it did, Braxton continued. "He destroyed her confidence step by step. It was classic."

At Krew's frown, Braxton explained, "I learned about it in psychology class. First, you isolate the person from everyone who cares about them. Then, you beat them down with your words. He criticized her constantly, put down her opinions until she felt she couldn't do anything right. We all walked on egg shells around him. The guy had a temper."

Braxton's eyes took on a distant gleam. "I never thought she'd kick him out, especially after she got pregnant with Axl."

"But she did."

Braxton nodded. "Then he got arrested and went to prison. He wanted Mom to come and see him and bring Axl. She refused. But he won't be in prison forever."

Krew shot the ball, and it swished through the net. "You think he'll come back around?"

"I think he'll do whatever he can to mess with her life." Braxton's face tightened into hard lines. "I won't let that happen. I'm bigger now. I'll keep him away from Mom and Axl. A man takes care of the ones he loves."

Braxton grabbed the ball from Krew's hands and set up for his shot.

A man takes care of the ones he loves.

The phrase continued to circle in Krew's head even after the game ended and they went inside to watch the pregame show.

When Krew saw Cassie down on the floor, playing tickle monster with Axl, his heart lurched. In that moment, he knew that Braxton wasn't the only one who would go to the mat to protect someone he loved.

Cassie expected Krew to make his excuses when the football game ended. Instead, he surprised her by agreeing to stay for butternut squash soup with herbed flatbread.

Afterward, the games and cards were brought out.

"Len and I could still use help with the puzzle," Anita told her family. "The one he brought today is a doozy."

"You're welcome." Len's wicked smile made her laugh.

The camaraderie between the two warmed Cassie's heart, but left her puzzled. She couldn't believe this wonderful man had asked her mother to marry him and she'd turned him down.

"I've got a couple of different decks of cards." Lindsay held three in her hand. "Uno. Go Fish. And a regular—" Lindsay frowned down at the third deck in her hand. "What the heck?"

Owen stepped to his wife's side and glanced at the cards. He groaned. "I thought you'd passed those on by now."

"I didn't have anyone—" Lindsay paused, her gaze settling on Cassie and Krew.

Crossing the room, Lindsay handed the deck to her sister. "These are getting-to-know-you cards. Also known as relationship cards."

Cassie pushed them back. "I'm not in a relationship."

Her sister's chin lifted in a stubborn tilt. "The way I see it, even if you aren't a romantic couple, you and Krew are now co-parents, which means your relationship is important. These cards are about strengthening relationships."

"I understand that, but—" Cassie began.

"You each answer three questions, and then you can get rid, ah, give them to someone else." Lindsay's eyes remained firm on hers. "Or are you scared?"

Cassie rolled her eyes. "Don't try that old trick. Just give me the stupid cards."

"Stupid, stupid, stupid cards." Axl spoke in a singsong tone while slashing his arm through the air as if brandishing a sword.

"*Silly* cards," Cassie said desperately.

"You said stupid." Braxton appeared amused. "You know the brat repeats everything."

"Axl," Krew said loudly, and the little boy whirled. "Do you want a new car to play with?"

The boy cocked his head, his gaze intense as he watched Krew pull a small red car from his pocket.

"It looks like your car, Krew," K.T. said as Axl snatched the car from him.

"What do you say, Axl?" Cassie prompted.

The boy held the precious car tight against his chest. "Thank you."

At that moment, Dakota strolled into the room. She eyed her mother. "What do you have in your hand?"

Casually, Cassie closed her fingers more tightly around the cards. If her purse had been nearby and it wouldn't have drawn more attention, she'd have dropped the deck into her bag. "Just some cards your aunt gave me."

"Playing cards?" Dakota asked, perking up.

"Not exactly," Cassie hedged.

"What are they, then?"

The question told Cassie that this girl was indeed her father's daughter. She was not going to give up until she had answers.

"They're getting-to-know-you cards." Falling back on Lindsay's earlier description, Cassie ignored her sister's smirk.

"I love that kind of stuff." Before she could stop her, Dakota swiped the cards from Cassie's hand.

Dakota turned to her brothers. "You guys want to play?"

K.T. glanced at his brother. "Since this is an electronic-free zone for the day and our other choice is a puzzle, I'm game."

Dakota motioned to Braxton. "You'll play, too."

"Will I?" Despite his words, the smile Braxton shot his sister was indulgent.

"Yes, you will." Dakota pulled a card from the middle of the deck, apparently not concerned about rules. Her lips curved as she read, "What's your favorite childhood memory?"

"You're the oldest, Dakota. You answer first," K.T. told her.

Dakota tapped her finger against her thigh, giving the question serious thought, not appearing to notice when her brothers dropped down on the sofa beside her.

Since it involved childhood memories, Cassie assumed it would involve Lindsay. Dakota and her aunt had always been close.

"I was five and it was summer. Mom was pregnant with K.T.,

and it was scorching in our apartment." Dakota slanted a glance in her mother's direction. "The window air conditioner had conked out. Remember?"

Cassie nodded, not sure where this was headed.

Braxton frowned. "I don't remember."

Dakota rolled her eyes. "You were, like, only two years old."

"But I was very advanced for my age."

"Hardly," Dakota teased. "You used to fart in our blow-up baby pool just to make bubbles. You'd say you were a motorboat."

Braxton grinned. "Told you I was advanced."

"So what's your memory?" K.T. prodded.

"Mom, Brax and I were walking to the park to cool off and so we could play. Someone had their oscillating sprinkler on, and the spray went over the sidewalk. I begged Mom to let us run through it." Dakota glanced at Cassie, and her expression softened. "The three of us ran through it holding hands. Because it was so much fun, we did it again. We were soaked and laughing so hard..."

Tears filled Dakota's eyes as she met her mother's gaze. "It was magical."

Cassie cleared her throat and nodded, not trusting herself to speak.

"You're up, Brax," Dakota said. "K.T., you're on deck."

"I got a rat for my birthday when I was ten." Braxton grinned at Krew's look of surprise. "His name was Nicodemus, and he was a good boy. Except for the one time he got loose in the house."

Dakota chuckled. "I saw him running down the hall and screamed."

"Anyway, Nicodemus must have been hiding under the sofa," Braxton continued, "because when Grandma came over, he decided to make a grand entrance. He poked his head out, then ran across her foot. She jumped up and screamed—"

"It wasn't funny," Anita called from the other room.

"It was very funny," Braxton called back.

"Good one, bro." Dakota shifted her gaze to K.T. and lifted a brow.

"Mine isn't funny. Mom took me to an art class at the Y when I was four." K.T.'s gaze sought hers, and she smiled, remembering. "It was one of those parent-kid classes. Moms and kids were asked to draw a horse. The instructor looked at Mom's and then at mine and accused us of switching. He was convinced she drew the one that I did."

All eyes turned to Cassie. She lifted a shoulder, let it drop. "Mine was pretty bad, while K.T.'s was amazing."

"I told the man he was wrong, that *was* my picture. He called us liars. Mom took my hand, and we walked out of the class." K.T. smiled. "And he never taught at the Y again."

"I don't get it." Krew's brows pulled together. "Why would that be a favorite memory?"

"Mom got a full refund on the class and used the money to buy me art supplies."

"You're right, K.T. It isn't funny, but it's a good memory. Let's do one more question." Dakota reached for the deck and looked at her mother. "This time, you and Krew have to answer."

Dakota slipped a card out from the middle of the deck. Red began climbing up her neck as soon as she scanned the card.

Braxton leaned forward. "What's the question?"

Dakota placed the card on the top of the deck and stood. "It's a boring one. Besides, you guys promised me a rematch at foosball. If we don't do it now, we won't have time."

The boys sprinted toward the stairs, Dakota close behind.

Krew turned to Cassie. "Why do you think she lost interest in playing?"

"No idea." Cassie scooped up the deck and flipped over the top card. Her eyes widened. "Oh my."

"What's the question?" Krew leaned close, trying to read the card.

She handed the card to him. "Take a look."

Cassie watched his eyes as he scanned the question. She knew he'd finished reading when he grinned. "Yes. I'd definitely be up for this. How about you?"

Even as fire scorched her veins at the suggestive image the words conjured up, Cassie laughed and waved away his question. Still, for the rest of the evening, every time her gaze locked with Krew's, the image of them together had heat surging.

As she gathered her purse at the end of the evening and saw the deck nestled inside, Cassie knew exactly what she'd dream about tonight.

From the look in Krew's eyes, she wouldn't be the only one.

"This has been one of the best Thanksgivings ever," Dakota declared, grabbing her oversized bag. "You know what would be the maraschino cherry on top of today's sundae?"

"You're a big nerd, Dakota," K.T. asserted. "Maraschino cherry, ha."

Dakota ignored her brother's teasing and focused on her father. "Will you come to my basketball game on Saturday? It's at one o'clock at the Y."

Krew's brow lifted. "I didn't realize you played basketball."

"It's just the Y," she clarified.

"Her team is currently at the top of the Y's intramural league," Braxton told Krew. "Dakota is their star player."

"Will you come? Please?"

Cassie didn't add her plea, knowing this was between Krew and his daughter. She only held her breath, knowing it would mean everything to Dakota to have him there.

It would indeed be the maraschino cherry on top of an exceptionally fine day.

Krew looked into Dakota's eyes and smiled. "I wouldn't miss it."

CHAPTER EIGHTEEN

The bells over the door jingled, and Cassie turned.

Her breath caught, and her heart pounded an erratic rhythm against her ribs.

"I didn't think I'd see you until Dakota's game tomorrow." She cursed the breathless lilt in her voice that made her sound like some NFL groupie or lovestruck teen.

Krew wore a forest-green parka today, and his dark hair was dusted with snow. "There's been a change in plans."

Something in his tone had her smile disappearing.

He gestured to a table near the front. "Can you sit for a few minutes?"

Cassie surveyed the room. It was midafternoon, and other than a group of women playing cards in the far back, the only other customers had earbuds in and laptops open. "Sure. I'm due for a break. I can sit for ten."

She sat across from Krew, hoping he'd explain his mysterious *change in plans* remark. When he remained silent, she took a moment to search his face. Lines of fatigue edged his eyes, and the spark that had been in them yesterday was gone. "What's wrong?"

"I just spoke with Dakota." He leaned back and expelled a breath. "She isn't happy with me."

That explained the look in his eyes. Cassie knew Krew would do anything to avoid disappointing his daughter. She reached across the table and placed her hand over his, not caring if anyone saw, wanting only to comfort.

His fingers closed around hers. "I told her I won't be able to attend her game tomorrow."

"Oh." Cassie stilled. "Did you explain why?"

"I told her I got a call from the front office." Krew met her gaze. "They want me to travel with the team for the game this weekend."

"You're going to play?" Cassie couldn't keep the shock from her voice. It was way too soon after his injury for him to be on the field. He could get hurt. Seriously hurt. "The doctors—"

"No, not to play." His eyes had softened at the distress in her voice. "I'll be on the sidelines, with the coaches."

Cassie let out the breath she hadn't realized she'd been holding. "Oh, that's good."

"Not according to Dakota." Krew gazed out the window. "She's right. I promised to be at her game. It's the one thing she asked of me."

"She was disappointed and caught off guard." Cassie offered a reassuring smile. "Trust me, once Dakota thinks it over, she'll understand and be happy for you. In terms of your future, this is a positive sign. They wouldn't want you there if they weren't serious about having you coach for them."

"That's what I thought, too." He rubbed his chin. "I couldn't tell them no."

"You could, but that would be stupid." Thinking of Axl, she amended, "Silly."

He smiled. The first genuine smile she'd seen since he'd walked through the door.

"I'm worried, Cassie."

"About?"

"What if I'm not cut out to be a father?" Krew's gaze met hers. "It hasn't even been two months, and I've already gone back on my word and disappointed our daughter."

"Sometimes, things come up and we have to disappoint our children. We don't like it when that happens, but usually if we explain why it's necessary, they understand."

He didn't appear convinced. "I suppose."

Cassie searched his face, memorizing every feature, knowing this trip with the team was the first step in him leaving Good Hope and returning to his other life. "I'll talk with her."

"Thank you. I—" His phone buzzed just then, and he glanced at the readout. "It's my agent. I need to take this."

"Get going." She pushed back her chair and stood. "Safe travels."

"You're the best." Krew answered the phone and was out the door in seconds.

Cassie watched him through the window until he disappeared from sight.

Krew was right about one thing. She *was* the best...at saying good-bye.

She should be.

She'd had a lot of practice.

Although Krew hadn't said where Dakota was when he'd spoken with her, Cassie knew it had to have been at Muddy Boots. Unless her daughter's schedule had changed, Dakota was working until eight.

Cassie planned on stopping by the café after she got off work, but when she saw the crowd, it was clear the day after Thanksgiving wasn't the best time for a mother-daughter chat. She texted Dakota, asking her to call after she got off work, but received a text back that her daughter was now working until close.

Perhaps that had been for the best, Cassie thought the next day as she sat in the stands of the gym. Time, and a good night's sleep, often had a way of putting everything in perspective.

She cheered loudly as Dakota stole the ball and moved it down the court. The game moved quickly, the teams evenly matched. Cassie wished Krew could be here. He'd be so proud.

Cassie jumped to her feet and cheered when Dakota sank another three-pointer.

Beside her, Axl abandoned his cars to clap along with the rest of the crowd.

Braxton and K.T. sat farther down in the stands with friends, but she heard one of them yell, "Way to go, Dakota."

Her field goal—with five seconds left—proved to be the winning shot.

"C'mon, Axl." Cassie opened her bag. "Put your cars in here. Let's go congratulate your sister."

When they reached the bottom of the bleachers, she lifted Axl in her arms so she could move more easily through the crowd. Cassie wanted to be there when Dakota exited the locker room.

She needn't have rushed. It felt like forever before Dakota stepped out, the strap of her gym bag slung over her shoulder.

"Kota." Axl ran to his sister, arms outstretched.

Dakota smiled and hefted her little brother into her arms, carrying him across the shiny linoleum to where Cassie stood. "I thought you'd be home by now."

"An incredible game, Dakota." Cassie patted her daughter on the shoulder. "You sure didn't get those mad athletic skills from me. Your dad would be proud."

Dakota's smile slipped. "I wish he'd been here."

Cassie knew Dakota was helping her grandmother at Crumb and Cake today, so there would be little chance for them to talk later. She gestured to a bench against a far wall. "Let's sit for five."

Dakota glanced at the door. "I promised Grandma I'd head to the shop right after the game."

"Take five minutes. Please?"

"Okay." Dakota crossed to the bench and dropped her bag to the floor with a thud.

Before sitting, Cassie pulled out a coloring book and crayons for Axl. "It would have been fantastic if your dad had been here to witness your stellar performance."

"He promised." Dakota's voice broke, and she looked away.

"Krew stopped by the Grind yesterday on his way out of town."

That got her daughter's attention.

"It was right after he spoke with you. He felt horrible about missing your game and disappointing you." Cassie sighed. "I have to admit, this whole thing made me wonder if letting him into our lives was a mistake."

A startled look crossed Dakota's face.

"Look how it's hurting you."

"He *had* to leave." Dakota rose to Krew's defense. "His future career is at stake."

"I know, but he broke his promise to you."

"I admit I was upset." Pink colored Dakota's cheeks. "I'm over it. You and I both understand how work can put you in hard situations. Krew is doing the best he can."

"Maybe."

"He is, Mom." Dakota's voice grew insistent. "Letting him back into your life—and mine—wasn't a mistake. It's funny, but I thought I was getting along just great without a father. But now that he's here, I can't imagine not having him around."

"He'll be leaving after the first of the year." Cassie voiced the thought that kept circling in her head.

"I know. I'll be gone then, too." Dakota reached out and gave Cassie's hand a squeeze. "We'll make time to connect."

Dakota's reminder that both she and Krew would soon be gone did little to buoy Cassie's spirits.

"You'll be starting your new career, too," Dakota reminded her. "Fresh starts all around."

Several days later, Cassie received a text from Krew informing her he was back in town and taking Dakota out to dinner. He didn't extend an invitation for her to join them, but that was okay. It wasn't as if they always had to do things together.

The next day, Cassie left work at four. She returned home to find Krew anchoring the sagging shutter. He stepped down from the ladder when she pulled up.

"You replaced the screen. And the shutter." For a long moment, she surveyed his work, her heart a sweet mass in her chest. "Thank you. It makes such a difference."

"I wanted to help." He gestured. "The driveway and sidewalks look good."

She smiled. "The boys are doing a good job keeping up with the snow."

"They're great kids." His gaze never left her face. "How've you been?"

"Good. How about you?"

"Busy."

"I can't wait to hear about your coaching adventures."

"I can't wait to tell you." He glanced at the dark house. "Where is everyone?"

"My mom and Len took Axl with them to do some Christmas shopping in Sturgeon Bay. K.T. is helping Lindsay at her shop, and Brax is at a friend's house."

"What do you say we go somewhere and grab a bite?" He offered a persuasive smile. "I've been wanting to check out that

Mexican place in Egg Harbor. If that doesn't sound good to you, we can go somewhere else."

"Are you asking me to have dinner with you?"

"I am."

～

Krew knew simply having a meal with a woman didn't qualify as a date. Still, tonight felt like a date. Which was ridiculous.

Or maybe not so ridiculous, considering how Cassie made him feel. The entire time he'd been gone, he hadn't been able to stop thinking of her.

Cassie took a sip of her margarita. "Did you enjoy your trip to Cincinnati with the team?"

"It was good to see everyone again." He washed a chip down with the rest of his soda, then grinned. "It was especially good because we won."

Being around the guys and other coaches had reminded Krew — not that he needed any reminders—just how much he loved the game.

After the win, he'd spent hours talking with the coaching staff. Not as a player this time, but as someone seriously considering joining their ranks.

"You understand why I had to go?"

"Your life isn't here, Krew. We all know and accept that."

"I wish I could have been at Dakota's game. She told me she hit the winning shot."

"It was very exciting. But there will be other games," she assured him. "Did you make any decisions about coaching?"

"I'm still considering." Krew realized they'd been talking about him since they'd left her house. "What about you? Did you take the licensing test?"

"Not yet."

"You said you were going to take it after Thanksgiving." He

forced teasing into his tone. "In case you hadn't noticed, it's after Thanksgiving."

"I know." She glanced down at her plate.

"If you need someone to quiz you or—"

"Thank you, but I think I'm ready." Her gaze lifted to meet his. "It's just, well, what happens if I fail?"

"You told me you'd take it again."

Her eyes widened.

"Not everyone scores a winning touchdown the first time out, Cass." He took her hand in his, locking his gaze on hers. "If you don't, you pick yourself up and try again."

She gave a little laugh. "You make it sound simple."

"It's not rocket science."

"Thank God." This time, her laugh was real and full-bodied.

"Think how good you'll feel when you pass and start your new career."

Her fingers tightened around his. "It's scary. I mean, I want to be a real estate agent, but—"

"But what?" he prompted when she didn't continue.

"What if nobody will list their home with me?" Cassie blew out a breath. "I don't have the best reputation."

Several heartbeats of silence settled over the table.

"I'm not going to sit here and say it'll be easy. I can tell you that anything worth striving for takes effort." Everything he was telling Cassie was true, but Krew could still see the fear and uncertainty in her eyes.

"I was afraid when I went off to college. Really afraid I was going to fail. I thought, then what would I do?" He tightened his hold on her hand. "For me, failure wasn't an option. Just like it isn't for you."

She blew out a breath. "I'll schedule the test."

"Will you let me know when?"

"Will you send positive vibes my way that day?"

"Absolutely." He grinned. "By the way, do you still have those playing cards?"

"Cards?" Cassie tried to play it cool. She lifted her hands, forced a sunny smile. "I don't know anything about any cards."

"I couldn't stop thinking about them. Or you." Krew leaned close. "Do you have the deck with you?"

It had to be the intoxicating scent of his cologne that short-circuited her good sense and had her answering honestly. "Yes."

"Pull them out. Ask me one of the questions." Krew's eyes glittered. "Or better yet, I'll ask you one."

Cassie shook her head.

"C'mon, it'll be fun."

"You know what kind of questions are in the deck." She wiggled her eyebrows. "Some of them are quite risqué."

"I remember. That's why I really want to play."

As much as Cassie was enjoying the banter, and she was enjoying it a great deal, the time had come to clarify. "The thing is, these aren't really getting-to-know-you cards."

He massaged her palm with his thumb while his gaze remained riveted on her face. "What are they, then, exactly?"

The look. The touch. Cassie struggled to form a coherent thought and answer the question.

"They're, ah, they're relationship cards. For, ah, for people in relationships."

The gentle caress continued.

"We're in a relationship of sorts. You're Dakota's mother. I'm her father. We're getting to know each other. Actually, I'd say we're in the middle of forging a relationship." He smiled. "Wouldn't you?"

It made so much sense when he said it. Or maybe it didn't. Regardless, Cassie found herself nodding.

"C'mon, Cass. Be a sport. Pull out the deck."

She assumed he'd let go of her hand. When he didn't, she was

REUNITED IN GOOD HOPE | 189

forced to forage through her purse on the floor with her free hand.

With her eyes still locked on his, she set the deck on the table.

"Would either of you like dessert?"

The server's voice was like a splash of cold water.

Cassie realized with sudden horror how this must look. Her hand in Krew's, gazing at him with some lovestruck puppy-dog expression.

She tried to jerk her hand free, but Krew merely held on and turned to Cassie.

"Dessert?"

"Not for me." Her words came out choked.

"Thank you." Krew smiled at the server. "No dessert tonight. Just the check, please."

When the server left, Krew turned back to Cassie. "Let's continue this discussion at my place."

Discussion? What had they been discussing?

His thumb continued to caress her palm, making rational thought difficult.

Cassie nodded and soon found herself in his sports car, on the way to his house.

Krew kept the conversation light, entertaining her with stories from his Cincinnati trip. By the time they reached the drive leading to his house, Cassie had almost convinced herself that being alone with Krew was no big deal.

Almost.

CHAPTER NINETEEN

Soon after they arrived at Krew's house, a fire was burning in the hearth, filling the air with the pleasant scent of applewood. Outside, big, fluffy flakes of snow fell into the quiet stillness.

Cassie gave herself an hour before she'd need to pick up Axl at her mother's house.

Krew settled next to her on the sofa facing the crackling fire, his fingers playing lightly with her hair. "You always smell so good, like vanilla."

She flushed. "It's my shampoo."

"Whatever it is, I like it." He gazed at her for a long moment, and her lips began to tingle. "Okay, pull out the cards."

She blinked. "You want to play cards?"

"Why do you think I invited you home with me?"

She might have believed him, but the twinkle in his eyes gave him away. Well, two could play this game. Cassie leaned over and took the cards from her purse.

"Pick a good one," he told her when she slid a card out from the middle of the deck.

Cassie flipped it over and read, "Has what you accomplished

in the last five years been what you wanted to accomplish?" She chuckled. "That's quite a mouthful."

His gaze grew thoughtful. "You go first."

Cassie leaned back on the plush sofa, liking the way his arm felt around her shoulders. The warmth of his body—or perhaps the heat came from the fire—completely relaxed her. The tension returned as she contemplated the question.

"I don't like looking back. The last five years hold some of the lowest points of my life." Cassie stared at the flames. "The positives are that I reconciled with my mother, I sought help from a psychologist—which I'd always resisted—and I now feel strong and hopeful."

Kicking Clint out—finally—and resisting his efforts to get her to visit him in prison had also been major accomplishments. But Cassie refused to let Clint be any part of this conversation.

"I'm proud of you."

She smiled. "I'm proud of myself."

The moment her eyes touched his, something inside her seemed to lock into place and she could not look away. The eye contact turned into something more, a tangible connection between them.

Cassie found herself filled with a longing so intense it took her breath away.

Then, because a strong woman took charge of a situation and asked for what she wanted, she gathered her courage. "I realize you haven't had your chance to answer, but I need to pick up Axl in forty-five minutes, so I'd like to ask a favor."

Obviously intrigued, Krew angled his head. "Anything."

Cassie swallowed, cleared her throat. "Instead of answering more questions, could we make out?"

The surprise that had his eyes widening would have been funny at any other time. "Ma-make out?"

"Just kissing." Though her voice remained steady, Cassie

could feel the heat rise up her neck. "I don't think I've ever just sat on the sofa and kissed a man. Not without there being an expectation of more."

Krew regarded her intently, then nodded. "I can do that."

"Only if you want—"

He chuckled, a low pleasant rumbling sound. "Oh, I definitely want."

Even before his mouth brushed hers, Cassie knew the feel of his lips, the softness and the warmth. He continued pressing his lips lightly to hers, teasingly, his mouth never pulling away. His lips were exquisitely gentle and achingly tender.

Winding her arms around his neck, Cassie embraced the pleasure, and her pulse became a swift, tripping beat. She planted a kiss at the base of his neck, his skin salty beneath her lips.

Cassie wasn't sure how long they kissed. All she knew was she'd never been kissed like this before. His fingers slid into her hair, his hands warm against her neck.

Unlike the night on the beach, his large hands, with their clever fingers, didn't roam. A feeling of gratitude washed through her for his patience. It was as if he knew just how much she needed this kind of closeness.

But when she opened her mouth, he changed the angle of the kiss, deepening it, kissing her with a slow thoroughness that left her wanting more.

More of him.

All of him.

Cassie moaned, a low sound of want and need.

His hand flattened against her lower back, drawing her up against the hard length of his erection.

A smoldering heat, urgent and hungry, flared through her and settled between her thighs.

At that moment, she wanted nothing more than to strip off her clothes, feel his bare hands against her skin and his—

"No." Krew jerked back, his breath coming hard and fast. "I promised you."

It took her several erratic heartbeats to find her voice.

"Y-you—" Cassie stumbled over the simple word, her brain caught in a lust-induced fog. What had she been about to say? *You didn't have to stop? You don't have to respect my wishes?*

Krew rested his forehead against hers. When he spoke, his voice was soft, reaching inside her to a raw, tender place. "I care about you, Cassie. So very much."

As he stood, he gently locked their fingers together and pulled her to her feet. "I think it's time to take you home."

Even as Krew sat in church on Sunday morning, an image of him and Cassie on the sofa pushed into his consciousness.

It didn't help that her leg was pressed against him in the tightly packed pew. She smelled terrific. How had he never known what an enticing scent vanilla shampoo could be? Her shiny blond hair hung loose to her shoulders and shimmered in the overhead lights.

Krew liked sitting beside Cassie and Dakota. And the boys, well, they were great kids he enjoyed being around.

"No, Axl, sit down." Cassie's urgent tone had him glancing at the little boy on her other side.

Axl's face took on a mulish expression that, even in the short time Krew had been in Good Hope, he'd learned to recognize as trouble.

When everyone rose for a pre-sermon hymn, Krew leaned close. "I'll take him out."

Her startled gaze searched his. "Are you sure?"

"No worries." Krew reached past Cassie and lifted the boy into his arms. For someone so small, the boy was built like a nose guard. "C'mon, Axl."

If the boy minded leaving his mother and brothers, it didn't show. He waved bye to them with the hand holding a plastic football.

Krew waited until they were in the lobby to set the boy down. Though it was probably sacrilegious to play a game of catch in church, other than running steps, he couldn't think of a better way to use up some of the kid's energy.

"Okay, Axl." Krew smiled. "Throw me the ball."

The child hugged the ball even closer and stared suspiciously at Krew. "My ball."

"I know it's yours. I'm not planning to keep it. You throw it to me. I throw it back to you." He took a step back and held up his hands. "Can you throw it this far?"

Axl studied him with suspicious blue-green eyes for several long seconds. Without warning, he heaved the ball in Krew's direction.

It hit the shiny linoleum several feet in front of Krew.

Taking a step forward, Krew reached down and caught it when it bounced. He grinned at the little boy. "Good job."

"Give me," Axl demanded.

"Are you ready?" Krew focused on the boy as if he were a wide receiver and they were about to go for the winning touchdown.

"Throw."

Krew grinned, liking the kid's style. Carefully judging the short distance that separated them, he lobbed the ball gently. It hit the boy right on the numbers.

For a second, as Axl fumbled with the ball, Krew thought they'd have an incomplete pass. Then the child gained control of the ball and hugged it tightly.

"Good job." He offered his fist, and Axl bumped his small one against it, grinning widely.

"Well, isn't this an interesting turn of events?"

Krew recognized the voice behind him immediately. He

swept Axl up into his arms. For once, the boy didn't squirm, but merely turned the football over and over in his hands.

"Mitch." Krew gestured with his head. "I didn't see you in there."

"I saw you." Mitch's eyes were bloodshot. Either he'd stayed up too late, or he'd drunk too much last night. Or maybe both. "You were all cuddly beside your baby momma."

When Krew didn't respond, Mitch gave a harsh-sounding laugh and shook his head. "I really thought the kid was mine. Thank God, she's not, but what were the odds…"

"If you really thought Dakota was your daughter, how could you ignore her all these years?"

"Oh, please." Mitch rolled his eyes. "Don't act so high and mighty. You wouldn't have played this any differently."

"You don't know me at all."

Mitch shrugged, pulled out a flask and took a swig. "I know it didn't take you long to get Cassie into your bed."

Krew held on to his temper with both hands. "C'mon, Axl. Let's go."

He'd taken only a few steps when Mitch called out, "How is she, by the way? Because back in high school, her, ah, skills left a lot to be desired."

Krew whirled. The straight-armed punch to the face had Mitch staggering backward, blood spurting from his nose. "You're—"

"We're done here." Krew hated that Axl had seen him hit someone in church, but the boy appeared unconcerned, his gaze still focused on the football in his hands.

Krew slid into the pew beside Cassie just as the sermon began.

"All good?" she asked in a low tone.

Krew ignored his aching hand and thought of Mitch. If he'd stayed in the lobby, the guy would likely have started with the legal threats. But Mitch wouldn't follow through. At heart, he was a coward.

Now, because of the punch, the man would steer clear of both him and Cassie. Which was the way Krew wanted it.

"It's all good," Krew told Cassie and focused on the sermon.

$\sim$

"You've got to come with us." Lindsay's voice turned pleading. "Everyone goes to Muddy Boots after church."

Not everyone, Cassie thought, mentally correcting her sister —every *couple* in Lindsay's social circle.

Though Cassie recalled being invited a time or two in the past, she usually hurried out of church the second the service ended.

Krew looked unconcerned, and she realized he was leaving the decision up to her. Cassie knew that his remaining time in Good Hope was limited. Sharing breakfast with these friends from the past was a good way to reconnect.

Still, she had Axl and—

"Has Axl ever gone to Little Fishes?" Prim Brody was one of the couples clustered around Krew and Cassie. The pretty strawberry-blonde held her youngest, Adelyn, a girl who must be six or seven months old by now. "I know Sarah Rose loves it. Doesn't she, Ami?"

Ami, who'd just walked up, holding hands with her husband, smiled. "Loves what?"

"I was telling Cassie that Sarah Rose loves Little Fishes," Prim explained. "Addie isn't old enough to go. It's for—"

"Children eighteen months to age four." Ami smiled at Axl. "He'd fit right in."

Cassie felt her arms tightening protectively around Axl. Which was ridiculous. It would be good for her son to play with other kids. Besides, once she started selling real estate, he'd have to go to day care on a regular basis. "Okay. We'll give it a try."

"I like the sound of giving something a try." Pastor Dan, Katie Ruth at his side, stopped by the group. "What is it you're going to try?"

"Axl is going to Little Fishes, and Cassie and Krew are joining us for breakfast," Lindsay announced.

"That is good news." Katie Ruth beamed. "I'm headed in that direction. I'd be happy to drop Axl off."

While a kind offer, it was obvious to Cassie that Katie Ruth didn't have children. There was no way Cassie would give Axl to someone he didn't know—no matter how wonderful and trustworthy she was—to then be left in a strange situation.

"Thanks, but if you point me in the right direction, I can find it." Cassie offered Katie Ruth a grateful smile.

"The Little Fishes room is at the end of this hall, last door on the right. Jackie White is the teacher."

"I'll walk with you." Krew dropped into step beside her while the others headed for the door, promising to save them seats.

"The man is completely oblivious to the way Katie Ruth looks at him," Cassie muttered once they were out of earshot.

"Who?"

"Katie Ruth. Didn't you see the way she looked at Dan?"

"Really?" Krew grinned. "You think she's got the hots for the preacher?"

Cassie swung Axl's hand wildly as they strolled down the shiny hall, making the boy giggle. "All I'll say is they'd be good together."

"That won't matter if there's no attraction on his part."

"Hold that thought." Cassie stopped in front of an open door, the sounds of young voices and laughter spilling out into the hall.

She strolled into the room with Axl while Krew waited in the doorway.

"Cassie." Jackie's smile widened when she saw her. After saying something to a girl who looked to be in middle school, Jackie hurried over.

Well, hurried as fast as someone using a cane could go. Jackie, tall and thin with reddish-blond hair, had been diagnosed with multiple sclerosis several years earlier. "You brought Axl."

The boy gave her four-pronged cane a suspicious look.

"This is my cane," Jackie said to him. "I need it to help me walk."

"I didn't call ahead and say I'd be bringing him. I hope it isn't a problem."

"No advance notice necessary." Jackie placed a hand on Cassie's arm, her eyes warm. "We're simply glad Axl is here."

Cassie noticed Axl was staring intently at where Sarah Rose and another girl were coloring. "Do you want to color, Axl?"

He nodded, not taking his eyes off the two.

"Mommy is going to leave, but I'll be back in an hour to pick you up." She kept her tone light and matter-of-fact. "Okay?"

"'Kay." He headed across the room without a backward glance.

Cassie didn't know whether to feel relieved or disappointed.

"We'll take good care of him." Jackie slanted a curious glance at Krew, who'd stepped just inside the room.

"Thank you." Just before she turned, Cassie pulled a piece of paper from her purse and scribbled a number, then handed it to Jackie. "My cell number. If you need anything, call and I'll come right away."

"Thank you. I'm sure I won't need it, but it's good to have."

For a second, Cassie wondered if she should go over and tell Axl good-bye.

Before she could give in to the impulse, Jackie made a shooing gesture with one hand and shot her a wink.

When she stepped out into the hall with Krew, he took her arm.

Cassie cast Krew a worried glance. "You think he'll be okay?"

"I hope so."

"I thought you might say I was babying him, but you're as concerned as I am."

"You're leaving the kid with a group of strangers. Of course you should be concerned."

She planted her feet and glanced back down the hall. "I should go back."

"No." He gave her hand a tug. "He's fine. In fact, I predict that when we pick him up, he won't want to leave."

Cassie exhaled a breath, knowing that was exactly how it would go down. "You're right."

On the drive to the café, they talked about Axl—mostly—and a little bit about the sermon, which had centered around forgiveness. No mention of last night's kisses.

"I know I should probably forgive my parents, but my dad was such a mean SOB." Krew's jaw tightened. "Especially when he was drinking."

The finality in his tone told Cassie he'd already made his decision, and it would take an act of God—ha-ha—to change it.

"I thought you admired your mom for how hard she worked to provide for you."

"I do, it's just, well, honestly, it's complicated for me. I know my mom didn't have it easy, but how could she stand by and let him hit and scream at us?" A muscle in his clenched jaw jumped. "Why didn't she leave him and get us out of there? It's not like it would have been any harder to provide for us. He certainly wasn't helping. It's like she chose him over her own kids."

Cassie felt as if water had filled her lungs, making breathing impossible. Panic had her heart skittering like a trapped bird.

"I admire you so much for your decision to focus on your family over men and dating." Krew shot her a wink. "Though I hope you're willing to make an exception for me."

Cassie could barely summon a smile at his teasing.

Each time she thought Krew might find out about the situation with Clint, she told herself he'd understand and forgive her.

She was only kidding herself. He wouldn't forgive her any more than she would ever forgive herself.

"What about you?" Krew asked. "Is there someone you have a hard time forgiving?"

Myself.

For a second, Cassie worried she'd spoken aloud, but Krew just continued to look at her with that curious gaze.

"I try not to dwell too much on the past." Cassie pointed to a truck backing out at the café. "Look there's a spot right in front."

Krew wheeled the car into the stall the truck had just vacated and cut the engine.

Neither of them made any move to get out of the car.

"What's wrong?" Krew's voice, so filled with concern, had an ache of yearning welling up inside her.

She was oh-so-tempted to come clean. Though it would be what she deserved, she wasn't prepared to have him take a big step out of her life.

Besides, now wasn't the time or place. Everyone was inside. Her sister was saving seats for them.

There would be time for confessing later. Maybe.

Cassie opened her car door. "I'm worried about Axl."

"We can go back and check on him."

Dakota had hit the jackpot in having this man for her father. And perhaps, if things had been different, Cassie and Krew might have been more than friends.

But that train had left the station long ago. Wishing, she'd learned, didn't change reality.

"I've got my phone." Cassie lifted it to show him. "Jackie will call if he needs me."

"Let me know if you change your mind."

Krew opened the door for an elderly couple, then motioned Cassie into Muddy Boots.

"Where are they?" Krew glanced around the crowded café. Laughter, conversation and the enticing scents of freshly brewed coffee and cinnamon filled the air.

"There's a large table toward the back." Cassie didn't even finish speaking before she started weaving her way through the tables.

Krew fell into step behind her.

His progress was slowed, because every couple of feet, he was stopped by someone wanting to comment on last week's game or ask him about his recovery.

When Cassie reached the table, she was alone.

Lindsay glanced around. Frowned. "I thought Krew was coming with you."

"He's here." Cassie gestured vaguely with one hand. "He has a thousand and one admirers in the restaurant. I think it's going to take a while for him to get free."

"But he's taking you back to pick up Axl, right?" Ami slanted a glance at her husband.

"I'll do what I can to extricate Mr. Football from his fans." Beck gave his wife's hand a squeeze and stood.

Cassie assumed that the two seats between Lindsay and Max Brody were for her and Krew. She took the one next to Lindsay.

"How did Axl do when you dropped him off at Little Fishes?" Prim asked.

Cassie glanced at Ami. "He was coloring beside Sarah Rose when I left."

"Jackie does such a great job with the little ones." Ami shook her head. "I don't know how she does everything."

"I saw she's using a cane now." Cassie nodded and pointed to her cup and Krew's when the waitress asked if she wanted coffee. "That's new since I last saw her."

"Yes. She's moving more slowly, but she's determined not to let her disability define her." Ami put her hand over her own cup. "None for me today, Helen."

"How are things going at the Daily Grind, Cassie?" Max, Prim's husband, asked. "You need to get Ryder to join us for breakfast. Every time I ask, he has some excuse."

"I have zero control over my boss," Cassie said as Krew dropped into the chair beside her.

"Who's the boss?" Krew asked, taking a gulp of the coffee Helen had just poured.

"I was telling Cassie she should try to get her boss to join us." Max, a good-natured accountant with a mop of blond hair, grinned. "He doesn't listen to any of us. We've been trying to get him here for months."

Krew cast Cassie a look she couldn't quite decipher. "He'll listen to you?"

"Yeah, right. The answer to that question is a big fat no." Cassie rolled her eyes. "I'm the employee. He's the boss."

"Not for long." Lindsay singsonged the words.

All of a sudden, Cassie found herself the focus of everyone.

Across the table, Eliza lifted a brow. "You're quitting the Grind?"

"I, ah—"

"She's taking her real estate licensing exam." Pride wove through Lindsay's words. "We're almost positive Tim Vandercoy will let her join his team."

"We don't know that for sure, Lin," Cassie protested.

Max glanced at his wife and received a nod. "If you decide to go out on your own, there's space in our office."

Cassie didn't know what to say to the generous offer. The building housing their accounting office was in a prime location.

Max lifted his cup and flashed that easy smile. "Just another option."

"Thank you." Cassie stumbled over the words. "That's so generous."

"Wait until you see what he plans to charge you in rent," Eliza warned. But her tone was joking, and once again, the laughter flowed freely.

Cassie felt tears sting the backs of her eyes. This suddenly felt real. It was as if she stood on the brink of a new life.

All she had to do was take the next step and be willing to risk failing...again.

CHAPTER TWENTY

The next afternoon, Krew read the text from Cassie telling him she'd scheduled the exam in Green Bay. Pride rushed through him. He knew, maybe better than most, what courage this had taken. Regardless of the outcome, taking this step was a huge accomplishment for her.

He texted back that he'd like to bring dinner by to celebrate. After telling him that wasn't necessary, she agreed.

Knowing the family's schedule—and how had that happened? —he timed his arrival so everyone was home before he pulled up with bags of food. Dakota pulled in behind him in a battered car that made Cassie's car look like a floor model.

"Hey, Dad."

Bent over the passenger seat, bags in hand, Krew froze.

He glanced up. Dakota might be smiling, but he saw the question in her eyes.

"I like the sound of that," he told her.

The tense set to her shoulders immediately relaxed. "I felt weird calling you Krew when you're my dad. But I didn't know if you'd mind..."

"I'm honored." His heart swelled with emotion, but he gestured with his head. "Thanks for picking up the cake."

"When you ordered it, I told Grandma I wanted to be the one to bake it." Dakota glanced down at the white box. "She insisted on doing her part. I did the baking, and she frosted and decorated it. I need to make sure to tell Mom that Grandma did part of it. I know that will mean something to her."

Krew cocked his head. "Red velvet?"

"With butter cream frosting." Dakota grinned. "Her favorite."

"What did she put on it?" Krew had left the wording up to Anita.

"You'll see," Dakota said mysteriously.

The boys, all three of them, were seated on the couch watching television.

Braxton shifted his gaze. "Mom said you're bringing dinner. What's the occasion?"

"Your mother scheduled her real estate licensing exam." Krew set the bags with the Muddy Boots logo on the card table. "I thought that was a cause for celebration."

Cassie appeared in the doorway. "I'm getting the plates and silverware out."

"Mom." K.T. turned to look over the back of the sofa at Cassie. "That's so cool. You'll ace the test."

"Absolutely," Braxton echoed.

"Your mouth, God's ear." Cassie smiled. "Dakota, I'm happy you're here. I thought you were working for your grandma tonight."

"I ran into this guy," Dakota jerked a thumb in Krew's direction, "at the Y when we were both working out. He told me what he had planned for tonight. When I mentioned it to Grandma, she gave me the time off. I didn't want to miss the celebration."

"It's not really a celebrat—"

"It is, Mom. Scheduling the test is huge." Dakota slanted a glance at Krew. "When Dad mentioned he was bringing dinner for a celebration, I wanted to be here. And I'll have you know I baked the cake he ordered, and Grandma did the frosting and decorating."

Dad. Krew saw that Cassie caught the change, but she didn't say a word. She had too many other questions. "Cake?"

Dakota glanced down to the box in her hands. "Red velvet with butter cream frosting."

"My favorite." Cassie's gaze sought Krew's, and he saw the question.

"Your mother told me." He gestured to the sacks. "We better eat before the burgers get cold."

"Burgers?" K.T. jumped up from the sofa.

"And broccoli," Krew added and watched the boy's smile fade. "It's good for you."

At his mother's warning glance, K.T. swallowed whatever he'd been about to say.

"Thanks, Krew." Braxton stood. "It's better than nothing."

"Braxton, manners," Cassie hissed.

"Oh, did I forget to mention the fries?" Krew dodged a punch in his good side from K.T. and watched the boys give each other a high five.

In a matter of minutes, they were seated at the table, or on the sofa, big, juicy burgers, broccoli and fries on the plates before them.

Krew hoped the kids truly understood what a big deal this was for their mother. Just in case they didn't, he'd help them out with a reminder. He thought about what Cassie had told him of the process. "I assume you've taken the sample test?"

Cassie lowered the burger in her hands. A smile tugged at the corners of her lips. She nodded.

"How did you do?" he pressed.

"Ninety-eight percent."

"Wow, Mom. You're a superstar," K.T. said.

At the word *superstar*, Axl clapped.

"What do you need to get on the licensing exam to pass?" Krew asked.

Her smile blossomed. "Seventy-five percent."

"You've nothing to worry about," Dakota said. "You're going to rock that test."

Braxton gave her two thumbs-up.

"Realtor Cassie Lohmeier for the sale." Krew spoke as if he were a sports announcer.

She brushed away the words with one hand, but her eyes were shining.

Their gazes locked, and a current flowed between them.

When had this happened? he wondered. When had she started to be so important to him?

By the time the cake was brought out, not a scrap of food remained. Dakota unpacked the cake, and Krew carried it to the card table.

Anita had outdone herself on the decorating. Her semicircle of cake sprinkles and pieces of rich dark chocolate left space for the words *We love and believe in you*. A smattering of red hearts surrounded the words.

Cassie stared at the cake for a long moment. Tears filled her eyes. She glanced at Krew, and the emotion shimmering in her gaze had his chest tightening.

"This is incredibly special." She cleared her throat. "Dakota, would you do the honors of cutting the cake?"

Dakota squeezed her mother's arm. "Of course."

"Give me an extra big piece," Braxton ordered.

"If he gets a big piece, I get one, too," K.T. said.

Cassie grabbed some dishes. "I'm going to put these in the sink."

Krew waited a second, then followed her into the kitchen. He found her with her hands on the counter, tears slipping down her cheeks.

"Hey." He spoke in a low tone. When she didn't respond, he

gently turned her to face him, wrapping his arms around her and pulling her close. "What's wrong?"

"I don't want to dis-disappoint you. Or the kids." She sniffled.

"You won't disappoint—"

"What if I fail?" Her voice was thick. "What if—"

"We've talked about this." He kept his voice stern, though he wanted nothing more than to soothe and comfort. "Half of winning is having a winning mentality. You've done the work. You're prepared. You will succeed."

"I hope so."

"I know so." He brushed a kiss across her hair and would have said more, but he saw Dakota standing in the doorway, watching them with an inscrutable expression. "Let's go and have some cake."

When Cassie stepped back from his arms, swiping at her cheeks with the pads of her fingers, Dakota was already back in the living room.

"This cake is amazing," Krew told his daughter fifteen minutes later when he finished off the last of his piece.

"Thanks." Her smile was quick and perfunctory, not reaching her eyes.

If something was bothering her, now wasn't the time to bring it up. Krew shifted his gaze to Cassie, who was letting Axl eat the last bite of cake on her plate.

"You're going to Green Bay on Thursday to take the test?" Krew kept his tone offhand.

She nodded.

"I happen to be going to Green Bay then myself." Until this moment, Krew had been content to let his agent handle the front-office negotiations. Now, it seemed prudent to be there in person. "What time is the test?"

"I can take it anytime between eight and five. The test itself can take up to four hours, so I want to start no later than one."

"My meeting is at two. We could drive there in the morning,

have lunch and I can drop you off where you need to be." He could almost see all the arguments against the plan winding their way through her brain, so he continued. "Mine won't last more than an hour. You can text me when you're done, and we can grab a drink to celebrate before heading home."

"Do it, Mom," Dakota urged. "Make this day special."

Cassie brushed back a strand of hair from her face and gave a little laugh. "You're all awfully confident I'm going to pass."

"You're prepared. You've done the work." Krew shot her a wink. "It's time to reap the rewards."

Cassie's text told Krew only two things. The test was over, and she was ready to be picked up.

As he drove the familiar streets of Green Bay, he realized she had been at the forefront of his mind since he'd dropped her off.

Though the test would be done on a computer, rather than face-to-face with professionals, she'd dressed as if she were headed for a business meeting, in dark pants, heeled short boots and a shirt that managed to look dressy but casual. She'd pulled her hair back into some kind of twist, as if worried it would get in her face and distract her.

It had taken every ounce of his self-control not to give her a kiss for luck. The last thing he wanted was to disrupt her concentration. On the drive from Good Hope, they'd talked about the exam, and over lunch he'd asked her questions from the sample test.

She was ready. He hoped she'd taken it to the goal posts.

Instead of waiting inside the building as he'd expected, she stood on the sidewalk, wearing that flimsy tan coat, her arms wrapped around herself to ward off the wind.

The second she saw his car pull up, she hurried to the curb and slid into the seat he had warming for her.

"How'd it go?" He kept the vehicle in park, making no move to pull away from the curb. Krew didn't want to be in rush-hour traffic if she was upset.

He'd promised her this morning that he would be here for her, regardless of the outcome. Krew had meant every word.

"I passed." She squealed the words and surprised them both by flinging her arms around his neck.

"Congratulations. I knew you could do it."

She lifted her face to his, her eyes sparkling like amethysts in the afternoon sunlight. "Thank you for your faith in me."

His heart suddenly squeezed tight in his chest. The intensity of the emotion welling inside Krew took him by surprise. It wasn't just desire he felt when he looked into those blue-green eyes, it went deeper.

This woman had captured his heart.

The certainty of it punched like a fist.

She'd chewed off the lipstick she'd put on this morning. Still, her lips were as plump and red as the strawberries he loved, and they called to him in a primitive way.

He should look away.

She should look away.

Instead, her breaths came in intoxicating little puffs, and his desire surged. But he was determined to not respond in the heat of the moment, giving her time to back off if she wanted to.

Cassie might have stared at him wide-eyed as his gaze traveled slowly over her face, but there was a knowing gleam in those beautiful eyes. He swore he could see his own desire reflected in her blue depths.

He bent his head and kissed her softly on the mouth, then leaned his forehead against hers. "I'm incredibly proud of you. I got you a congratulatory gift."

"You did?"

"If you're going to show homes in Wisconsin, you need to be prepared." Krew reached into what passed for a backseat in his sports car and handed her the beautifully wrapped package with a big silver bow.

"This is lovely." Cassie fingered the bow, her gaze firmly fixed on him. "What's in it?"

"Open it and find out."

She hesitated. "This is a loading zone. We shouldn't—"

"No one else wants this spot." Even if they did, Krew wanted to be stationary when she opened his gift.

"When did you get this?"

"I went shopping while you were taking your test. I'll have you know I picked this out myself."

"That makes it even more special." With trembling fingers, she carefully removed the wrapping paper, then opened the box from one of the finest women's stores in Green Bay. "Oh, Krew."

She pulled the charcoal-colored coat out of the tissue and stroked the fabric. "It even feels warm."

"It's alpaca, so it should keep you plenty warm. I told the clerk you were tall and slender, and she recommended this tailored cut."

"It's beautiful...and way too expensive." With a sigh, she laid the coat back into the box. "I couldn't accept—"

"Take the coat, Cassie." There was a hint of desperation in Krew's tone. "Please. For me."

Her fingers returned to the soft fabric. "I would look pretty snazzy showing homes wearing this coat."

He grinned. "Extremely snazzy."

"Thank you." Her gaze met his, and when she spoke, it was like a vow. "I'll think of you every time I put it on."

"That's the plan." Slowly, he lowered his head and covered her mouth again, kissing her with a slow thoroughness that left them both vibrating with desire.

It was crazy how, after all these years, the taste of her, the way her mouth moved so innocently under his, the way she made the blood burn in his veins was so familiar.

As they kissed, she caressed the back of his neck, twining her fingers in his hair as if they had all the time in the world.

Krew realized that, while they might not have forever, they had today. There was no real rush. Not like there had been that night on the beach.

Krew tucked a stray silky curl behind her ear and caught the faint scent of vanilla. Did she have any idea the power she had over him?

He was determined to take his time, wanting to savor this moment, but when she moistened her lips with the tip of her tongue, a smoldering heat flared through him.

"There's a hotel a couple of blocks from here." The words came out on a husky rasp as need gripped his body.

The second he spoke, he wanted to take back the words.

"I-"

Krew didn't have a chance to get anything more out, before she pulled his head down and gave him a ferocious kiss.

Dazed and breathing hard, she pulled back. "I want you."

He cupped her face with one hand and gazed into her eyes. "I want you more."

She shook her head, a smile on her lips that were already swollen from his kisses. "What was that thing your coach used to say?"

He cocked his head, not following.

"Sometimes you have to move forward."

The words finally clicked. "Push forward."

"Let's push forward."

"You're sure?"

The look she shot him fried every brain cell he possessed. He didn't ask again.

CHAPTER TWENTY-ONE

When Cassie walked into the recently restored downtown hotel, holding hands with Krew, part of her wondered what in the heck she was doing. The other part wished they were already in a room.

Stepping to the desk, Krew flashed his heart-stopping smile at the woman behind the gleaming wooden counter. "We'd like a suite."

Cassie's heart danced against her rib cage. The thought of being with Krew—naked with Krew—had her feeling woozy.

"I'm sorry, sir, but our suites are fully booked."

To her credit, the pretty blonde in the crisp navy suit appeared contrite.

Cassie attempted to step back and make a break for the door, but Krew's hand, now on her arm, held her in place.

Unlike her, he didn't appear to have any intention of leaving.

"Is the manager available?" Krew might have worded it as a question, but it sounded more like a summons to Cassie.

It must have sounded that way to the blonde, because she smiled brightly. "I'll get him for you."

"We don't have to—" Cassie began in a hushed whisper, but

she stopped speaking when a balding man in a dark pinstripe suit hurried over.

"I understand there's—" The manager paused as recognition lit his eyes. With a broad smile, the man rounded the desk and moved to Krew, his hand extended. "Krew Slattery. It's an honor to have you stay with us this evening."

"Thank you." Krew swept the lobby with one hand, encompassing the glimmering chandelier, mosaic tile floors and arched windows. "You've got a beautiful place here. This will be my first stay here since the team had the celebration in the ballroom."

"A lovely event. Your MVP award was well deserved." The manager rubbed his hands together. "What seems to be the problem?"

The blonde shifted from one foot to the other, the perky smile still on her face. Still, Cassie could see that the dynamic she witnessed between the two men had her worried.

"No problem." Krew's easy smile was back. "I was hoping you'd have a suite available."

"Of course." The manager turned to the blonde. "Put Mr. Slattery and his guest in the VIP suite on ten."

"Thank you," Krew glanced down at the man's nametag, "Harold."

"Always a pleasure to host one of the team." The man's eyes glittered with curiosity. "I hear you may be making the switch to the coaching staff."

Krew lowered his voice to a confidential whisper. "It's definitely something I'm considering. Let's keep that just between the two of us."

Harold beamed and made a zipping motion across his lips. He turned back to the blonde and held out his hand for an ornate metal key. "Gillian, please have a bottle of champagne sent up to the suite. My compliments."

"Yes, sir." Gillian's gaze shifted from Krew to Cassie.

Cassie saw her puzzlement. It was obvious she couldn't figure out what the gorgeous sports star was doing with someone like her. The truth was, Cassie was having difficulty figuring that out, too.

On the elevator ride to the tenth floor, Cassie forgot her reservations when Krew pulled her to him for a scorching kiss. By the time the door opened, she wanted him with every fiber of her being.

The kisses continued as they walked down the carpeted hall to the door to suite ten.

Cassie thought it sweet that it took Krew three tries to get the key in the lock. Once he did, they tumbled inside, the kisses growing more urgent by the second.

In this moment, her blood was on fire, the way it had been that first night. She'd never experienced this all-out longing for anyone since that time. If it wasn't flat-out crazy, she'd think a cosmic connection existed between them.

Her coat was on the floor and his had just dropped beside it when a knock sounded at the door.

Krew cursed. "The champagne."

"Just a minute," Cassie called out when the knock sounded again.

Her breath came hard and fast, and her knees felt as shaky as a newborn colt's, but Cassie covered the few steps to the door, opening it only slightly.

A young man dressed in black pants and a spotless white shirt stood beside a cart. There was a bottle of champagne chilling in a silver ice bucket, as well as a tray of assorted cheeses and fruits.

"I—" Cassie began. "We—"

"I've got this." Krew, back in control for the moment, opened the door wider. "Please, come in."

Cassie glanced at the floor, but in the mere seconds it had taken her to open the door, Krew had picked their coats up and draped them over the sofa.

"Where would you like me to put this, sir?" the young man asked.

"By the window would be fine."

Once the cart was placed in position, the man removed the wrapping over the fruit and cheeses and inclined his head. "Would you like me to uncork the champagne?"

"Not necessary. I can do that."

"Very well, sir." The man, who couldn't have been much older than Dakota, offered a polite smile to Cassie, then to Krew. "Enjoy your evening."

Krew walked the man to the door, pressed a large bill into his hand, then shut and locked the door.

The interruption had given Cassie time to think. She moved to the window and stared out over downtown Green Bay. "Is this wise?"

Krew didn't immediately answer. Instead, his arms slid around her from behind.

Perhaps she should have pulled away. It would certainly be easier to think when his strong arms weren't holding her close. She could feel the heat of his body all the way to her core.

"I'm so afraid of making a mistake." The words tumbled out before Cassie could stop them. "I told myself I wouldn't get involved with a man, but this isn't really getting involved, is it?"

"This is whatever you want it to be." His lips brushed against her hair. "At its heart, this is a celebration of you, of what you accomplished today. We can order up dinner, enjoy the champagne and fruit and talk. We don't even have to take off our clothes."

Cassie laughed. "Shedding my clothes as quickly as possible was the only thing on my mind a few minutes ago."

Krew turned her in his arms so they faced each other. "As frustrated as I was at the interruption, I think it was a good thing."

"You do?"

"I don't want to rush you into anything you're not ready for." With gentle fingers, he pushed back a strand of her hair and studied her face, his eyes dark with need. "I know how you feel about getting involved with anyone at this point in your life."

"Have you really accepted the coaching position?"

Surprise had his eyes widening. "You want to talk about my career now?"

She could see the moment he understood.

He expelled a breath. "Yes, I'll be returning to the team in a coaching capacity after the first of the year."

Okay, Cassie thought, they had that covered. This wouldn't be a relationship. He would be gone, and this, whatever it was, would be over--after the holidays.

The thought didn't make her as relieved as she'd thought it would, but she pushed forward.

"When we return to Good Hope, this," she waved her hand vaguely in the air, "won't continue."

"Are you referring to the sex?" he asked in a measured tone, "or our friendship?"

"Do you consider me a friend?"

He slowly nodded, and she saw the question in his eyes.

"I consider you a friend, too." She chewed on her bottom lip for several long seconds. "We could still be friends, just not, you know…"

"Sleep together."

"Right." She gave a decisive nod.

"Why is that?"

"You know why." Frustration edged her voice. Why was he making this so hard?

Needing to put some distance between them, Cassie crossed to the sofa and dropped down.

The move ended up being pointless when he took a seat beside her.

"If I knew," he told her, "I wouldn't have asked."

Cassie blew out a breath, familiar shame splashing over her like dirty water. "My reputation in Good Hope is in the gutter."

Why, after all this time, did saying the words still hurt so much?

"You think being with me will make you look bad." A muscle in his jaw jumped.

"No." She flung out her hands in frustration. "I'm trying to rise above my past, to get people in Good Hope to see me in a different light."

"You think if they find out we're involved physically—"

"They'll roll their eyes and think, 'Same song, different man.'" Just saying the words brought an ache to Cassie's heart, because she knew what existed between her and Krew *was* different. That didn't change the fact that when he returned to Green Bay, she'd be left to not only deal with the gossip, but to piece together the shattered bits of her heart.

"Then if this afternoon is all we have, it will have to be enough."

But I want more.

Like a willful child who suddenly finds herself deprived of her greatest wish, Cassie was seized with the desire to stomp her foot. Which was ridiculous, considering Krew was giving her everything she asked for, everything she said she wanted.

She'd have his body, but not his heart.

Just like before.

"Cass?"

He spoke her name in a tone as soft as a caress.

"I don't want champagne. Or fruit." She angled toward him and looped her arms around his neck. "I just want you."

Krew's eyes darkened. Without saying a word—or perhaps in answer—he planted kisses along her jawline.

She arched back, giving him greater access, then jerked straight up, nearly clipping him on the chin. "Do you have protection?"

He smiled and kissed her lightly on the mouth. "Absolutely."

"Enough?"

As he pulled her close, she felt a chuckle, warm and deep, rumble through his chest. "Yes."

"We're going to take this real slow." He nuzzled her neck. "There's no reason to rush."

His lips roamed over her face and neck, stopping to linger on her mouth.

Cassie's blood began to hum.

This time, she wouldn't be an inept participant. She would focus on his pleasure, too.

When his lips covered hers, she opened her mouth, pressing more tightly against him, sliding her fingers inside the collar of his shirt.

By the time they came up for air, every inch of her body tingled. Cassie wanted more and she wanted it now.

She began unbuttoning his shirt.

Bemused, he watched her trembling fingers struggle. "Do you want me naked?"

She nodded, narrowing her gaze on a particularly obstinate button.

"Sweetheart, you only had to say the word." He stood, and in seconds he wore only navy boxers.

Cassie's mouth went dry as she drank in his physical perfection. The broad shoulders, the lean hips and the muscular legs covered in a light dusting of hair. She frowned. "You're not naked."

"I'm closer than you are." He pulled her to her feet, and the scent of his shampoo, soap and cologne had her heart rate going into overdrive.

His fingers moved to the top button on her blouse.

"I can undress myself." She gazed into his eyes and made no move to push his hands away.

"I know, but I've been wanting to do this since I first saw you."

He made quick work of the shirt, sliding it off her shoulders and gazing appreciatively at her lace demi-bra. Her navy pants were dispensed to the floor in short order.

He stepped back to study her, and Cassie was tempted to cover her belly with her hands. She supposed the slight pooch was unavoidable after four pregnancies, but she wished she could be perfect for him.

"You're gorgeous." The assessing gleam in his eyes was tempered by humor. "You're also overdressed."

She laughed. "Yeah, right."

"May I point out that you have two pieces of clothing on while I only have one?"

Cassie could see where this was headed. Excitement skittered up her spine.

"Do you want to pick which item to discard?" He cocked his head, a smile playing at the corners of his mouth. "Or shall I choose?"

Cassie brought a finger to her lips and pretended to think. "You pick."

Pleasure blanketed his face, along with a wicked grin. He stepped even closer.

Her heart hammered so loudly, she wondered if he could hear.

With one flick of his fingers, the front closure of her bra opened. Her breasts weren't large, more like tangerines than melons, but the flare in Krew's eyes said he liked what he saw.

Cassie's breath came in short puffs, and her nipples, now free from restraint, formed hard little points. She ached for his touch.

He kept her waiting, kissing her long and deep and with such passion, it was as if she'd never been kissed before. The feel of the hard length of him pressed against her had her knees going weak.

Just when Cassie wondered how much longer those weakened knees could hold her, Krew took her trembling hand in his large one and led her into the other room.

The bed, massive with at least ten pillows propped against the headboard, had Cassie's pulse quickening.

"I'd like to just kiss for a while," he said as he brought the hand he held to his mouth and placed a moist kiss in her palm before lifting his eyes to hers. "If that's okay with you?"

He wasn't going to rush her, push her to go harder and faster than she was ready to go.

She nodded and glanced at the bed. "Can we lie down? I don't think my legs will hold me for much longer."

His eyes twinkled. "Are you saying I make you weak in the knees?"

She laughed. "Something like that."

Still clad only in her panties, Cassie pulled back the covers and moved to the middle of the bed. When Krew settled beside her, she expected him to start kissing her right away, maybe even pull off the last scrap of lace.

Again, he surprised her.

His hand was gentle as he pushed back a lock of her hair. "Let's get one thing clear." His voice was as soft and soothing as his touch. "You don't need to ask me if we can do anything. What you want is what I want. Tell me what you want."

"I want to kiss you—"

"I hear a but in there." His gaze searched her face.

"I also want you to touch me." The heat burned as it traveled up her neck to her face. "I really want you to touch me."

His smile eased her fears. "I'm glad, because I want to touch you, too."

When his lips closed over hers, his large hand, capable of plucking a football out of midair, closed around her breast. As they kissed, his thumbnail flicked over her nipple, sending shock waves of feeling to the very core of her body.

His tongue swept her lips, and when she opened and he plunged inside, feeling and need wrapped around her and squeezed tight. Breathing became difficult.

She wanted...

She needed...

As if sensing her struggle to hold on to control, he moved his hand to stroke her back. That sensual hand slid past her hips, then back up the side of her body, fingers brushing lightly against her breast before beginning their downward descent.

Her breathing evened out.

Then his lips were on hers again, offering soft, warm kisses full of emotion and promise. The desire that surged this time built slowly, and she found herself leaning into it instead of pulling back.

Krew's lips trailed from her mouth to her neck, where he lingered before heading lower. His hands were back on her breasts, stroking, kneading, until they ached for more. When his mouth replaced his fingers and he suckled, she came up off the bed.

He pulled back ever so slightly.

"No," she pleaded. "Don't stop."

"Never."

As his mouth continued its downward journey, Cassie was pummeled by all the feelings. This was more than sex. This was making love. She'd been around the block enough to appreciate the difference.

Never, not ever, had it been like this.

When he left the bed to grab a condom, she had the feeling it would never be like this again.

Not with anyone else.

Only with him.

CHAPTER TWENTY-TWO

"Tell me about the test." Krew turned onto Highway 57 with more than a little regret. He and Cassie would soon be home all too soon.

Cassie leaned back in her seat, looking tousled and tumbled and very pleased with herself. "What would you like to know?"

"Were the questions as difficult as you thought they'd be?"

"You really want to talk about me?"

"Of course." Something in her voice had Krew curious. "Why does that surprise you?"

"I thought you'd want to talk about your meeting. You know, with the front office."

"We can talk about that later." He took her hand, playing with her fingers. "This was a big day. I know that you passed, but not much else."

Krew wanted to hear all about the test. Without him asking direct questions, she probably wouldn't tell him much. From what he'd observed, Cassie had become adept at putting everyone else's needs before her own.

It was time that stopped.

"Don't spare the details."

"I thought I'd be more nervous." She flashed a smile that managed to look both proud and shy. "I told myself to take my time, to read each question carefully."

Any other time, Krew might have jumped in and taken charge of the conversation, firing questions at her. It was his natural tendency. But this was her story to tell. In her own time. In her own way.

"About halfway through, my heart started beating so fast I thought my chest was going to explode." The delightful flush he found so charming colored her cheeks. "You know what I did?"

He shook his head, loving the excitement in her voice.

"I focused on my breathing until I felt calmer." She smiled at his obvious confusion. "Dr. Gallagher has me meditating each night. He says focusing on your breathing helps you be present in the moment. It sounds crazy, I know."

"It doesn't. Not to me, anyway." Krew slowed the car as they approached Sturgeon Bay. "In the past few years, the team has worked with players on what they call mindful meditation."

"Really?" Cassie shifted in her seat, appearing intrigued.

"As you might suspect, everyone who reaches the NFL is very goal-oriented. The problem is, it's difficult for such personalities to stay in the moment. Instead, players and coaches are always focusing on past missteps, or they're looking ahead to where they want to be in the future."

Cassie's nod of understanding had him continuing.

"It's not a new concept," Krew explained. "Bill Belichick has been spouting 'do your job' with his teams for years. There's just more focus now as the game continues to change and evolve."

"Is the mindful meditation something you'd be involved with as an assistant coach?"

Though Cassie's obvious interest pleased him, Krew didn't want to talk about the future. A future that would involve them seeing each other only sporadically, if at all.

Just because he'd maintain his relationship with Dakota didn't mean that would include her mother.

"I'm not sure." He redirected the conversation back to her. "So, what's the plan now that you can get your license?"

"Well," she took a moment to consider, "I need a sponsoring real estate broker. I'm hoping Tim will sponsor me."

"Your mother's old boyfriend."

"Tim is extremely successful. I think, I hope, he'll take me on."

"Have you ever considered moving to a bigger market?"

She shook her head. "I don't like big cities."

Krew thought how wonderful it would be to have her in the same town. "Not a big city. Perhaps a town the size of Green Bay."

The more Krew thought about it, the more jazzed he was about the idea.

Cassie apparently wasn't seeing it as she gave her head a slow shake. "The idea of being in a new community and starting fresh is appealing. If I was single. But I have the kids to think of. Not to mention, it's expensive to relocate."

"True," Krew conceded, resisting the urge to push hard. "Though bigger schools would have a lot to offer both Braxton and K.T."

"I don't want to sound like a user." Cassie spoke slowly. "But in Good Hope I have friends and family. People I can call on if I get sick or need help."

Krew thought of all the years he'd had to worry only about himself. Cassie had never experienced that freedom. From the time she'd been fifteen, she'd had to take someone else into consideration.

"What about Clint?"

A startled look crossed Cassie's face. "What about him?"

"Is staying close to where he's incarcerated part of the consideration because he's Axl's father?" Just thinking of Clint ever touching Cassie had Krew's jaw tightening.

"No." Cassie's voice turned hard. "Actually, I'd love to be farther away from him than I am."

"Do you hear from him much?"

"More at first, but I heard from him just last week. He offered to relinquish his parental rights to Axl for a thousand dollars. Apparently, he needs it in order to hire what he calls a 'real' attorney, which I took to mean one who isn't court-appointed."

"Are you going to do it?"

"I looked into the possibility." Cassie gazed down at her hands before looking up. "I don't want him being any part of Axl's life. When I mentioned something to Beck—who's an attorney— about Clint's offer, I discovered termination of one parent's parental rights isn't usually granted without an accompanying stepparent adoption."

"That seems strange."

"I thought so, too. Beck says the state feels that a child is entitled to have two legal parents to support them." Cassie lifted one shoulder and let it drop. "I would have had to try to borrow the money, anyway."

Krew thought of Axl. The kid was spirited but as sweet as they came. What would happen to that childish innocence when Clint Gourley got out of prison and asserted his parental rights?

Clint *would* come around, Krew had no doubt of that, if only to make Cassie's life miserable.

"You could marry me. I'd adopt Axl, and then you'd be free of Clint forever."

Cassie inhaled sharply, then gave a soft laugh. "I believe that's the most generous offer anyone has ever made me. But I have to say no."

Krew had shocked himself with the proposal. The words had been out of his mouth before he'd had a chance to fully consider what he was offering.

Marriage? Adopting a child? What about the older boys? They would be part of the package, too.

When Cassie touched his arm and gave him a shy smile, Krew fought a surge of emotion that told him maybe asking her to marry him hadn't been such a crazy idea after all.

"Thank you," she whispered, even though they were the only ones in the car.

"For what?"

"For caring." Her eyes grew misty. "For just being you."

The seven-foot Douglas fir Krew had personally picked out that morning showed up, as promised, on his porch at noon.

Krew stared at the perfectly shaped tree positioned in front of the window. When he and Tessa had been kids, they'd begged for a Christmas tree. His dad had considered them a waste of money, preferring to spend any extra cash on another bottle of cheap whiskey.

None of the teammates Krew had lived with had been into holiday decorating, so they'd never bothered with a tree.

His fingers stroked the surprisingly soft needles. He hoped to get Cassie, Dakota and the boys to help him decorate.

Krew had discovered Dakota possessed a love for the holidays. She and Cassie were alike in that regard. When he'd dropped Cassie off yesterday, there had been no tree in their living room. Then again, there was really no room for one.

Cassie had done her best to make the house look festive by draping red and green rings of construction paper that Axl had obviously glued together around a sad-looking plant.

Pulling out his phone, Krew texted Cassie.

Got a tree today.

Tree?

Xmas tree. Want to bring kids & help decorate tonight?

Do you have decorations?

He didn't, but he could pick some up today. *Yes.*

He pictured Cassie in his living room handing ornaments to Axl to hang on the tree. Laughing with Dakota and teasing Cassie's sons. Krew thought how nice it would be to watch Cassie put a star at the top.

He wanted her here. Wanted all of them here.

Sure.

He smiled. *Plan on seven. I'll have food.*

Krew glanced at the bare tree. If things went as he hoped, tonight it would be festooned with strings of lights and ornaments.

The holiday was off to a great start.

Cassie couldn't believe she would see Krew three days in a row. Tomorrow night, she'd go with him to Rakes Farm to sing Christmas carols and drink hot apple cider. Tonight, they would decorate his Christmas tree.

At the moment, her heart simply overflowed with holiday cheer.

"Do you think he's getting pizza?" Braxton asked from the passenger seat.

"If he does, I bet it's pepperoni." K.T. spoke from behind her. "Krew knows it's our favorite."

"All I know is there'll be food." Cassie added a bit of warning to her voice. "Regardless what it is, we'll say thank you."

"We know, Mom," Braxton said. "But if he got hamburger, we have to give him grief."

"Brax." She said his name in a low growl.

"He expects it, Mom."

"Yeah," K.T. agreed. "He'd wonder what was wrong if we didn't razz him."

Cassie didn't know how to respond to that, so she focused on the road. She couldn't recall the last time they'd decorated a

Christmas tree as a family. Her mother always ordered a flocked tree and had it professionally decorated.

"Our thanks will be to toss some ornaments on his tree," Braxton said.

"Even for pepperoni, I draw the line at singing Christmas carols," K.T. asserted. "Just sayin'."

The pronouncement drew a harsh intake of breath from his big brother.

"Is that even a possibility?" Braxton's tone held horror.

Cassie laughed and turned into the driveway, parking behind a shiny red Honda that looked brand new. "It's going to be fun."

When Dakota had said she'd meet them at Krew's home, Cassie had assumed Krew was giving her a ride. She hadn't considered Dakota would bring a friend.

"Whose car is that?" Braxton asked.

She wasn't the only one who was curious.

K.T. wiped the condensation off the window and gave a low whistle. "That is one sweet ride."

"I wanna see." Axl began jumping up and down in his car seat, as far as the restraints would allow.

"We'll find out who it belongs to soon enough." Cassie spoke in a matter-of-fact tone. Years ago, she might have envied the person who owned such a beautiful vehicle. Now, she was simply thrilled to have a car that ran. "K.T., can you carry your brother to the house?"

"That's okay, Mom." Braxton's lips quirked upward. "I think I can walk."

The two teens started laughing like hyenas at his little joke. Even though Axl didn't understand, he laughed along with them.

Cassie only shook her head, but a warmth flowed through her at their easy camaraderie. The boys might bicker at times, but they were good friends and they had each other's back.

Dr. Gallagher had told her to embrace her successes. Her children's closeness was a small one, but she'd take it.

Glancing at the grand house awash with lights, Cassie felt her heart lighten.

A Christmas tree.

An evening with her family.

Krew.

Her life couldn't get any better.

CHAPTER TWENTY-THREE

The door swung open when Cassie and the boys reached the porch. Dakota and Krew stood with welcoming smiles on their faces, motioning them inside.

Cassie handed her coat to Dakota and exchanged a glance with Krew.

She resisted the urge to wrap her arms around him and pull him close. Cassie had hoped their lovemaking would quench her desire for him. Instead, she'd dreamed of him last night and had awakened this morning aching for his touch.

When his eyes locked on hers, she saw the same flicker of want.

"Whose car is that?" Braxton's gaze scanned the room to see who else was at the party.

"It's mine." Dakota now held Axl, who'd buried his head in the curve of her neck.

"You can't afford a new car." The blunt words popped out before Cassie could stop them.

"Dad bought it for me." Dakota smiled at Krew. "He wants me to have reliable transportation when I go back to school."

Cassie whirled, fixing her gaze on the perpetrator of this

unwelcome surprise. "You never mentioned you were even considering buying her a car. Have you given one thought to what the insurance on a new car will cost? Because let me tell you, it's expensive."

Practicality was a necessity in Cassie's world. While a new vehicle was nice, having an older car was a plus when it came to insurance rates. Especially with a teen driver on the policy.

"I see the car and covering the insurance as part of paying for her education."

Dakota appeared as puzzled as Krew. "Why would he need to explain anything to you? This is between him and me."

Cassie opened her mouth, but Krew spoke first.

"She's right that I should have mentioned it to her before I bought it for you. In my eagerness to do this for you, I forgot that important step." Krew's tone remained calm. "Your mom and I are your parents, which means we're a team. Team members work together, not in isolation. Understand?"

"I guess so." Dakota glanced at Cassie.

"It's a beautiful car." Cassie knew when to let something go. "I hope you'll give me a ride in it sometime."

"Sure." Dakota shoved her hands into the pockets of her cardigan. "It's not frivolous, Mom. Having a car will give me more options regarding part-time jobs when I return to La Crosse. And I won't have to look for someone to give me a ride home on breaks."

"Is anyone hungry?" Krew asked, obviously done with the car conversation. "I have pizza."

Braxton and K.T. exchanged glances.

"Pepperoni?" Cassie voiced the question she knew they wanted to ask.

Krew lifted his hands and shot the boys a wink. "Is there any other kind?"

The two boys high-fived each other.

Cassie opened the pizza boxes while Axl sat on Krew's lap and the older children vied for Krew's attention. It didn't bother her, Cassie told herself. Well, maybe just a little. Despite arriving late in the game, Krew had slipped so easily into her children's affections.

Didn't they realize he'd soon slip out of their lives just as quickly as he'd slipped in? Perhaps she should have done a better job at keeping him away from—

"Let the feasting begin," Krew announced, and everyone cheered.

In addition to the pizza, there were glasses of ice and bottles of brand-name soda, even a new sippy cup filled with milk for Axl.

This time, they ate around a sleek table with a glossy ebony lacquer finish and enough chairs for everyone. The boys' questions had Krew regaling them with tales from his years in the NFL.

Though most were humorous, it was clear he'd worked hard for his success. Just like what he'd told her, anything worth achieving didn't come easy.

"This is nice." Impulsively, Cassie leaned over and gave Dakota a hug. "I'm glad we can spend this time together."

Dakota hugged her back. "Me, too."

After they'd eaten their fill of pizza, followed by sour cream brownies so rich, Cassie could eat only one, Dakota pushed back from the table.

"I'm going to put on the Christmas music," she announced. "Perhaps we can sing some carols later."

Braxton choked on his last bite of pizza.

K.T. laughed and pounded his brother on his back.

Dakota, apparently oblivious to his distress, grabbed Braxton's arm. "You've got to see the sound system. It's amazing."

"I want to see it, too," K.T. called to their retreating backs before scooping up Axl and hurrying after them.

Cassie waited until she was certain she and Krew were finally alone to speak. "I'm happy about the car, Krew. It's a load off my mind knowing she'll have a dependable vehicle. I just wish you'd discussed it with me first."

"I don't know why I didn't think to mention it. But, Cass, if you truly recognize me as Dakota's father, you can't expect me to ask your permission for everything." Krew blew out a breath. "This is a father taking care of his child, something I should have been doing for the past nineteen years. The thing is, you're operating under an old model where you had to do it all alone. That isn't true anymore. You can share that load with me. Does any of this make sense?"

Cassie sighed. "It does."

"I am sorry that it caught you by surprise." Krew slung an arm around her shoulders. "Forgive me?"

"Oh, I suppose."

He smiled when he saw the teasing smile tugging at her lips.

His gaze lingered on her mouth, and her lips began to tingle. She lifted her face, ready for his kiss.

Strains of Mariah Carey's version of "All I Want for Christmas is You" filled the air as their lips melded together in an all-too-brief moment. Before she could fully step out of his arms, footsteps echoed on the hardwood.

Cassie turned, Krew's arm still around her shoulders, to see Dakota skid to a stop.

Her daughter glanced from her dad to Cassie.

"Where are the boys?" Cassie took a casual step away from Krew, traitorous heat firing in her cheeks.

"Nosing around the house." Confusion furrowed Dakota's brow. "What are you two doing?"

"Talking." Krew turned to Cassie. "Will picking you up at seven tomorrow work? Or is that too late?"

"Tomorrow?" Two tiny lines formed between Dakota's brows.

"I invited your mom to join us at Rakes Farm tomorrow."

"What about Axl?" Dakota inclined her head. "That's pretty late for him to be out."

"His brothers will watch him."

Dakota frowned. "You've been leaving him a lot lately."

The blow hit its target. Cassie had to have caregivers for Axl when she worked; there was no getting around that. But Dakota was right. These other activities were unnecessary.

"I hardly think Axl is suffering." Krew glanced at the little boy, currently giggling while being held upside down by Braxton as he strolled into the room. "Your mother has a right to get out, too."

"I think you forfeit that right when you have children." Dakota's eyes narrowed on Cassie. "Your child should be your priority, not your social life. Or your boyfriend."

If Krew thought Dakota was speaking about him, he was mistaken. The look in her daughter's eyes told her exactly who Dakota was talking about.

She'll never forgive me, Cassie thought. Ignoring the stabbing pain in her heart and stealing a page from the Krew Slattery playbook, Cassie changed the subject. "I can't wait to decorate the tree."

K.T., the artist, took charge of the lights. "I did my research. We need three sets of one hundred lights each for every foot of the tree."

"This is a seven-footer," Braxton announced after surveying the fir, his thumbs hooked in the belt loops of his jeans.

Dakota glanced at K.T., who was pulling packages of lights out of a sack, then back at her mother.

For a second, Cassie thought Dakota would return to their conversation, but Dakota shifted her focus back to K.T. "Do we have enough?"

"We can always get more—" Krew began.

"Nope. We have just enough." When Dakota reached for a

package, K.T. hugged some light sets to his chest. "You can't just start tossing these up there, Dakota."

"I wasn't going to toss them up there. I was going to start at the bottom—"

She made another grab, but K.T. turned and blocked her.

"You don't start at the bottom." K.T. blew out a breath.

Dakota put her hands on her hips. "Then tell me, smart guy, how do you do it?"

"You start at the top near the trunk," he began, while Braxton returned to the table for another brownie.

"...three triangular sections."

Cassie was distracted from the sibling squabbling when Krew stepped close.

"Okay, so you wrap around the tree from the top. Got it."

"You're not listening." K.T. swatted Dakota's hand away when she once again reached for the lights. "You weave the lights back and forth across the triangle."

"Oh, come on, K.T. You're making this way too complicated."

Braxton stood back, feeding Axl bits of brownie.

"Are they always like this?" Krew asked Cassie.

"Sometimes it's worse," Braxton said as he handed Axl to Krew.

Recalling Dakota's earlier words about her pawning off her youngest to anyone and everyone, Cassie held out her hands. "I can hold him."

Axl's only response was to wrap his arms around Krew's neck. "Dad."

Cassie froze for just a second. But it was long enough for Axl to lean back in Krew's arms, look him straight in the eyes and pat his cheeks with both hands. "My dad."

Braxton rolled his eyes.

K.T. and Dakota continued their conversation, though Cassie noticed they'd moved on to stringing the lights.

"I'm sorry," Cassie said to Krew before focusing on her youngest. "Axl, this is Krew. Can you say Kr-ew?"

The little boy studied her for a long moment, then patted Krew's cheeks again. "Dad."

Krew chuckled. "It's okay."

"It's not okay."

"He's a little boy, Cass." Krew's eyes met hers. "I don't mind. Really."

She remembered the offer he'd made when they were in Green Bay. He would marry her and adopt Axl. He hadn't been serious, of course.

What an odd thing to think of now.

"If I call you Dad, will you buy me a car?" Braxton somehow managed to keep a straight face, but Cassie saw the laughter in his eyes.

Krew swung the little boy in his arms down before answering, "I believe it's time to get out the ornaments."

~

Cassie stood back as Axl studied one of the unbreakable ornaments that Krew had purchased specifically for the little boy.

Her youngest had already placed a wooden reindeer, a ball and a penguin on the lower branches. This ornament was even more appealing—a bright green race car with wheels that actually moved.

Axl's face scrunched up as he pulled the car tight against his chest. "Mine."

"Axl, honey." Cassie kept her voice calm, knowing it was past his bedtime and a wrong move would ignite the tantrum simmering just below the surface. "That's for the tree."

Dakota crossed to her little brother in several long strides and scooped him up. "Would you like your car to be on a branch way up high?"

"Nooo. I want it." Axl struggled in her arms until Dakota had no choice but to set him on the floor.

Fueled by fatigue and sugar, Axl was now, officially, out of control. Before Cassie could reach him, he flung himself back, his head smacking against the hardwood. His cry of outrage changed to shrieks.

Cassie was to him in seconds, scooping the screaming boy up into her arms. Her gaze shifted to Krew. "Do you have an ice bag?"

Worry raced through Cassie as she felt the knot already forming at the back of his head. "Axl, sweetie, let Mommy check..."

He screamed even louder as she separated the hair to see if he was bleeding. No blood, just a knot that seemed to be growing larger by the second.

"Will this work?" Krew returned and knelt beside her.

"Yes. Thanks." Cassie pressed the ice bag firmly against the back of Axl's head. "Braxton, get the phone out of my purse and turn on the flashlight. Check his pupils while I hold him."

"I can do it," Dakota offered.

"I know the drill." Braxton squatted in front of Axl, whose sobs were now more of the hiccup-ping kind. "Hey, brat, I'm going to shine this light in your face. Pretend I'm a policeman."

Cassie might have found the remark humorous at another time. Not now.

Despite his lighthearted tone, Braxton's expression turned serious as he flashed the light.

Almost immediately, Axl began to squirm. "I wanna play."

Braxton met Cassie's gaze. "All good."

"Are you sure?" she asked.

"Equal and reactive," Braxton confirmed.

"You really do know the drill," Krew said to Braxton, appearing impressed.

Cassie released her hold on the struggling boy, and Axl scrambled to his feet.

"Should we take him to the hospital? Just to be sure?" Krew glanced worriedly at the boy

Slowly rising to her feet, Cassie gestured to her youngest, who was now pointing to the car near the top of the tree, which Dakota immediately retrieved for him. "He took quite a hit, but it doesn't seem like he has a concussion. He isn't bleeding, and he wants to play."

"All good signs," Braxton added.

At Krew's look of surprise, Braxton grinned. "I have two younger brothers. This sh—ah, stuff, happens all the time."

Dakota found another car in the pile of ornaments and handed it to Axl. "Look, Axl. Now you have two cars."

"Mine." Axl held out one of the cars to her, then quickly pulled it back out of reach.

Cassie noticed that even Dakota smiled at the classic Axl move.

The rest of the decorating went smoothly, with K.T. trying to direct the others to put the ornaments where his artistic eye thought they would look best.

His brothers and sister ignored him. K.T. finally gave up and joined the fun.

Cassie was conscious of Krew's every move. The rich, intoxicating scent of his cologne wrapped around her each time he lifted a hand to place an ornament on the tree. The sounds of applewood crackling in the hearth provided the perfect accompaniment to the Christmas melodies wafting from the home's stereo system.

The tree grew more beautiful with each colorful bulb added to its branches. Happiness bubbled in Cassie's veins as her children laughed and joked with her and Krew. Axl continued to add some of the unbreakable objects to the bottom of the tree and hoard others in a pile he'd started by the sofa.

"It's beautiful." Dakota took several steps back, her gaze traveling up and down the massive fir.

"It turned out better than I imagined," K.T. admitted. "It still needs something at the top."

"I have just the thing." Krew pulled a brilliant silver star out of a sack that Cassie hadn't noticed before. "I think your mom should place it."

"Works for me." Braxton glanced at K.T. and Dakota, who both nodded.

Axl had decided it was time to play with all the ornaments, er, toys he'd been hoarding.

"Me and Brax thought we might check out the pinball machines we spotted in the game room." Though a statement, Cassie saw the question in her son's eyes.

The boys would stay while she put the topper on the tree, if that's what she wanted. But this night was as much about them having an enjoyable evening as it was about her.

"That's fine. Thank you both for the stellar job you did on the tree," she told them. "It's been fun."

"Yeah," Braxton conceded. "It was."

"Can I play pinball, too?" Dakota asked, then glanced at her mother. "Or do you want me to keep an eye on Axl?"

"No. Krew and I will keep an eye on him."

"This has been really nice." Dakota's voice thickened. "I only wish Axl hadn't gotten hurt."

"He'll be fine." Cassie gave her daughter a hug. "Beat the socks off your brothers."

Dakota laughed. "I'll do my best."

Cassie turned back to Krew.

He'd pulled a small stepladder close to the tree. When he held out a hand to her, she couldn't help but smile.

"This has been a wonderful evening." She placed her hand in his and felt the surge of heat. "Thank you."

"It isn't over yet." His gaze lifted to the top of the tree. "When I spotted this tree, it was you I saw placing the star at the top."

The air turned thick, and Cassie had trouble catching her breath. Her smile was wobbly, and she felt not quite steady as she placed a foot on the small ladder and began to climb.

She paused when she reached the top step, the shiny star clutched tightly in one hand. Krew released her hand and settled both of his on her waist.

It took her several seconds to secure the star at the top and then to attach it to the string of lights. Finally, she nodded in satisfaction and looked down with a triumphant smile.

"Beautiful." Krew's eyes were dark as he gazed up at her.

Cassie flushed. Why did she have the feeling he wasn't speaking about the star?

Her gaze locked with his. Energy surged, and the air pulsated. Once again, Cassie felt breathless and a little giddy.

She glanced around the living area as she slowly stepped down. From the dinging of bells and shouts of triumph, her children were enjoying the game room immensely.

Axl appeared totally absorbed with his toys.

For the moment, it was just her and Krew. The attraction that had only continued to build since they'd returned from Green Bay reached a fever pitch.

When her feet hit the hardwood, Krew remained where he was, not giving her room, but not crowding her, either. His eyes remained watchful.

"I'm glad you came tonight." His voice was low and husky. When he tucked a strand of hair behind her ear, she suppressed a shiver.

As if on autopilot, her arms rose to encircle his neck. "I'm glad, too."

His lips closed over hers, and every worry Cassie had disappeared in the rightness of that moment.

CHAPTER TWENTY-FOUR

Instead of riding to the party with her parents, Dakota drove her new car to Rakes Farm. She wanted to show off her ride to her friends who were home for the holidays.

The majority of attendees at this event were as old as her parents. Which was why, two hours later, she stood alone in Jeremy and Fin's grand home wondering why she was still here. The outdoor activities had ended an hour ago. Her friends, after oohing and aahing over her car, had left.

Anita, vibrant and festive in red, stood by the fireplace beside her boyfriend.

Her mother and Krew were laughing with Owen and Lindsay about something that was obviously uproariously funny.

Bored, Dakota studied her mother. Cassie had mentioned wanting to go for a ride in her new car.

Dakota crossed the room, emboldened by her mother's welcoming smile. She was struck by the thought that her mom was pretty. Maybe it was the bright smile or the fact that Cassie wore a blue sweater that flattered her coloring. Whatever the reason, tonight she looked pretty, happy and surprisingly young.

"Hey, sweetie." Cassie leaned over and kissed her cheek. "Are you having fun?"

Krew shot Dakota a wink, then returned his attention to something Owen was saying.

"I thought maybe I could take you for a ride in my car." Dakota spoke quickly, wanting to get all the words out. She willed her mother to see just how much this meant to her. "You've been wanting to take a ride, and we haven't had much of a chance to talk recently."

While Dakota had grown to love her father, it seemed to her that her mom spent a lot of time with him and very little with her. Surely her mother would understand just how important this girl time was to her. Especially since she'd be leaving for college in a few weeks.

"Oh, Dakota, I'd really love to go, but—" Cassie glanced at Krew.

When they exchanged a smile and his hand stole around her mother's waist, Dakota's anger meter shot into the red zone. Some of the temper came from sleeping poorly last night, upset and worried about Axl and his injury. Then she'd started thinking about returning to campus a whole semester behind her friends. Would everyone treat her differently when it came out that Krew Slattery, NFL superstar, was her father?

There was so much she wanted—needed—to discuss with her mother. Her mom had a knack for quieting her fears.

"How about we do it tomorrow?" Cassie inclined her head. "Do you have to work? I'm sure we can find—"

"A man always comes before me." Dakota pushed the words past suddenly numb lips.

Cassie straightened away from Krew, clearly alarmed.

For some reason, her mother's concern over what others would think only fueled Dakota's rising anger.

"I find out I have a dad, and instead of giving me a chance to get to know him, you're all over him. You—"

"Dakota." Krew saying her name in that disappointed manner was the last straw.

"You think you know her. You maybe even like her." Dakota was aware she spoke too loudly. She was also aware of the sudden hush that fell over the room. But she was too far gone. "I'm betting she hasn't told you how she nearly served me up on a silver platter to Clint Gourley."

Out of the corner of her eye, Dakota caught the questioning look Krew shot her mother, who stood unmoving, as stiff as a statue.

Good, Dakota thought. *He deserves to know what kind of woman she is.*

"When I told her Clint Gourley wanted to have sex with me, she defended him." The last words came out on a shout, surprising even Dakota. She heard the gasps, but barreled ahead, her gaze focused on her mother. "You didn't even try to protect me. I had to protect myself."

Cassie's face blanched white.

"Dakota." Lindsay's calm voice filled the sudden silence. "This is not the time or the place for this."

"Come to our house." Owen added a persuasive smile. "We can all talk there."

Dakota ignored them both.

Anita tried to put a hand on Dakota's shoulder, but Dakota shrugged her off. She brought a clenched fist to her chest and continued to glare at her mother. "You took his side against your own daughter."

Anita again tried to intervene, but Cassie shook her head and motioned for her mother to step back. She moved toward Dakota and met her steely look.

"You're right. I made a horrible mistake, and you have no idea how much I regret it. However angry you are at me will never compare to how angry I am at myself."

Tears filled Dakota's eyes. She pressed her lips together to still the trembling. Her mother's response surprised her. It had never occurred to her that her mother gave what happened with Clint any thought at all.

"It's no secret I screwed up many, many times. I'll never forgive myself for some of my choices. I will never forgive myself for what I nearly let happen to you. *Never.* But some of those choices…" Her mother's gaze slipped to Krew. "Well, I can't regret all of them, because they resulted in something great, like you and your brothers."

When Cassie touched her arm, Dakota jerked away.

Though her mother's face held lines of strain, she kept her composure and her voice remained even. "You have every right to your anger, Dakota. Every right. I was dead wrong, and I'm so sorry I put you through that. I'm so sorry I didn't protect you the way a good mother should. I thank God every day your grandmother and aunt were there for you when I wasn't. And I don't expect you to forgive me. I mean, how could you *ever* forgive me? But know this—I will *never* again stand by and let someone hurt you or threaten to hurt you. I will protect you with my life, because I love you, Dakota. I love you more than you will ever know."

Dakota glanced around the room and saw the concerned faces of her grandmother and Len, of Lindsay and Owen and everyone else still at the party. What was she doing? Why had she brought this up now? Her head ached, and nothing made sense except the pain. That was real, and memories of those horrible months pummeled her.

Dakota wrapped her arms around herself, and tears slipped down her cheeks. She shivered, cold to the marrow. She couldn't remember ever feeling so alone.

Then her mother's comforting arms were around her, like they'd been all those times when she'd skinned her knee or a friend had hurt her feelings.

A second later, Krew's arms were around both of them, and Dakota found herself wrapped in the warmth of their love.

She felt her father's lips brush her hair. "Let's go home."

Krew didn't say a word on the drive to his house.

"Can I get you something?" Cassie asked Dakota once they were inside. "Maybe a glass of warm milk? Or I could draw you a hot bath?"

Dakota shook her head and avoided Cassie's concerned gaze. "I just want to sleep."

Dakota didn't look at either of them as she climbed the steps to the bedrooms.

Cassie dropped down on the sofa and stared into the dark hearth.

Krew started a fire, more to steady himself than for the warmth. Instead of sitting beside Cassie, he chose a nearby chair. "I need to know what happened with Clint."

It took everything in Krew to keep his voice calm, to not give in to the anger rising inside him...and the guilt. He should have been there to protect Dakota. She was his child, and he hadn't been there for her.

"Dakota never liked Clint." Cassie expelled a shaky breath and swiped a hand across her eyes. "He had a job when he moved in, but then he wrecked his motorcycle and claimed his back hurt and he couldn't work. He got even more mean then, if that was possible."

That sounded like the Clint he remembered. The one who'd faked nose bleeds to get out of gym class and who'd beaten a possum to death with a baseball bat.

"Clint was fascinated with Dakota." Despite the roaring fire, Cassie wrapped her arms round herself as if she was freezing.

"He was always giving her compliments, telling her how sexy she looked."

A muscle in Krew's jaw jumped. "How old was she then?"

"Sixteen. No, she'd just turned seventeen." Cassie blinked rapidly, and he watched her fight for control. "She came to me, told me that the way he looked at her made her uncomfortable. She said she'd overheard him telling a friend that as soon as he got the chance, he was going to—"

Cassie repeated the words in a voice barely above a whisper.

Krew cursed. "I hope you threw his ass out."

"I didn't. I stood up for Clint. I told Dakota to quit flirting. I warned her not to screw it up for me with her lies."

Krew stared, incredulous. No wonder Dakota was bitter and angry. Her mother, the person who was supposed to protect her, had all but tossed her to the wolf.

"Dakota went to her school counselor, who called me. When the woman called me, I told her Dakota was jealous of the new baby and making things up. That put Dakota in a horrible position. And Clint knew at that point he could do whatever he wanted to her, and no one would believe her. I wouldn't believe her."

"What happened?" Krew ground out the words between clenched teeth.

"Dakota was—is—a strong girl. She took charge. With Beckett Cross's help, she maneuvered it so she could live with Lindsay that last year in high school. Eventually, I kicked Clint out, and he was arrested later for multiple burglaries."

Krew clenched his jaw so tightly it ached. "If I'd been there, I'd have protected Dakota."

Something in the simple statement must have hit a nerve. Cassie's head jerked up, and sparks shot from her eyes. "Well, you weren't here, were you? It's easy to say that you'd have been perfect when you come in after the fact and play Dad for a couple weeks. You order a few pizzas, throw your money around, and suddenly you know everything about parenting. Well, I didn't know anything about parenting. I was alone and screwed up and scared and desperate and, yes, a bad mother. But I plan to make that up to Dakota and my boys every day for the rest of our lives, not just until the end of the year."

Krew recognized the truth in her rant. Her words cut him off at the knees as surely as if she'd chop-tackled him.

Cassie gave a little laugh that ended in a hiccup. "I was afraid for you to find this out because I know how much your mother's actions hurt you. Now that it's out in the open, I don't have the emotional energy to worry about what you think. All I can care about is Dakota and helping her deal with what happened and my betrayal. So if you want to judge me, go ahead. It doesn't really matter, since you'll be doing it from a distance, anyway."

Again, all true. Krew scrubbed his face with his hands and wondered how his perfect life could have gotten so messed up.

Krew was in the kitchen making breakfast when he caught sight of Dakota in the doorway. She was wearing the same clothes she'd had on last night. Her hair was a tangled mass around her shoulders.

She offered a wan smile when their eyes met.

"Breakfast is almost ready." He gestured toward the table where he'd set out the cups, plates, and silverware.

"I'm not hungry." After picking up a mug from the table, she wandered over to the coffee maker and poured herself a cup. "Where's Mom?"

"She took a cab home."

Dakota frowned. "Why didn't you take her?"

"I didn't want to leave you here alone."

Ignoring the table, she dropped down on a stool at the bar. "I'm not a kid. Leaving me here would have been okay."

"I didn't want you to wake up and find yourself alone."

Dakota gave a jerky nod and gulped coffee.

"Your mom told me all about Clint. We fought about it." Krew turned off the burner and set the skillet aside. He sat on the stool next to her. "I'm sorry I wasn't there to protect you, Dakota. I'm angry that your mother wasn't there for you."

Dakota lifted one shoulder, let it drop and took another long drink of coffee.

"I want you to make your home with me in Green Bay."

Confusion furrowed her brow. "I'm going to school in La Crosse."

"I mean for holidays and breaks and in the summer," he said. "You can put Good Hope, your mom, and Clint behind you."

"Who are you to judge my mom?"

Krew blinked, startled by the vehemence in her tone.

"I have my reasons for being angry at her, but what right do you have? You abandoned her. You got a fifteen-year-old girl pregnant and then left her. How would you feel if some guy did that to me? I never really thought about it before, but if some guy did that to me, I don't think I'd ever be able to look at him again. Yet my mom has spent all this time with you because I asked her to."

"Dakota, please—" He touched her arm, but she shook him off.

"I thought she was choosing you, but she was just doing what I asked. And now you want me to abandon her like you did? Leave my brothers, my whole family to run off with you? I'm not going to repeat either of my parents' mistakes. I'm not going to blindly follow a man I just met, and I'm not going to turn my back on people I care about. I'm also not going to hold on to all this toxic anger and judgment. My mom has made mistakes, and she's struggling with the consequences, which I didn't realize before. But I do know that she's been really trying to do better.

And no matter what I said to her last night, I love her and I know she loves me."

Krew stared at his daughter. He'd thought he was being supportive of her, but it appeared he was wrong. Maybe he wasn't cut out to be a father.

Maybe they'd all be better off if he left and just sent money.

CHAPTER TWENTY-FIVE

Cassie told herself to wait until the afternoon to try to contact Dakota, to give the emotions from the evening before time to settle. But she couldn't wait. She feared she'd already waited too long.

She called and discovered her daughter was still at Krew's house. When she asked if she could come over so they could talk, Dakota agreed.

Cassie reminded herself that she had no control over Dakota's reaction, or Krew's. All she could do was speak from the heart.

Krew opened the door and stepped aside to let her enter. "Cassie."

"Hello, Krew. Thanks for letting me come over."

His gaze remained impassive, providing no clue as to his feelings. She told herself to be glad he wasn't openly hostile.

"Mom." Dakota stepped into the room. "I thought I heard the bell."

Her daughter looked the same as she had at the party, except she'd washed her face and her eyes were still red-rimmed.

"I was hoping we could talk." It was a stupid thing to say. Wasn't that what they were doing now?

Dakota gestured toward the sofa.

Cassie glanced at Krew, who watched, arms crossed, from several feet away.

"Do you mind if Dad stays?" Dakota asked.

"Whatever you want."

"Stay," Dakota said to her father. "Please."

He nodded and took a seat in the chair, while Dakota sat on the sofa.

Cassie opened her mouth, but Dakota spoke first.

"I'm sorry about bringing up all that stuff at the party last night." Dakota's gaze met hers. "You've been doing so much better lately, and the last thing I want is to derail—"

"Don't worry about me." On impulse, Cassie took her daughter's hands. Tears stung her eyes when Dakota didn't pull away. "I let you down, Dakota. You deserve a better mother than the one you got. But I love you, and I want to be a part of your life. If that's too hard for you, I'll understand."

"I love you, Mom." Tears now filled Dakota's eyes. "So, you're not perfect. Well, neither am I. I think it's time we move on from the past."

"I am sorry, Dakota."

"I know." Dakota squeezed her hands. "The thing with Clint, it's behind us now. I forgive you, and I hope you'll forgive me for bringing it up last night in front of everyone."

"There's nothing to forgive." Cassie expelled a breath. "I'm just sorry I didn't have the strength to talk to you about it before. I was terrified of losing you."

Then her daughter was in her arms, and Cassie's arms tightened around her girl. They'd found their way back to each other, and this time nothing would tear them apart.

~

Watching the two women cling to each other and cry, Krew wished he was anywhere else.

His feelings for Cassie had been so clear before last night. He'd been falling in love with her, dreaming of a future with her. Now he wondered if he ever really knew her.

Had he simply gotten caught up in the idea of being part of a family?

Krew was suddenly glad he would be leaving Good Hope at the end of the month. Moving into the coaching ranks would demand his total concentration. The way things stood now, he wouldn't have anything other than football on his mind.

At the sound of the two women standing, he pulled to his feet.

Cassie's eyes met his. "I told Dakota I'd drop her off at Jeremy and Fin's so she can pick up her car."

"I left my purse upstairs. Be right back." Dakota tossed the words over her shoulder as she rushed up the stairs.

An awkward silence descended like a shroud over the beautiful space.

If Krew didn't know what to think, he certainly didn't know what to say.

Cassie left a wide berth between them. Her lips trembled, but the gaze that met his was steady.

She waited.

He waited.

For what, Krew wasn't sure.

They both turned at the sound of Dakota's feet on the steps.

"I'm sure you'll be busy until it's time for you to return to Green Bay," Cassie said to Krew. The smile she offered was in sharp contrast to the bleak look in her eyes. "Good luck with the coaching."

"Thanks. Good luck with your real estate career."

"It'll be tough, but I'll persevere."

Tough, Krew thought, was an understatement. With her sordid past being brought to the forefront again, it was likely that her new career had tanked before it'd had a chance to begin.

Cassie knew that, too. He could see it in her eyes. Still, she was keeping up a brave front.

Krew was seized with the sudden urge to pull her into his arms and tell her this revelation about Clint changed nothing between them. Tell her he loved her and wanted to be with her. Tell her that she and the boys could move to Green Bay with him, and they'd start a new life together.

Instead, he walked her and Dakota to the door.

"Wow." Cassie shivered as a gust of wind hit them. "The wind has really picked up."

"Drive carefully," he told them. "It looks like the snow is starting up again."

He couldn't believe his relationship with Cassie had been reduced to discussing the weather.

"Thank you." Dakota wrapped her arms around him in a fierce hug.

"For what?" he asked.

"For being there for me last night." Then her gaze shifted to her mother. "I'm ready to go."

The week before Christmas, Krew accepted an invitation to meet Owen at the Flying Crane. He was still trying to figure out what he was going to do about Christmas Eve. The fact that he'd promised Dakota a family Christmas weighed heavily on him.

Krew knew he and Cassie needed to talk, at least one more time, before he left town. He wasn't sure what to say to her.

Dakota had forgiven her mother.

Forgiveness didn't come easily to Krew. Not surprising, since he still hadn't forgiven his parents. Not that they would ever ask for his forgiveness. In their minds, providing a roof meant they had done their part.

As soon as Krew entered the waterfront bar, he spotted Owen seated at a table near the far wall. He must have been watching the door, because he raised a hand when Krew walked in.

Out of the corner of his eye, Krew saw Mitch at one of the barstools, talking with what looked like a fellow city parks worker. Mitch didn't look in Krew's direction, for which he was grateful. The man's actions toward Cassie had left a permanently sour taste in Krew's mouth.

"Hey, man," Owen greeted him with a big smile. "I'm glad you could make it."

"Thanks for asking." Krew sat across from Owen and signaled for a beer. "Dakota has been so busy working that I've been at loose ends."

If not for the promise he'd made to his daughter, Krew would already be back in Green Bay.

"I ran into Braxton." Owen paused while the server dropped off Krew's beer. "He told me about the work you and the boys have been doing on Cassie's place."

"It was something I promised." Krew lifted the pilsner glass and drank. "The place looks a little better."

"I drove by. It looks amazing." Owen shoved the bar mix in Krew's direction. "I should have fixed that shutter and torn screen a long time ago. I should have helped Cassie more."

"You've got your own family."

Owen stared into his beer. "I'm not going to screw up this time around."

Krew frowned. "What are you talking about? You didn't screw up. You and my sister, you just weren't right for each other."

"Did Tessa tell you I told her to stay away from Mindy?"

Krew released his handful of snack mix back into the basket. "Why did you do that?"

He was aware his sister hadn't seen much of her daughter

after Owen gained sole custody. But Tessa had never mentioned being told to stay away.

"Tess would promise to come and Mindy would get excited. Then something with her job would come up, and she'd cancel at the last minute." Owen shifted his gaze for a second to the television over the bar before refocusing on Krew. "I'd had enough of seeing my daughter cry. In my righteous anger, I told Tessa to stay away. I said she was hurting Mindy. She argued, but finally agreed."

"Tessa loved Mindy. And Mindy loved her. Why would she have agreed to stay away?" None of this made sense to Krew.

"Your sister and I talked in October when she was back in Good Hope." Sorrow filled Owen's eyes. "I hurt our child. I told Tessa that I was sorry."

"What did she say?"

"She had her own regrets. She was sorry she agreed and sorry she stayed away." Owen shook his head. "We were both at fault."

"People make mistakes." It was an inane comment, but the best Krew could come up with. Though Krew didn't agree with what Owen had done, his former brother-in-law was a stand-up guy and Krew had always liked him.

Though, it baffled him how Owen could have done this to Tessa and Mindy.

"You're right. *Everyone* makes mistakes." Owen met his gaze, and suddenly Krew knew where this was headed.

"You're saying I should forgive Cassie and move on."

"Or forgive and hang around." Owen shrugged. "Tessa forgave me. I forgave her. I like to think Mindy, with her big loving heart, forgave us both."

"My situation is different." Krew leaned forward, resting his arms on the table. "How could Cassie not stand up for Dakota?"

Owen's gaze narrowed, turning sharp and assessing. "How could you not stand up for Cassie?"

"What do you mean?" Krew's voice rose. "You think I should have gotten between her and Dakota at Rakes Farm?"

Owen swiped the air with his hand, as if brushing aside a pesky gnat. "I'm talking way back. You had to wonder if the baby was yours when you heard Cassie was pregnant."

"I thought it was Mitch's."

Owen's gaze, fixed on Krew's face, never wavered. "You're telling me you were one hundred percent convinced the child she was carrying wasn't yours?"

Krew hesitated, wanting to be honest. "Maybe not a hundred percent."

"Do you ever wonder how you could justify leaving a young girl all alone to face a pregnancy she sure as heck hadn't bargained for?"

"I told you, I thought the baby was Mitch's." Krew jutted out his jaw, as if daring Owen to take a hit.

"You said you weren't positive." Owen cocked his head. "I bet having a baby would have screwed with your college and pro dreams."

"Big-time," Krew responded, then cringed as he realized how that sounded.

"We all make mistakes. We all do things we regret." Owen swallowed convulsively, as if his throat had suddenly gone bone-dry. He took a long drink of beer. "You and I, we can't change history. But we can forgive ourselves and others and make better choices going forward."

"I don't know if I can forgive Cassie for not believing Dakota when she complained about Clint's actions. He could have..." God, he couldn't even say it.

"There's no way to know if Cassie would have stepped up before that happened. Let me say it one more time: We all make mistakes." Owen grabbed a handful of the snack mix. "Last week, Pastor Dan said, and I quote, 'Let he who is without sin cast the first stone.'"

"You've made your point," Krew grumbled.

"Good. Enough about that. What teams do you think we'll see in the Super Bowl this year?"

Krew could talk football in his sleep. While he chatted with Owen, his gaze slid to Mitch. He thought how he'd left Cassie alone to deal with someone who knew just how to manipulate her innocence and destroy her confidence.

Let he who is without sin…

That wasn't Krew, not by a long shot.

He'd made his share of mistakes, including pulling away from Cassie when she needed his support the most.

That ended today.

CHAPTER TWENTY-SIX

Cassie worked until five o'clock Sunday afternoon. Ryder brought in extra help for the Christmas Stroll, so she was able to leave at the end of her shift. She should head straight home. That would be the smart thing to do. In a household of four, there was always laundry to do and a house to clean.

Or, she could sit in her car, plan the week's meals, then stop at the market and pick up groceries. The boys, who had absolutely no interest in strolling, were home with Axl. Not knowing if she'd have to stay late, Cassie had the evening meal in the refrigerator. All Braxton had to do was nuke it.

Feeling decidedly impractical, Cassie buttoned the coat Krew had bought her all the way to her chin, wrapped a scarf around her neck and pulled on her gloves.

When she'd been in high school, the Christmas Stroll had been a rite of passage. Shops were open late and served specialty foods. Most teenage strollers didn't care about picking up a slice of kringle from the bakery or a bit of mistletoe from the Enchanted Florist.

See and be seen was the purpose of the stroll when you were young. Her mother had promised Cassie that once she turned sixteen, she could stroll with her friends. By the time that birthday rolled around, Cassie had had a baby.

Tonight, she sauntered down the sidewalk, reveling in the cold, crisp air and the heavenly smell of evergreen. She decided to make Blooms Bake Shop her first stop. No one made kringle as delicious as Hadley Chapin, Ami's second-in-command. But when Cassie saw the place packed with high school-aged boys and girls, she hesitated.

"Quite a crowd."

The familiar masculine voice had her turning her head and gazing into Krew's beautiful eyes. Though Cassie had accepted that the closeness she and this man had once shared was over, her traitorous heart obviously hadn't gotten the message. It slammed against her ribs, then began an erratic rhythm.

"I think this is the busiest I've seen Blooms." Cassie forced her attention back to the bakery and considered how badly she wanted that slice of kringle. "Good luck braving the crowd. I'm going to pass."

Wiggling her fingers good-bye, Cassie began walking.

To her surprise, Krew fell into step beside her. Cassie saw the assessing glances slanted their way and understood what this was about.

She lowered her voice to a hushed whisper. "You don't have to do this, Krew."

"Do what?"

She couldn't keep the exasperation from her voice. "Show your support."

Her foot slipped on the sidewalk, and she suddenly found her arm tucked firmly around his. One touch was all it took for yearning to rise up and strangle her heart.

"You have my support, Cassie." His voice was low and husky. "I should have made that clear before now."

Cassie's heart rose to her throat as they strolled past store-front windows rimmed in brightly colored lights. On the doors, evergreen wreaths with bows and ribbons added an extra holiday punch. Banners hanging from vintage street poles and proclaiming "Seasons Greetings" and "Deck the Halls" complemented the heartwarming scene.

Whether it was the warmth of his hand or the companionable silence between them, Cassie began to relax.

"When I was a girl, I dreamed of walking these streets with a handsome boy." She gave a little laugh. "Or I saw myself with a pack of girlfriends on the hunt for a hot boy."

"I ruined those dreams for—"

She stepped in front of him.

Only quick reflexes kept him from plowing into her.

"The time for regrets and looking back is over, Krew." Cassie met his gaze, her voice firm. "Life is too short for either of us to stay mired in the past."

Admiration filled his eyes. "You're an amazing woman."

When she found herself tempted to argue with him, Cassie took her own words to heart. She grinned. "Yes, I am."

"Would you stroll with me, Ms. Amazing Woman?" He surveyed her with a lazy smile. "I'm a hot guy, and I feel naked without a hot girl on my arm."

"It's too cold to be naked." Cassie shot him a wink. "Muddy Boots is selling cups of peppermint hot chocolate. Let's get some."

"Before we head there, I have a question for you. I'd like it if we could all be together at my house on Christmas Eve." Krew held up a hand. "Full disclosure. This would also involve attending church and caroling in the town square. Dakota really wants church and caroling."

Cassie smiled. He wasn't telling her anything she didn't already know.

"So you'll come?"

Knowing what spending more time with him would mean to

all her children, Cassie didn't hesitate. "The boys and I would love to spend Christmas Eve with you and Dakota."

When he smiled, Cassie went warm all over.

"I'll be returning to Green Bay soon."

It took everything she had to not let her smile slip. "Are you excited?"

"I'm eager to get started. But I'm going to miss everyone." His gaze lingered on her for an extra heartbeat.

Cassie was glad the scarf hid the red creeping up her neck.

"How's the real estate business going?"

"Could be better." Cassie tried to sound upbeat. "Tim assures me December can be a slow month. Buyers are often more focused on the holidays than they are on looking for a new home or selling their current residence."

Cassie realized they'd passed Muddy Boots and had made it all the way down the street to Swoon, a local boutique and bridal salon. Her gaze was drawn to the dress in the window, a gorgeous white gown with fur around the bodice and wrists.

When she glanced back and found Krew staring, Cassie lost her train of thought. "What were we talking about?"

Krew studied her with inscrutable eyes. "Real estate."

"Oh, yes. I've been answering phones at Tim's office as much as I can, hoping to pick up a new client of my own. So far, nothing." She shrugged. "It makes me glad I kept my job at the Grind."

"You could consider moving to a bigger market…"

"Like Green Bay?" Cassie forced a teasing tone, though she knew that was no longer a possibility, not that it had ever been one.

"It's a great town." Krew's expression was serious as he took her hand. "About Clint—"

She pulled her hand back. "Not going there. Remember?"

"I should have called the second I heard you were pregnant."

Cassie experienced whiplash at the subject change. "What are you saying?"

"I'm saying you're not the only one with regrets."

She gazed into his eyes. In that moment, she understood that, just as she'd forgiven him, he'd forgiven her.

Cassie wondered if he had any idea that this was the best Christmas gift he could have given her.

On Christmas Eve, Krew glanced around his living room and watched the boys distribute the gifts. Cassie's gifts to her children were already at her mother's home, ready for Christmas morning. What surprised Krew was the growing stack of presents at his feet. He hadn't expected them to bring him gifts.

Having Cassie, the boys, and Dakota here with him was gift enough. He wanted this woman and her family to be his, but sensed Cassie wasn't ready for such a commitment.

Long ago, Krew had learned the value of patience, both on and off the field. Though he'd be leaving at the end of the week for Green Bay, Krew reminded himself that Good Hope was only a short drive away.

"What's in this big box?" Cassie's hand caressed the shiny red paper, then fingered the starched white bow.

"I guess you're going to have to open it and see." He waited for her to rip off the paper, but she didn't make a move.

"Oldest to youngest, them's the rules," Braxton declared. "Which means, old man, you go first."

"Open mine first, Dad." Dakota pointed to a box decorated with dancing penguins and topped with a candy-striped bow.

Krew lifted the small box, shook it, then smiled at his daughter. While everyone watched, he tore off the paper.

Inside was a picture frame decorated with words like *Good Hope, fun, daughter, dad* and other words. The picture was of him and Dakota, his warm gaze filled with pride and her looking up at him with an adoring smile.

He cleared his throat. "I love it. Thank you."

Dakota flushed. "Brax took the picture, and K.T. made the frame. I thought you could put it on your desk at work. Or maybe at home. I hope every time you see it, you'll think of me."

"It's a wonderful gift. Thank you. I'll definitely find a special place for it." His gaze settled on Dakota, and Krew was struck again how lucky he was to have her in his life. "Even without the photo, I'll always think of you."

He shifted his gaze first to Braxton, then to K.T. "Thanks for your parts in this gift."

Braxton grinned.

K.T. gave him the thumbs-up.

Krew moved on to his other gifts. He received lightsaber chopsticks from Braxton, a painting of the screaming heads alley art project Krew had admired from K.T. and a picture of everyone in the "family," drawn by Axl in bright purple crayon.

Each gift brought a lump to Krew's throat.

He opened Cassie's present last, a sports whistle set. She'd had his name monogrammed on the side of the whistle with a simple message engraved on the box: *Push forward.*

The woman knew him so well.

He turned to her and smiled. "Thank you. It's perfect."

"Mom was all worried about what to get you," K.T. told him.

"Yeah, money is a little tight right now, and—" Braxton stopped at the look Cassie shot him.

Krew met Cassie's gaze. "I really do love it."

He experienced a surge of satisfaction when her smile blossomed. It took every bit of his self-control not to pull her into his arms and show her just how much he liked it…and her.

Cassie went next, saving his box until last. Her fingers trembled as she lifted the two gift certificates from the tissue. One was for Swoon and the other for the consignment store she'd mentioned in Sturgeon Bay. Her gaze sought his. "This is too much."

He waved away her concern. "You need clothes for your new career. This will give you a good start on that wardrobe."

She opened her mouth as if to argue, but Dakota pointed to the gift at her eldest brother's feet. "Braxton, you're up. K.T., be ready."

"You're next, Dakota," Braxton reminded her.

"I already opened my gift." Dakota pulled the latest iPhone from her purse and shot a sunny smile at Krew.

Braxton ripped off the paper on his gift.

"Oh, man, these are sick." Braxton reverently lifted one of many AR/VR gadgets from the huge box. "Thanks, Krew."

Cassie took one look at the gift and raised her brows, obviously having some idea of the cost.

When K.T. opened his gift—raw pigments and a grinding set —he looked at Krew, wide-eyed. "I can make my own paints."

"That's the idea." Krew breathed a sigh of relief. The person he'd spoken with at the art store in Green Bay had said a serious artist would appreciate such a gift.

"I've been wanting these for so—" K.T. paused to clear his throat. "Thanks, man."

"You're welcome."

"Hey, brat." Braxton tousled his little brother's hair. "Your turn."

The child tore at the paper on his gift, flinging it and the bow aside. He pointed at the picture of the car carrier truck on the outside of the box. "My truck."

"Yes. Your truck." Krew sat on the floor beside the boy and helped Axl take out the toy.

The boy squealed when he saw not only a truck, but the cars that went with it. In seconds, Axl was pushing the truck all over the hardwood floor, making zooming noises.

Krew looked up to find Cassie gazing at him with misty eyes. "It's not much."

"You know what he likes." Cassie's gaze slid around the room, pausing on each of her children.

Dakota scrolling on her phone.

Braxton checking out the VR goggles.

K.T. intently studying his paints.

"What they all like," Cassie added.

"What about you?"

"It's too much money, but I know you won't take it back."

"We know each other so well."

After a moment, she nodded. "I believe we do."

He and Cassie—with Dakota's help—cleaned up the wrapping paper and boxes. Once that was done, they toasted marshmallows in the fireplace and made s'mores.

"I'm going to take Axl with me to Gram's," Dakota told her mother when the child's eyes began to droop. "She and Len have this whole big thing planned in the morning."

"I heard Len is going to dress up as—" Cassie stopped, as if conscious of little ears.

Dakota nodded. "Are you sure you don't want to come and spend the night? She's got enough room for all of us."

"I already told Mom the boys and I will sleep in our own beds and then head over there bright and early."

"We told Grandma we'd sleep over, too," Braxton announced.

Cassie frowned. "When did you tell her that?"

"This afternoon when she called." Braxton's gaze dropped to his gift. "Len is going to think these are so cool."

"Grandma told me she'd make a batch of my special cookies if I spent the night," K.T. added.

Dakota rose and glanced pointedly at her brothers. "You guys can ride with me. That way, Mom doesn't need to rush off."

In a matter of minutes, Dakota was pulling her car out of the driveway.

"I should be heading home, too." Cassie might have said the words, but she didn't move from her position on the sofa.

Krew stood. "What's the rush?"

"You have to leave in the morning."

They'd all thought Krew had until the end of December to report, but holiday time was football time and the coaches wanted him there as soon as possible.

Tomorrow would be a walk-through, and then his life in Green Bay would get crazy.

"Stay and keep me company a little longer." Krew patted the spot beside him on the sofa.

"I can do that." Cassie dropped down next to him.

"There's something I've been meaning to ask you."

She shifted to face him, her gaze curious.

"I don't want this to be good-bye." Krew reached out and ran his thumb lightly over the back of her hand. "Green Bay isn't far. I'd like for us to still see each other."

"You'll be busy."

"I make time for what's important." Krew couldn't resist any longer. He brushed her lips with his. "You're important to me, Cassie."

She sighed and leaned her head against his shoulder.

He placed his arm around her and gazed into the fire. "New Year's Eve is coming. Then it'll be Valentine's Day. Do you have plans for either?"

Cassie shook her head. "There's lots of women in Green Bay, Krew."

"I want only you, Cassie." Krew rested his head against hers. "There's no one else. Not for me."

CHAPTER TWENTY-SEVEN

Nearly two months later, Cassie opened her front door and found Lindsay on her stoop, a florist box cradled in her arms. "I didn't expect to see you before the party tonight."

"An order came in that I wanted to deliver personally." Lindsay brushed past Cassie, her large belly leading the way.

"Are those for me?" Cassie couldn't imagine another reason her sister would take time on Valentine's Day to stop by.

"Who else?" Lindsay spoke in a cheery tone.

"I never got flowers before."

It would be another first for her, Cassie thought. Like dating. Or kissing the man she was falling in love with under a glittery chandelier at the stroke of midnight on New Year's Eve.

"Well, enjoy." Lindsay presented the box with a flourish, then handed Cassie the accompanying card.

After setting down the box, Cassie opened the tiny card with eager fingers.

My darling Cassie,
Happy Valentine's Day.
In you, I've found someone I can't live without.

Love, Krew

Her heart gave a solid thump in her chest. She traced the words with her finger.

Lindsay grinned. "He told me what to write and how he wanted it signed."

Cassie slid off the ribbon. She opened the box to reveal two dozen long-stemmed red roses interspersed with baby's breath and greenery.

"They're gorgeous." Cassie lifted her gaze to her sister. "How much did these set him back?"

"Always so practical. Well, I'm practical, too." Lindsay opened the huge bag she carried and brought out a crystal vase in bubble wrap. "I doubted you'd have a vase big enough to hold these beauties."

Once the flowers were arranged and sitting on the kitchen counter, Lindsay met Cassie's gaze. "Do you know what you're going to say when he asks?"

"He won't—"

"He's going to ask you to marry him. The signs are there." Lindsay waved away her protests. "He's spent the past two months courting you. Taking you on dates and to parties. Spending time with you and the boys."

"He lives in Green Bay."

"Which is just down the road."

"The boys—"

"Adore Krew. They may be excited to move." Lindsay shrugged. "You need to ask them."

"But—"

"If you want to marry and build a life with him, say yes." Lindsay squeezed Cassie's hand. "If you're not sure, tell him you don't want to rush into anything."

"I love him." The words felt right on her lips. "I want to be with him."

"You have your answer." Lindsay pulled Cassie in for a hug. "Trust me, there isn't anything more wonderful than being in love with a man who loves you back."

∼

Cassie wore the red dress she'd bought with the Swoon gift certificate Krew gave her, supplemented with some of the money she'd earned from the first house she sold after getting her license.

She'd splurged on a pair of nude-colored heels. A recent haircut by Marigold had her hair lying in soft waves to her shoulders.

When the doorbell rang, Cassie felt like a nervous high schooler.

Taking a deep breath, she opened the door.

His coat was open, and the sight of him in a suit had her mouth growing dry.

"You clean up well."

"So do you." Before stepping inside, he leaned over and kissed her.

The intoxicating scent of his cologne wrapped around her like a lover's hand.

"Please, come in."

His gaze searched the room, settling on the vase of flowers.

"They're absolutely lovely," she said in answer to his questioning gaze. "I was going to text you my thanks, but I wanted to tell you in person."

"I'm glad you like them."

"I love them." Her voice sounded quite breathless, even to her own ears. "And the card."

Something flickered in the depths of his eyes. "Good."

"Hi, Krew," Braxton called from his position on the couch.

K.T. strolled in from his bedroom, a sketch pad in hand. "Hey, man, good to see you."

"Daddy." Axl, who must have been in the bedroom with K.T., ran to Krew, who lifted him high in the air and had him giggling in seconds.

Cassie sighed heavily. She'd tried to get Axl to call Krew by his name, but her youngest had a stubborn streak. Thankfully, Krew didn't seem to mind.

"Thanks for watching him," Cassie told the older boys. "I'll probably be late—"

"Why don't you just spend the night at Krew's place?" Braxton suggested. "That way, you won't wake up the brat by coming in once he's asleep."

Cassie stilled. Krew had signed another short-term lease on the house on Millionaire's Row. When he was in town, he stayed there.

Not once had Cassie stayed overnight, though she'd found herself hoping he'd ask. Now, it was as if her sons were forcing the question.

"What a good idea." Krew shot the boys a wink. "Maybe we can all go out for breakfast in the morning."

"Works for me." Braxton slipped on his VR goggles.

K.T. was able to pull a clinging Axl from Krew by promising to play trucks with his younger brother.

By the time they reached the party at Eliza and Kyle's home, Cassie's insides shook. She told herself Lindsay had it wrong. Krew wasn't going to ask her to marry him.

But a part of her, the romantic part, the part that all the setbacks of the past twenty years hadn't been able to completely eradicate, still hoped.

She and Krew had grown close over the past couple of months, building a strong friendship. There wasn't anything she couldn't tell him.

She'd given a lot of thought to why he hadn't slept with her again. If she read the situation right, it was because he wanted to give her back that time in her life when she could date and have fun with a guy without it being all about sex.

Still, she desperately hoped tonight would be the end of her unwanted sexual fast.

She pressed herself more fully against him on the dance floor, wanting him with every fiber of her being.

"Don't you two make a nice-looking couple?"

Gladys stopped them with a tap on Krew's back in the middle of the dance floor. Cassie recognized the other woman's partner as an older man who worked with Kyle.

"You look lovely this evening, Gladys," Krew said gallantly.

The caftan Gladys wore, in shades of red, black and silver, suited the woman.

"There's a full moon this evening," Gladys informed them. "There's a perfect view of it from the alcove off the second parlor."

"Good to know." Cassie offered a polite smile.

"You simply must check it out," Gladys insisted. "It's not just full; it's a Lovers' Moon."

"I don't believe I've heard that term." Instead of polite, Krew sounded surprisingly interested.

"Perhaps you know it as a Strawberry Moon or Rose Moon?"

Cassie and Krew exchanged a glance and shook their heads.

"Well, such a moon is known for bringing with it the energy for love, marriage, and success." Gladys placed a hand over her heart. "My dear Henry proposed during a Lovers' Moon, and we had a wonderful life together."

When Cassie and Krew remained where they were, Gladys made a shooing motion.

As soon as the couple disappeared from the room and Gladys bid her partner adieu, Ruby slipped out from her spot behind a potted plant.

"I heard what you told them." Puzzlement blanketed Ruby's face. "I thought a Strawberry Moon occurred only in June."

"Gladys isn't one to worry about pesky details." Katherine joined them, offering a wry smile. "Something tells me her husband also didn't propose during a Lovers' Moon."

"If there had been one in the sky that night, I'm sure Henry would have seized the moment." Gladys gazed in the direction of the second parlor. "Let's hope Krew Slattery takes the hint."

Cassie stood beside Krew and gazed through the window at the darkened sky made brilliant by the light of the moon. "Gladys was right. This spot provides a perfect view."

"These short bits of time we spend together aren't enough for me."

Her heart plummeted. Not sure how to respond, Cassie settled for a nod.

"I've thought, and I still believe, that you deserve to be properly wooed. Getting pregnant at such a young age took all those opportunities from you." His eyes were dark and intense. "I've wanted to give that to you. And I've wanted to give us time to reconnect and really get to know each other."

"What are you saying, Krew?"

"I'm making a mess of this." Krew started to pace. "This is coming out all wrong."

"Speaking from the heart is never wrong." She clasped her hands together to still their trembling. "Whatever you have to tell me, just say it. A Band-Aid always comes off easier if you just rip it off."

A strange light filled his eyes, and he chuckled. "I never thought I'd hear a proposal compared to ripping off a Band-Aid."

"A-a proposal?" Cassie swallowed past the lump forming in her throat.

Krew stood in front of her now and took her hands, prying them apart. "I love you, Cass. I think in some way I've always loved you. But during our time together, I've grown to know the woman you are deep down."

As if he knew the direction her thoughts were taking, he jiggled her hands. "Neither of us is perfect, but who'd want to be with someone who's perfect? What we do is fit together... perfectly. As corny as it may sound, you really are the half that makes me whole."

"It's not just me, Krew. I have three boys still at home."

"I know. They make this even better."

She looked surprised, and his smile widened. "You already know how I feel about Dakota. And the boys, well, I love them as if they're my own. If you and they are willing, I'd like to adopt them after we're married, all three of them. And then we'll pay off Clint and get him out of the picture for good."

"You'd do that for me?"

"I'd do that for us and for our family."

Tears slipped down Cassie's cheeks. "If this is a dream, I don't want to wake up."

"Stick with me a little while longer." His expression turned serious. "I know you love Good Hope, but Green Bay isn't far. We'd come back as often as possible."

"You want us to live there."

"I'd like you to consider the possibility. Bigger schools with more opportunities for the boys. More opportunities for you to further your real estate career, if that's what you want." Krew expelled a breath. "The thing is, coaches work a lot of hours. It'd be more convenient for me if we lived there. But if you want to stay here, that's what we'll do."

"I don't how the boys would—"

"I spoke with Braxton and K.T. and got their blessing."

"What did they say?"

"They're willing to move right now, though they'd prefer to

finish the school year here." Krew's gaze never left her face. "Marrying and moving in May should work. It'll give us time to plan the wedding."

"Wedding? I thought we'd just go to the courthouse."

"If that's what you want, we can do that. But I'd like you to have all the hoopla. I'd like *us* to share that moment."

She nodded, trying to still the rapid beat of her heart and failing miserably. "A May wedding with hoopla it is."

"Let's make it official." Krew dropped to one knee, one hand still holding hers. "Cassie Lohmeier, it may have taken us time to find our way back to each other, but it was worth the wait. The story of our love is just beginning, and I can't wait to write our happy ending. My life won't be complete without you in it. I know I can meet any of life's challenges if you're with me."

His voice cracked, and he paused for a heartbeat before continuing. "I love you more than I thought it was possible to love someone. I love Dakota and the boys, and I even kind of like your mother."

Cassie laughed. Who but Krew would bring Anita into a marriage proposal?

With his free hand, he pulled out a jeweler's box and flipped it open. A large diamond surrounded by four semiprecious stones winked up at her.

"The diamond represents us, and the gems surrounding it are the birthstones of our four children."

"It's beautiful." Her voice turned husky with emotion. "It's perfect."

"Will you marry me, Cassie? I promise no one will try harder to make you happy or cherish you more than I will."

"Yes. I'll marry you." Her heart swelled until she thought it would burst. "I love you, Krew, so very much. There is no one for me but you. There's never been anyone else in my heart. Only you."

He slid the ring on her finger, then rose and pulled her to him.

When his lips settled over hers, Cassie knew she was finally where she was meant to be.

The kiss sent fire coursing through her veins. The last time they'd made love had been at the hotel in Green Bay, and that seemed like eons ago.

"Come home with me."

Cassie only hoped he planned to do more than kiss once they got there.

"I want to make love to you," he continued, "all night."

Relief skittered through her. "Why haven't you asked me before? You have to know how much I want you."

"It killed me. I swear, waiting nearly did me in." Krew's expression softened as he brushed his knuckles against her cheek. "I thought you should have the experience of dating without the pressures of sex. Now that we're engaged, I have something special to suggest for this evening."

Cassie perked up. "What is it?"

"Remember the relationship cards?"

Cassie made a valiant attempt to keep the smile on her lips. "You want me to answer questions?"

"Only one." Krew pulled a card out of his pocket and held it out.

Cassie read the words. She wiggled the card in the air. "Are you asking if this is something that appeals to me?"

He nodded.

She grinned. "Race you to the car."

Gladys didn't mind that Cassie clipped her slightly on her way out the door. When she hesitated and began to apologize, Gladys waved her on, noting with satisfaction the large diamond on her ring finger.

She smiled when Krew sped by after his fiancée.

Once they were gone, she and her friends gathered in the alcove and stared at the moon.

"You were right." Katherine lifted her glass of champagne in a toast. "It really is a night for lovers."

Gladys glanced over to where Katie Ruth stood alone near the punch bowl, trying to appear unconcerned that her date had deserted her.

"If there's one thing I love more than a happy ending," Gladys clinked her glass against Ruby's and Katherine's and took a sip of the very excellent champagne, "it's a new challenge."

Thank you for coming along on Cassie and Krew's journey. I hope you enjoyed reading this book as much as I loved writing it.

The next book in the series brings together Dan Marshall and Katie Ruth Crewes. This story shows that a person is more than their past mistakes. I really think you're going to love it!

Pick up your copy of this heartwarming story now. A Match Made in Good Hope (or keep reading for a sneak peek):

Chapter 1

Valentine's Day sucked.

Katie Ruth Crewes was no stranger to this particular holiday gone bad. It was her own fault she felt so low. She'd set her hopes too high for tonight.

Not that she expected a rom-com-worthy Valentine's Day. Just a nice night with an old friend, maybe ending in a sweet good night kiss at the door. But this was shaping up to be the worst Valentine's Day ever.

No, not the *worst*. That title would always belong to the holiday eight years ago when she'd been part of a Valentine's Day bachelorette weekend in Vegas that had gone very, very wrong.

The bride had gotten alcohol poisoning, the maid of honor lost a small fortune in the casino, and Katie Ruth had—

She shut her eyes against the memory. She'd been a different person back then. Those wild and crazy few years were definitely in the rearview.

Tonight's Valentine's disaster was still very much front and center.

The fact she had a date for the party at Kyle and Eliza Kendrick's home had itself been a cause to rejoice. Last year, when she turned the big 3-0, she'd spent V-Day alone with a pint of Ben & Jerry's, watching *Shakespeare in Love* for the zillionth time.

The sad part was, that had been a better night than some of the ones she'd spent with a man.

She slanted a glance at Dexter Woodard, her date for the evening's festivities. He and Beckett Cross—attorney and restaurateur—were currently engaged in a deep conversation about something to do with physics and mass transfer.

Katie Ruth, well, she was pretending to be interested.

When Beck's wife, Ami, strolled up with two glasses of fruit punch, Katie Ruth flashed a relieved smile. The cavalry had arrived.

Ami handed a crystal cup to Katie Ruth. She listened for a second to the conversation between her husband and Dexter. Then she stepped back and made a come-with-me motion. Apparently, Katie Ruth wasn't the only one bored by biotechnology chatter.

"You look ready to pop." Katie Ruth widened her eyes at the sight of Ami's pregnant belly, covered by the soft red fabric of a wrap dress. "I'm surprised you came this evening."

"It feels good to be out instead of sitting at home wondering if today's the day." Ami, her blond hair pulled back from her face with two sparkling butterfly clips, rested a hand on the mound. "We're all excited to meet him or her."

All, Katie Ruth knew, included soon-to-be big sister, two-year-old Sarah Rose.

"I wonder if it'll be a boy or girl." Though Katie Ruth didn't have any children, many of the women she'd gone to high school with were having babies this spring. They usually loved talking about their children or their pregnancies.

Which was why Katie Ruth was surprised when Ami waved

the topic aside and leaned close, her voice barely above a whisper. "Eliza mentioned you were bringing a plus one. She didn't say it was Dexter."

Katie Ruth understood Ami's interest. Dexter had gone to high school in Good Hope. Then he'd left for college and built a life elsewhere.

Ami's eyes sparkled with curiosity. "When did he get back?"

"A couple of days ago." Katie Ruth took a sip of fruit punch and kept her tone matter-of-fact. "His mom was recently diagnosed with cancer. Dexter wanted to be here when she has surgery on Monday."

"I hope she'll be okay." Ami's green eyes clouded. "I really like LaDonna. I don't think I've ever seen the woman without a smile on her face."

Katie Ruth nodded. "Dexter has nice parents."

Parents who'd never said a word to Katie Ruth about the scandal affecting her own family.

"I have to say," Ami's red lips curved, "I'm impressed."

Confused, Katie Ruth inclined her head.

"You move fast." Ami chuckled. "The guy barely hits the city limits, and you snag a date for the most romantic evening of the year."

"You misunderstand." Katie Ruth spoke quickly. Knowing how easily rumors could take hold and spread, she needed to make it absolutely clear this wasn't a date. They were simply two friends from high school attending a party together. "It's not like that."

"Not like what?" Eliza Kendrick, hostess of the party and Ami's BFF, interrupted without apology.

Like Ami, Eliza was pregnant, though not due for a couple of months. Instead of looking like a beach ball beneath her stylish black cocktail dress, Eliza's baby bump was more like a cantaloupe.

"Katie Ruth was about to spill how she and Dexter hooked up tonight," Ami told her friend.

Katie Ruth stifled a groan.

Eliza's gray eyes shifted to the man still in conversation with Beck, now gesturing excitedly with his hands as he made a point. "He's certainly changed since high school."

That was the understatement of the year. The tall man, with his athletic build, dark wavy hair and brilliant blue eyes behind stylish eyewear, bore no resemblance to the boy. Back then, Dexter had been a beanpole with glasses that were always slipping down his nose, and he'd had an awkwardness around anyone of the female persuasion.

He'd also been scary-smart and fascinated by anything to do with science and math. He—like Katie Ruth—had led a comfortable existence on the outer fringe of the popular crowd.

As if sensing their assessing gazes, Mr. Geek-Turned-Hunk turned to direct a megawatt smile at their hostess. "Eliza Shaw. Thank you for allowing me to crash your party."

"It's Kendrick now." Eliza smiled even as she continued to openly study him. "And you didn't crash. You came with Katie Ruth."

Dexter offered Katie Ruth a quick smile, then immediately refocused on Eliza. "That's right. Kendrick, not Shaw. I heard you'd gotten married. Congratulations."

"Thank you." Eliza's gaze strayed to where her husband stood, surrounded by friends. She smiled, and any hard edges softened when her gaze settled on Kyle. "It's been an exciting year."

Beck moved to Ami's side and slid an arm around her shoulder. The light kiss he brushed against his wife's cheek had Katie Ruth swallowing a sigh.

The gesture was so sweet.

So romantic.

Dexter remained where he was, a good foot separating him

from Katie Ruth. No one looking at them now would think they even knew each other.

"I heard your husband is part of Kendrick Inc." Dexter's tone was one of respect. "That's a huge operation. They've got their fingers in a lot of pies."

Pies that obviously interested—and impressed—Dexter.

Eliza waved away the comment. "I was sorry to hear your mother is having health issues."

"The doctors are hopeful that once they take out the part of the kidney where the tumor is, she'll be fine." Though Dexter's tone remained light, the worry in his eyes had Katie Ruth's irritation easing.

"We'll be keeping her in our prayers," Ami assured him.

Katie Ruth nodded.

Dexter rocked back on the heels of his Ferragamos and cleared his throat. "I appreciate that."

"Now, tell us." Eliza swept a hand in Katie Ruth's direction. "How did you two get together?"

Dexter blinked. "We're not really—"

"She means tonight," Katie Ruth clarified.

"Oh, yes, of course. Katie Ruth and I have kept in contact through social media. And I subscribe to the Open Door." Dexter slanted a glance at Katie Ruth as he mentioned the e-newsletter she edited. "When I mentioned I was coming back to Good Hope for a week, she asked if I wanted to come with her tonight and reconnect."

"Reconnect?" Eliza arched one dark brow, a teasing glint behind her sharp and assessing gaze. "That sounds…intriguing."

Dexter had had the unfortunate tendency to blush when he was younger, Katie Ruth suddenly recalled. Though he kept his composure, she saw the tips of his ears turn red. "That was poorly worded."

"Eliza." Katie Ruth spoke sharply. The woman was toying with him, much like a cat played with a mouse merely for the sport of it. "Cut the guy a break. You knew what he meant."

"Katie Ruth assured me there'd be a lot of people I knew from high school here tonight." Regaining his composure, Dexter gave Katie Ruth a mock salute. "She delivered."

Katie Ruth might not have had any romantic fantasies where Dexter was concerned, but did he have to make it sound as if she was nothing more to him than a vehicle for a party invitation?

Don't be ridiculous, Katie Ruth told herself. She and Dexter were friends. Hadn't they chatted comfortably on the drive over to Eliza's house? If he'd failed to offer any compliments about her appearance, well, it was because he saw her as his friend, not his date.

Dexter's gaze slid around the room and came to an abrupt stop. His eyes widened as his gaze shot back to Eliza. "I thought your brother no longer lived in Good Hope."

Ethan must have spotted Dexter at the same time. He grinned and lifted a hand in greeting to his former Science Olympiad partner.

"He's been back for—"

"I'm going to say hello." He was across the parlor before anyone could blink.

"Like Dexter said, tonight is, ah, all about reconnecting." Katie Ruth managed to keep a smile on her face. "If you'll excuse me, I think I'm going to grab more of this amazing fruit punch and mingle."

Katie Ruth took her time refilling her cup. She would admit, just to herself, that while she hadn't assumed—or expected—Dexter to be glued to her side, she *had* thought they'd spend *some* of the evening together.

Right now, she felt like a lonely only in a room full of couples. A pint of Ben & Jerry's and a movie were sounding better by the second.

Across the room, Katie Ruth caught Gladys Bertholf studying

her. The ninety-some-year-old knew everything that happened in this small community on the Door County peninsula. Because Katie Ruth had her pride, she abandoned her solitary stance at the punch bowl, smiled brightly at no one in particular and sauntered over to a group gathered by the food.

Eliza and Kyle had gone all out for this party, not only bringing in a bartender and wait staff, but filling the two parlors and foyer with a plethora of roses.

When Katie Ruth had stepped through the door earlier this evening, the sweet scent wafting in the air struck her as oh-so-romantic. Now, the cloying fragrance had her stomach churning.

Out of the corner of her eye, Katie Ruth saw Dexter was now in the midst of a flirtation with Greer Chapin.

Greer's gray silk was the perfect foil for her dark hair. Katie Ruth could see why Dexter appeared mesmerized.

"If you wanted to spend the night talking to everyone else, why did you come with me?" Katie Ruth muttered. It might not be fair, but she wasn't feeling particularly generous right now.

"Pardon?"

A curse rose to Katie Ruth's lips. She immediately swallowed it as she turned to greet Dan Marshall.

Pastor Dan Marshall.

A godly man who'd likely never uttered a foul word in his life.

"Did you just arrive?" Despite her almost faux pas, Katie Ruth relaxed, and the smile she offered was genuine.

Dan was a solid guy whom she knew well from her volunteer work at the church. With him, there was never any game-playing. What you saw was what you got. And what you got from this man was all good.

"I walked through the front door less than five minutes ago to find the party in full swing." The minister's brown eyes were warm, and his normally messy cap of brown hair had been recently cut and combed.

"I wasn't sure about coming, but I ran into Kyle earlier today.

He made me promise to stop by." He gestured with one hand to the group by the bar. "It feels strange attending a Valentine's party alone."

"Surrounded by couples." Katie Ruth glanced around the room and resisted the urge to sigh.

"You look lovely this evening." Dan studied her short, black-lace sheath dress with a flirty scalloped hem.

The chill, which had seeped into her when Dexter hadn't commented on her new outfit, disappeared in a warm rush of pleasure.

"Thank you. You're looking spiffy yourself." The second the words left her lips, Katie Ruth wished she could pull them back.

The exercise class she'd started teaching at the Good Hope Living Center was clearly having an impact. Seriously, did anyone under the age of eighty even know what *spiffy* meant?

Not to mention there was probably some sort of biblical canon against complimenting a minister.

Dan glanced down at his dark pants and gray shirt. "I should have worn a suit."

Katie Ruth made a dismissive sound. She'd spent her childhood surrounded by men in suits. Dark suits and conservative ties were de rigueur in the death care industry. Until she'd left for college, her parents had owned and operated the Amigone Funeral Home. The funeral directors, including her dad, wouldn't be caught dead in anything but a suit. Pun intended.

Thinking about those days still brought a smile. The mortuary had been called Amigone when her parents had purchased the business, and they'd kept the name. Her parents' quirky sense of humor and love of the absurd were only two of the many reasons she adored them.

Dan glanced around the room as if to reassure himself he fit in, or maybe he was seeing who was here that he knew. Which, if she had to hazard a guess, was probably close to everyone.

Dan shifted his gaze to the bar. They watched business owner

Ryder Goodhue down a shot of whiskey, then immediately hold it out for the bartender for a refill. "What's with him?"

With Dexter busy mingling with everyone but her, Katie Ruth had plenty of time to study the rest of the party guests. "Something is definitely troubling him."

Dan's brow creased in concern as Ryder tossed back the second shot.

Katie Ruth wondered how long it would be until the minister left her to check on Ryder.

"Engaging in a little partner switching this evening, Ms. Crewes?" Dexter's drive-by shot, coupled with a wink and a thumbs-up, had Katie Ruth sucking in a breath.

She didn't have a chance to respond, because Dexter disappeared into the crowd. Feeling Dan's assessing gaze, Katie Ruth rolled her eyes. She'd had lots of practice controlling her reactions to such comments. Still, hearing the barb come from Dexter's lips had been a surprise.

He'd never teased her about her parents. Not once.

Why now?

Beside her, Dan furrowed his brow in confusion. "Who is he?"

"Dexter Woodard. He's an old high school classmate." Katie Ruth fought to keep her tone nonchalant. "We rode to the party together."

Katie Ruth hoped that would be the end of it, but she hadn't realized Ruby and her two friends stood close enough to hear.

The older woman placed a hand on Katie Ruth's arm, her bright blue eyes filled with sympathy. "I'm sure Dexter didn't mean it the way it sounded."

"The way it—" Katherine Spencer, Ruby's close friend, frowned as if not making the connection. Then her eyes widened. "Oh. Oh."

Gladys Bertholf, elder statesman of the threesome at ninety-seven, stepped forward. "The man is a cad. Eliza should toss him to the curb."

"It was a careless remark," Katie Ruth began, but Gladys waved an impatient hand.

"Careless remark, my ass," Gladys muttered.

"Gladys." Ruby gestured with her head toward Dan. "Man of God."

"Don't make a scene." Katherine, steady as they came, gave her friend a warning glance.

"I'm not following." Dan glanced at Katie Ruth, appearing even more puzzled.

Katie Ruth hesitated, then gave a little laugh. "It's nothing. Really."

"Daniel." Gladys fixed those pale blue eyes on him. "Why don't you and Katie Ruth grab some food and enjoy this lovely party?"

"Ah, sure." Dan offered a tentative smile, glanced at the empty glass Katie Ruth held tightly gripped in one hand. "Would you like more punch? Or something to eat?"

The kindness in those dark depths had her returning his smile. It was the question she saw lingering there that had her making the decision to explain.

"I'd love some. While we eat, I'll tell you a story." When her knees went suddenly weak, Katie Ruth slipped a hand around Dan's arm. "Once upon a time…"

This is just the book to bring some warmth and kindness into your life. Grab your copy and dive into this uplifting story. A Match Made in Good Hope

ALSO BY CINDY KIRK

Good Hope Series

The Good Hope series is a must-read for those who love stories that uplift and bring a smile to your face.

Check out the entire Good Hope series here

Hazel Green Series

Readers say "Much like the author's series of Good Hope books, the reader learns about a town, its people, places and stories that enrich the overall experience. It's a journey worth taking."

Check out the entire Hazel Green series here

Holly Pointe Series

Readers say "If you are looking for a festive, romantic read this Christmas, these are the books for you."

Check out the entire Holly Pointe series here

Jackson Hole Series

Heartwarming and uplifting stories set in beautiful Jackson Hole, Wyoming.

Check out the entire Jackson Hole series here

Silver Creek Series

Engaging and heartfelt romances centered around two powerful families whose fortunes were forged in the Colorado silver mines.

check out the entire Silver Creek Series here

Made in the USA
Las Vegas, NV
28 June 2022

50819844R00173